Mrs. Rachel Rhoads

Poems: A Series of Tales in Verse

With a Variety of Lyrical Productions on Chosen Themes ..

Mrs. Rachel Rhoads

Poems: A Series of Tales in Verse
With a Variety of Lyrical Productions on Chosen Themes ..

ISBN/EAN: 9783744788120

Printed in Europe, USA, Canada, Australia, Japan

Cover: Foto ©Andreas Hilbeck / pixelio.de

More available books at **www.hansebooks.com**

POEMS:

A SERIES OF

TALES IN VERSE,

WITH A

VARIETY OF LYRICAL PRODUCTIONS ON CHOSEN THEMES,
INTENDED TO PLEASE THE MANY
AND OFFEND NONE.

BY

MRS. RACHEL RHOADS,

("THE AMERICAN HARP,")

AUTHORESS OF "THE MINSTREL LYRE," "ZIMLUKA," ETC.

PHILADELPHIA.

J. B. LIPPINCOTT & CO.

1863.

PS2698
.R42

24202

CONTENTS.

————※※————

(v)

Poems.

NAPOLEON AND JOSEPHINE.

WHAT form is that, 'neath many a velvet fold
Of gorgeous hangings, wrought in threads of gold,
With features fair, most beautiful and bland,
As though just sculptured by some master-hand?
Within those eyes, what depths of flashing light
Shine from their fringes, like some orb of night
Beaming in silent grandeur from above,
While each expression tells of hope and love!

'Tis Josephine, the beauteous child of wrong,
Whose name will ever grace the poet's song;
Her jeweled arm supports her classic head,
While memory wanders o'er bright moments fled,
And marks the vista of unfolding years,
Which may prove joyous—or be wrung with tears—
Should Time his golden honors still display,
And Fortune crown her conquering Hero's way.

With what affection and what anxious soul
She counts the varied moments as they roll,
Leading her proud and nobly-gifted sire,
At every turn, in martial glory higher.

2   (9)

She hears the loud, the clarion tongue of Fame,
From shore to shore resounding with his name;
High deeds of valor and victorious sway
Have gained him all the honors of the day.
The laurel rests upon his lofty brow,
While hopes exulting in his bosom glow;
With pride he views the golden trophies won
On Egypt's plains, beneath a burning sun.
What cares he now for Infidel or Moor?
A crown is won! a kingdom made secure!
Devoted France must succumb to his power,
And claim Napoleon as its emperor!

Not clamorous councils sitting in debate
Could hope to turn him from his lofty state
When once his bold, aspiring motives rose
To grasp the reins and quell his envious foes.
For proud ambition led the hero on,
From conquering deeds to mighty empires won,
Till nations trembled at the dread of war,
And thousands bled beneath the victor's car.

But view again that beauteous, loving form,
Whose bosom thrills with sweet emotions warm;
What anxious thoughts inveigh her precious mind
While brooding o'er her hero, brave and kind!
She hears the shout of honor and applause
Soar on the air, and well divines the cause;
She knows the nature of her valiant sire,
Whose heart and hopes to kingly deeds aspire.
Vive Napoleon! Yes, she greets the sound
That now ascends from countless voices round,
While throngs confused rush madly to and fro—
Some drunk with joy, some too with bleeding woe;

For strange reverses must in main appear,
Now that her lord the jeweled crown must wear.

But does the .smile of bliss illume her brow?
Doth golden dreams across her vision flow,
While grand results seem crowding o'er her fate
And glorious honors all her steps await?
Ah, no! A veil dark as the pall of night
Intruding, shrouds all gladness from her sight;
Looming and mournful thoughts unbidden rise,
And prompt the tear to glisten in her eyes.

Alas! that dreams foreboding thus should pain
A heart so pure, so void of passions vain;
A soul to every gentle virtue given,
As though a daughter well approved of Heaven.
But while the shout went up upon the air
In honor of her brave and valiant sire,
She felt emotions that too plainly told
Peace was not won by earthly fame or gold.
A thousand fears possessed her generous mind
In princely halls she would no pleasure find;
She cared not for the pomp of regal state,
But loved a virtuous and more lowly fate;
Nor could her loving, faultless lips refrain
From kindly warnings, o'er and o'er again,
To him who held her destiny in hand,
Her love, her peace, her life too, at command.
Fain would she curb his proud, ambitious views,
And have him still a humbler pathway choose;
But no! On, on, through martial storm and toil
Napoleon dashed, resolved to win the goal!

True, the fair Josephine, while with anxious heart,
Saw her loved lord pursue his glorious part,
Could not avoid a sense of inward pride
To hear his praises deeply multiplied.
Ah, no! she was not proof against the power
Of deeds heroic that then came crowding o'er;
She loved, adored his grand and master mind,
Nay, worshiped—if so it may be defined—
His every look; each accent from his tongue,
Like music on her gentle hearing hung.

The die was cast! We see the conqueror come
To share the honors of his regal home!
The palace halls now ring with festive mirth,
As though a day was born to bless the earth,
And mighty schemes were waiting to unfold
Their wealth of wonders, as in times of old;
Yes, times when Rome her Cesars brave could boast,
And martial armies, numbered by the host,
Spread their vast phalanx o'er Pharsalia's plains,
To pour out there the blood of proudest veins!

Another Cesar! yes, but greater far
Was brave Napoleon's mighty feats of war!
What tottering kingdoms felt his potent sway,
What empires raised or crushed within a day!
What hosts of valiant sons obeyed his call,
Resolved to conquer or most nobly fall!
See what success attends his martial reign—
Each battle fought is never fought in vain,
For victory is the shrill, the battle cry,
We go to conquer, or we go to die!

Ambitious man! What deep, insatiate thirst
Burned in thy breast, e'en from the very first,
To grasp the world, and bring submissive down
Imperial nations, subject to thy crown!
'Twere not enough to raise in might and power,
And have thy name to sound from shore to shore;
Too great, I wot, thy greatness fain would be,
Too hardly earned thy immortality.

But let us pause in this thy vast career:
Oh! couldst thou but have been contented here—
But no! more brilliant hopes and schemes were thine;
Thou didst aspire to raise a kingly line;
A throne so bravely and so hardly won
Must not be minus of a royal son!
If ever hell a thought revealed to man,
'Twas this to spoil thy every future plan;
For glory and success, by Heaven's decree,
From that foul moment never followed thee.

What! leave that angel wedded to thy fate,
Whose soul watched o'er thy early hours and late
With trusting love, and confidence so true,
That spirits from the upper world might view,
And sanction with recording voice and pen,
As worthy of the greatest, best of men!
What! leave that partner of thy griefs and fears,
Thy joys and prosperous dreams, and kingly cares,
To take another to thy regal arms,
Whose soul possessed not half her glowing charms?
Shame on the hour! yes, sorrow veiled the day
That thou didst cast thy Josephine away!

An heir was born! But oh! the bitter thought,
With that fond gift a solemn change is wrought;
Can that pure wife, of sweet, neglected love,
Rejoice o'er this young treasure from above?
For thus it seemed that Heaven did grant thy prayer,
Proud monarch, and bestowed a royal heir!
But mark the turn of fortune and of fate,
What sorrows o'er thy dooming steps await!
For God had sent abroad his wise decree,
That what Napoleon aimed at ne'er should be;
No regal son should mount that earthly throne
Which proud ambition had so darkly won,
Nor joy could bloom in that young mother's breast,
Who robbed another of her wedded rest;
For worlds united should not tempt a heart
To act so callous and so base a part!

Poor Josephine! I see thy beauteous mien,
Through vision, as thou erst had often been
In happier mood, arrayed in jeweled tire,
For wondering hearts to honor and admire,
Nor dreamt so sad a change would mark thy fate,
And trials fall with overwhelming weight
Upon that bosom which so fondly hung
To hopes elate, then left it rudely wrung.
No wonder that thy frenzied feelings strove
In vain to cancel chaste, enduring love,
Toward the object of thy spirit's choice,
Who won thee by the music of his voice,
For vows exalted met thy gentle ear,
Nor couldst thou doubt those breathings were sincere.

But oh! the burning burst of agony
That overwhelmed thy queenly destiny,

When he, with dauntless lips, could fain impart
What well he knew would break thy gentle heart!
But now the deep, the tragic dream is past,
And long consigned to dark oblivion's waste,
Save the lone herald of historic fame,
The page that points to each immortal name!
Speaking of martial glory won and lost,
Ere the proud victor was an exile tost
On Saint Helena's barren sea-girt shore,
To die a victim through tyrannic power.

Alas! what thoughts were thine in bitter mood,
In this, thy lonely, august solitude;
For though surrounded by a peopled soil,
Thy feelings mingled not with busy toil;
For weary, sorrowing, did thy spirit yearn
For freedom, and to home again return.
'Twas all in vain, and echo answers why,
The royal captive was sent there to die!

THE OLD MAN'S STORY,

OR,

HOW BLESSINGS COME IN DISGUISE.

"Come hither, my boy!" said a weary old man,
    As he sat on the turf near his own cottage door;
"My morning is past, and life's but a span,
    And soon will its lengthened out moments give o'er.

"But listen and learn while youth's on thy brow,
    For changes and scenes may appear
Not dreamt of, to darken thy sunny heart now,
    For strange is our mortal career.

"Yea, thou art so young! but time hurried flies,
    And spring's early bloom fades away,
And manhood and vigor successively rise,
    And spread their bold front to the day.

"Then let gentle counsel, like seed in good ground,
    Take root in thy juvenile brain;
That when a few seasons have traveled their round,
    Instruction has not proved in vain.

"When I was a youth, as thou art, my boy,
    With feelings as generous and bold,
I lived but in scenes that were lit up with joy,
    Nor dreamt of the time to grow old.

"My parents were wealthy, were proud of their son,
    And oft would they pat my white head,
And smile o'er the wonderful freaks I had done
    When among my brave play-fellows led.

"But, ah! what a change came over my doom;
    My father was called to the field,
And battle soon gave him a warrior's tomb,
    And the fate of the future revealed.

"And now what I wish soon to show you is this,
    Though my story in pain may be drest,
That changes in life, when robbed of all bliss,
    May happen, my son, for the best.

"My father now dead, the first blighting scene
    Burst over my infantile view,
For kindest of parents that father had been,
    And kind was my dear mother too.

"Alas! when I turn to those moments long gone,
    When the spring of my childhood was beaming
With blessings that fell as seasons rolled on,
    And life was with fairy dreams teeming,—

"And think of the trouble and deep folding gloom
    That fell like a pall of death o'er me,
For scarce had my father sank down in the tomb,
    Than death from my mother dear tore me!

"We wept o'er our loss, for we felt it too sure,
    For the sun of our day dream was clouded,
And ills like a tempest, too much to endure,
    O'er the hopes of the future were clouded.

"Too much was the grief; like a canker it hung
    O'er her bosom so noble and kind,
Till the last gentle chord of her heartstrings was wrung,
    And left me an orphan behind.

"Oh! blighting regret! oh! moments of pain!
    What anguish, what bursting of feeling,
Were never before, nor can be again,
    As when by her corse I was kneeling!

"Oh! shade of my mother! thy last holy prayer,
    As breathed when thy spirit departed,
Still sounds in its tenderest tones on my ear,
    And makes me once more infant hearted.

"But then, my dear boy, I dash off the tear,
    Forgive an old man for this token,—
When memory reverts to those hearts that were dear,
    Its fountain is sure to be broken."

THE BOY'S REPLY.

"Dear father," said now the young lad, as he wept
    To see age in tears, "I feel pained;
Nor can I discover in all that's past yet,
    That blessings were thus to be gained.

"You told me that all you would deign to relate
    Should prove a broad lesson, to test
That all that occurred in the scenes of one's fate
    Would happen perhaps for the best.

"Was it good that your parents were taken away,
    And sorrows shed gloom o'er your head?
I am sure if I had, sire, but one word to say,
    'Twould be misery placed in its stead. ·

"Blest! that word is so ample, I cannot conceive,
    When dangers and trials draw near,
Why your generous feelings were taught to believe
    That bliss in disguise would appear?"

THE OLD MAN.

"Well, hearken, my boy," said the reverend sage,
    "I've not told you half of my ditty;
Though the scenes of my youth fill up many a page,
    We must mingle delight with our pity.

" 'Tis true I was of both my parents bereft,
 And I, to a stern guardian's care
A poor little friendless orphan was left,
 With none my affliction to share.

" But evil seemed brewing in destiny's mould,
 To fashion my future career;
My guardian laid claim to my silver and gold,
 And left me a beggar boy here.

"Divested of all that was needful on earth
 To render me happy, I found
The fate of the future was like to give birth
 To many a dangerous wound.

"Some years fled apace; to manhood I grew;
 A slave on the galleys I dwelt:
And as for vicissitudes, naught else I knew,
 Nor aught but keen sorrow I felt.

" I bore with all patience the weight of my toil,
 As well as my nature could bear,
Yet often, while forced from my own native soil,
 I drank of the cup of despair.

"I now 'gan to murmur at Heaven's decree,
 That my fate to misfortune was chained,
When sudden a change was extended to me
 That little I dreamt to have gained.

"By a skirmish of war, I was cast on a shore
 That was strangely savage and wild;
But soon I perceived there were blessings in store
 For the slave and the poor ocean child.

"Being blest with some knowledge acquired in youth,
    Which I ever most jealous retained,
And languages many I studied forsooth,
    Delighting to have such explained.

"For on these vast galleys all nations and tongues
    Appear to exist, that is true;
And each seem quite sensible too in their way,
    From the Turk to the Babylon Jew.

"Thus learning, dear boy, was a blessing, to bring
    My friendless heart to a station
That soon was decreed by the generous king
    To make me the chief of a nation.

"So pleased was his royal affection for me,
    That he proved a kind father and friend;
And as a reward for my services, he
    His daughter bestowed in the end.

"Yes, yes! the fair Tama, an angel of love,
    Was given to me for a bride,
Who was all that my holiest hopes could approve,
    With honors and riches beside.

"Some years, they rolled by, the king was no more,
    Yet blessings and wealth were our claim:
A son and a daughter were joined to our store,
    And grateful were we for the same.

"And now I proposed to the bride of my soul—
    As I longed for my own native land—
To come with our children and dwell on the soil
    Where freedom and liberty stand.

" She consented with joy, for I was her guide,
 Her being, her happiness, all.—
Thus soon we were borne on the deep ocean wide,
 Nor did tempest or danger befall.

"And thither we came; though now we are old,
 Yet blest are we still in our store;
Our children are settled: we gave them our gold,—
 They are happy, we ask nothing more.

" The very best children they are too, I own;
 In yonder gay mansion they live ;
And we feel, and we know we are not left alone,
 For blessings they constantly give.

" Enough we have got of our own, very true,
 This beautiful cottage and lawn,
And means that are plenty still break on our view
 From night till the sweet morning dawn !

" Their home too, is ours ; but we now delight
 To live in simplicity's style;
The gay things of splendor we do not think right,
 Lest our old feeble hearts they might spoil.

" So now, my dear boy, was it not for the best,
 That afflictions and sorrows were mine?
For had I not been on a slave galley prest,
 I'd have missed cunning Fortune's design.

"My guardian a wretch of the vilest became,
 In the midst of his ill-gotten prize ;
He murdered himself on the strength of his gain,
 For conscience they say never dies.

"But thinking me lost, or a wanderer doomed,
  He left his possessions to be,
If e'er I returned, all the wealth he'd assumed,
  With his own to be given to me.

"And thus you perceive that fate was still true;
  For had he not robbed me, I ne'er
Should have got my own fortune, with his, my boy, too,
  And perhaps would have never been here.

"And now, let me tell you, whatever in life
  You find to go gloomy and wrong,
Bear patient each ill, each unfavoring strife,
  For some blessing may to them belong.

"Believe me, I deem it exceedingly wise
  To be both enduring and kind,
For blessings, my boy, often come in disguise,
  That joy in the end we may find!"

BOY.

"Thanks, sire, for all you have told me; for now
  I will profit by counsel so wise;
Submissive to fate I will humbly bow,
  And trust Father Time as he flies."

OUR COUNTRY.

LAND of sweet liberty, land of the West,
The home of the weary, the brave, and oppressed,
What glory, what honor, what martial renown,
Around thy bright altars are proudly thrown!

We look on thy triumph through years that are gone,
The loud clang of battle, and victories won,
And see our proud banner with beauty unfurled,
As a signal of joy to astonish the world.

How late, in primeval grandeur, was seen
Tall forests, bright, waving in rich flowing green,
Where now stands our city, exalted and free,
Whose goddess and glory is famed Liberty?

Sweet land of devotion, of honor, and peace!
Long, long may thy bountiful borders increase
In science and knowledge, in wealth and in power,
Till time gives its mystical changes no more.

Yes! long may thy banners, white, scarlet, and blue,
Wave over the beautiful, gallant, and true,
Inviting all nations to come and behold
Our gardens of freedom, our portals of gold.

'T is here that the weary and stricken may come,
And share in the joys of our heaven-born home,
Where dark usurpation and tyranny ne'er
Sent its wild screams of famine and woe on the air.

But honor and plenty, with union and love,
We cherish as bountiful gifts from above;
And proud as a nation that's gallant and free,
We glory in triumph and famed Liberty.

———◦◦◦———

MORNING.

AWAKE! awake! the blushing sky
Is tinged with many a rosy dye,
        For day is gaily gleaming!
And weighty floods of golden light
Descend in all their beauty bright,
        And on the waves are beaming.

The tuneful zephyr steals along,
And birds renew their early song,
        And cheerful is the morn;
The sweetest flowers bloom fair and gay,
With foreheads open to the day,
        While dewdrops kiss the thorn.

Awake, my muse! nor silent prove,
While nature breathes its hymns of love,
        And light and beauty glow
O'er every feature, far and near,
That flourish through the rolling year,
        And God's own wisdom show!

Trace but His mighty wonders o'er,
That spread abroad from shore to shore:
        The deep his power proclaims—

Beneath whose lofty, rolling waves
Are coral groves and diamond caves—
   There august silence reigns.

Awake! awake, my muse! the chime
Of morning bells tune forth the time,
   And nature all looks cheering;
The towering woods, and flowerets young,
With every trembling leaf a tongue,
   Behold in praise appearing.

Shake off, shake off each drowsy power,
And mingle with the joyous hour—
   Come join the happy strain!
Till time's uncertain numbers they
Shall set in life's declining day,
   To rise and shine again.

GENIUS IN BUD.

Genius, like germs from some fair-spreading tree,
   Shoots forth in swelling grandeur from the mind,
And proves in time what erst its fruits will be,
   By memory's templed gods to be enshrined.

Like the sweet olive, in luxuriant pride,
   That nobly decks the rich and sunny soil,
Is growing genius, spreading far and wide,
   While glory crowns the subjects of her toil.

   3*

THE DAWN OF LIGHT ON HEATHEN NATIONS.

HAIL, Asia! to the dawn of light
   Which o'er thy heathen temples shine!
'Tis glory breaks the spell of night
   That round your classic pillars twine.

Omnipotent the morning breaks
   O'er superstition's fated land;
And many a weary pilgrim seeks
   The Christian brother's heart and hand.

Round heathen temples green and dark,
   Where once Mohammed led his train,
We can the Christian progress mark,
   For Gospel efforts proved not vain.

Where now, ye worshipers of fire,
   Whose kindling altars fearful glow,
Or ye who build the funeral pyre,
   For sacrifices here below,

Will stand your mockery's direful aim,
   To lead the human heart astray,
When He who is the great I AM,
   Ye and your soulless gods shall slay?

Pale memory turns, with soul aghast,
   To scenes upon the Ganges' side,
Where solemn deeds of worship cast
   Your victims to its rolling tide.

What whitened bones beneath its waves,
　　Will ne'er be told on history's page,
Lie bleaching in their watery graves,
　　Frail martyrs to the darkened age.

And view abroad, o'er Hindoo plains,
　　Where many a ghastly skull appears,
Where Juggernaut's dark spirit reigns,
　　And there his demon temple rears.

Bleaching beneath the burning sun
　　The bones of countless mortals lie,
Whose frantic souls once heedless run
　　Beneath his chariot wheels to die.

Then hail to India's dawning hour,
　　When glory burst the gates of night,
And Gospel eloquence and power
　　Essayed to spread its holy light!

Down to the shades of darkest void
　　May superstition e'er be hurled,
Till naught but righteousness enjoyed
　　Shall flood and inundate the world.

When He whose majesty supreme
　　Shall wave His sceptre and His rod,
And wake creation to a scene
　　That claims and knows no other God!

TO THE SUN WHILE SETTING.

In purple and gold thy beauty is setting,
   Thou glorious orb of day!
And dewdrops the lovely flowers are wetting,
   As thy last dying streak fades away.

'Tis a season of calmness and pleasure,
   When the heart loves to muse o'er the past;
When moments of peace were a treasure,
   As though they forever would last.

But pleasures are fickle and fleeting,
   As zephyrs that float through the bower;
You scarce give them joyful greeting,
   Than they perish and fade in an hour.

But oh! for that beauty unbroken,
   That never shall wither or die;
That blissful and glorious token
   That beams from God's portals on high.

When the light of the Spirit Eternal
   Rolls on through immensity's space;
Nor needs thy effulgence diurnal,
   To illumine the heavenly place.

That home of the just and the weary,
   Where blessings undying remain,
Where beauty can never grow dreary,
   Nor the soul be unhappy again.

A TRUE FRIEND A BLESSING.

How sweet to find a generous heart
   While roaming through life's giddy throng,
A soul devoid of guile or art,
   To whom all virtuous traits belong.

A firm, a brave, devoted mind,
   Who changes not when ills oppress;
Never ceasing to be kind,
   And then if poor ne'er loves you less.

Ay, when misfortunes shade the brow
   And veil the trusting soul with care,
'Tis sweetly soothing then to know
   You have a friend those woes to share.

But vain and fickle often prove
   Those whom we deem the most sincere;
We find their pity and their love
   As fleeting as the desert air.

THE OLD GARDEN WALL.

DEAR ruin, how I love thee, in thy ivy-mantled power,
For thy beauty now reminds me of many a gone-by hour,
When youth and hopes were brightest, and life was free
      as air,
And visions hung the lightest o'er the brow that knew
      no care!

Thy old gray arches tell me of many a fairy scene;
Though changes have befell me, sad changes they have
          been;
The mind, with fond devotion, loves to linger o'er the
          past,
For memory, like the ocean, swells and surges to the
          last.

What sunny days of pleasure hang around the spring of
          youth,
When innocence, sweet treasure, lights our pathway up
          with truth,
And friendship smiles endearing give rapture to the
          heart,
Each passing moment cheering, free from all disguise or
          art !

Remember do I truly, when my romping days were done,
And I ceased to be unruly, who my first affections won;
It was my own dear Jesse, the fair boy at the mill,—
He was the youth to bless me, and I think I see him still.

How oft at twilight hour, when the summer skies were
          clear,
And many a beauteous flower sent its odors through the
          air,
Have we wandered through the wood, through the bower
          and the hall,
And many a time we stood 'neath thy ivy-mantled wall!

And many a shining cluster of rich and purple fruit,
The brightest we could muster, our happy hearts to suit,
Would we gather all so merry, then hasten to the bower,
To sip the lucious berry and talk friendship by the hour.

But dreams of youth are winning, as moments steal
  apace:
All things have a beginning in every sphere or place;
And thus our hearts united from friendship into love,
Till Jesse dear invited me his honored bride to prove.

And many are the hours long gone or past away,
Since joyous youth and power gave its vigor to the day;
Yet seasons though they vanish and changes still appear,
There is naught our love can banish though our age is in
  the sear.

And still we love to wander 'neath the dear old garden
  wall,
At its climbing beauties wonder, and heavy moss withal,
Yet think the glowing tracing in its twining, tottering
  age,
Is like myself and Jesse — sinking, slowly from life's
  stage.

----- ⚘ -----

WHAT WOULDST THOU HAVE?

WHAT wouldst thou crave? would riches be
· A source of light and joy to thee?
    I pray thou wilt beware!
  They are allurements truly vain,
  That many a noble heart hath slain
    And doomed to deep despair.

Wouldst thou have honors in the field,
Where deeds of valor often yield
    A gory, ghastly sight?

'Tis not the clarion blast of war
That can make bright thy setting star,
   Or cheer death's coming night!

Wouldst thou to festive scenes repair,
To find unshaken pleasures there?
   A phantom thou wilt find:
Not all the gilded rosy hours
That fain would strew thy path with flowers
   Will yield thee peace of mind.

'Tis not in homes of stately form,
Or kindling smiles of friendship warm,
   Can render sweet repose;
Not palaces, nor wealth, nor power,
Nor martial mighty deeds of war,
   Thy hours in peace will close!

Alas! how vain are fleeting joys,
Which rolling time so soon destroys!
   They vanish like a dream.
A few short changes mark our day,
When life is found to ebb away
   Like snowflakes on a stream.

Then let us turn with feelings true,
While holy wisdom guides us through,
   To that sweet Lamb of Love!
Who calls in bleeding mercy still,
That all obedient to His will
   May share His bliss above!

THE ANGEL'S CHOICE.

A SPIRIT of bliss, in a curtain of light,
Came down on the voiceless bosom of night
And wandered invisible, searching to find
A subject most holy and pure to her mind.

She traversed the earth in a passion of love,
Such as the bright order of angels approve,
And touched her light foot with a magical bound
Where she thought the sweet treasure of bliss might be
    found.

The world was all hushed in its dreamy repose,
And scarcely a sound on the deep silence rose,
Save the hum of an insect or evening bird,
In the lonely night watch, was now to be heard.   .

She paused as she gazed on the slumbering world,
Then pressed her bright brow with glory impearled,
Invoking instruction which way to pursue
To find what was beautiful, perfect, and true.

She listened, a sound came up on the air—
It was a sweet maiden in wrestling prayer—
From the chamber of death where a dear mother lay,
Whose spirit was rapidly ebbing away.

Her features, like marble, were chaste to behold,
For Heaven had formed her in beauty's own mould,
Were bathed in a deluge of beautiful tears,
As bright as the dew of the morning appears.

4

Then silent and noiseless the messenger flew
From the chamber of death, her way to pursue,
For she found the fair maiden, though truthful and pure,
Was not the bright tribute she wished to secure.

And now with a trip that was light as the air
That tunefully sweeps o'er the gossamer's snare,
She flourished her plumes, then winged her lone way
To search for the treasure without more delay.

And soon a grand palace arose to her view,
And thither the heaven-born messenger flew,
For there the soft echo of music arose,
Like the harp spirits song over midnight repose.

For there as the lingering melody hung,
It told a sweet story of two beings young,
Whose union of bliss Hymen's fetters had wove,
And joined in a triumph of holiest love.

Affection so pure was a beautiful theme,
Yet was not the spotless treasure supreme,
The angel of glory would hold as a prize
To carry exulting away to the skies.

Then again the sweet messenger turned from the sphere
Where music and harmony hung on the ear,
And hastened to where a bright, loved infant lay,
As fair as the beauties of opening day!

On the breast of the mother the little one slept,
While an innocent smile o'er its fair features crept,
She thought in a transport the boy had been given
As one of the holiest gifts under heaven.

She gazed on the stainless creature, and soon
She made up her mind it would be the right boon,
When, waving her wing o'er its slumbering brow,
She bore it away from this dark world of woe.

The mother now knew that her darling was blest,
Though hastily wrung from her unconscious breast,
For lo! the bright morning revealed to her sight
Her beautiful offspring had died in the night.

VALENTINE FAIR,

OR

LOVE IN DISGUISE.

SAID Mary to Minty, "I tell you what,
    While you are thus moping there,
You have in your indolent mood forgot
    To day is the Valentine Fair!

"The beaus and belles are tripping away
    To the village behind the hill,
To purchase a ribbon or billet-doux gay,
    With a merry and right good will.

"For now is the time for hearts and darts
    And Cupids with golden wings,
For Love knows how to carry his arts
    'Neath paper and silken strings.

"Such billing and cooing, in earnest or fun,
    Is pleasing enough to be sure,
But as for a beau, you or I have got none,
    'Tis horrid the thought to endure!

"Then let us away to the Valentine Fair,
　　Nor mope in the cottage forever;
Who knows but a happy gallant may be there
　　That may think you or I very clever?

"And thus ere the sun shall sink in the sky,
　　And nature is hushed to repose,
A billet of love to our cottage may fly,
　　Bound up in some blessing—who knows!"

"Oh! hush, dearest Sis! how little you know!"
　　The innocent Minty replied;
"I've got something here I could very soon show,
　　Which caused me to laugh till I cried.

"Don't measure my fate by your own,
　　Or think I no lover can find;
If we do live secluded and lone,
　　I've long found a youth to my mind.

"And here near my heart is his vow,
　　In a valentine penciled in gold;
I received it, my sister, just now,
　　When you were not here to behold."

"A valentine! sister, you joke!
　　It cannot be true what you say!
If so I am ready to choke,
　　That you would be sly in this way!

"For never a man has been here
　　To tarry an hour, you know,
Save the young village pastor, Moclear,
　　And he never came as a beau."

"Yes, yes, but he did, sister mine!
　He loves with a bosom sincere;
The same way my feelings incline,
　And thus we're a lovable pair."

Oh! horror of horrors! the frown
　That rose to that petulant brow,
Told Mary was near overthrown,
　Yet to hide it she could not tell how.

For long she had loved in disguise　.
　The parson, yet never dare name
A passion so hopeless, unwise,
　Lest she would be scorned for the same.

A dream the most foreign, ne'er told
　Her heart that the pastor would deign
To choose from so humble a fold
　A damsel to love and maintain.

Thus terrible was it, to hear
　That Minty had gathered the prize,
Would be married in less than a year
　To one who was holy as wise.

Poor Mary from that very hour
　Felt all her hopes wither and fade;
She ne'er spoke of valentines more,
　And died in the end an old maid!

4*

THE TRIUMPH OF GENIUS.

GENIUS! thou fair and early boon of Heaven,
Bestowed on man while yet the world was young,
The kindest and the holiest treasure given
Since light hath over God's creation hung!

When first the morning stars together sang
With joy exulting o'er the birth of time,
And heavenly courts with rapturous praises rang,
Thyself was heard to join the hymn sublime.

The muses, in their youthful beauty, flew
From plains celestial to this new-born sphere,
While God Apollo soon the graces drew
Around his heart by music soft and clear.

And who had taught the winning god to charm
The lovely nymphs by sweeping thus his lyre,
Or thrilled their spirits with devotion warm
By sacred breathings of poetic fire?

'Twas thou, fair maid, in classic glory dressed,
Taught him the tuneful honors and the bliss
Of gaining votaries, which the god caressed,
Thus won his laurels in a world like this.

A boon of Heaven we call thee: so thou art,
A portion of the deity divine!
He whose broad wisdom formed creation's chart
Crowned thee the goddess of fair learning's shrine.

And thy first impulse given unto man
    Was in blest Eden, God's own planted bower,
When Adam craved thy skill, and formed the plan
    Of sewing *fig leaves*, in his erring hour.

Since then what vast advances hast thou made,
    As time has winged his rapid course along!
What greatness and what triumph own thy aid!
    And often hast thou graced the poet's song!

The gods have mused thy lovely wonders o'er,
    Ere mighty Greece and towering Athens rung
With heathen fables, or with ancient lore,
    And praised the music of thy gifted tongue.

Ere learning swelled the scientific page,
    And, like a sea, o'er lofty cities spread,
Thou hadst walked forth on nature's glowing stage,
    And glory followed where thy movements led.

Yes, ere Olympic ages sought to rule,
    Or empire greatness rose with strength unfurled,
Thy power in nature's young and modest school
    Was destined to arouse, amaze the world!

Bright were the flashings of thy beauteous eye,
    Dispelling gloom that hung o'er Egypt's plains;
Before thy form did fabled darkness fly,
    And superstition burst her slavish chains.

Thus, while Olympic greatness and renown
    Through empires spread, and walked the courts of
        kings,
'Twas thou, fair goddess, ruling from thy throne,
    That scattered wisdom from thy classic wings!

And taught the heroes in fame's early school
    The daring feats of chivalry and pride,
And though the power of tyranny would rule,
    New elements of learning were supplied,

Till valor bore the impress of thy sway,
    And dextrous freaks were but too proudly won,
When the brave gladiator gained the day,
    Or to the earth a lifeless corse was thrown.

And then what noisy shoutings, long and loud,
    Went up upon the hot and stifling air
From the assembled, dark, admiring crowd,
    In vain applause to greet the dying ear!

For, Genius, thou hadst lent thy civic art,
    And led to combat frames with vigor strong;
Each gladiator practiced well his part,
    But then if vanquished, felt too deeply stung.

And now we trace thee to the plains of war ·
    Of Thessaly, or ancient Greece or Rome,
Where loud was heard the eagle's screams afar,
    That told of bloody and of darkening doom!

Yes, Rome! fair city of exalted might,
    Whom classic Greece had gladdened with its lore,
Where virgin graces moved with sweet delight
    Among thy temples crowned with civic power.

The wars of ages are a mournful theme
    Which bards have sung in rolling seasons past;
But thou, O Rome! was foremost in the scene
    Which hath a gloom upon thy history cast.

Thy fallen temples and thy mystic shrines
  Long crumbling in the dust of ages gone,
Or ivy now each mouldering ruin twines
  With foliage rank, deserted and alone,—

All tell a tale of solemn usage fled,
  When Genius there reigned lofty and supreme,
When deeds of valor crowned the victor's head,
  Who did with bright and noble honors teem.

Loud from the Forum rang brave Cicero's voice,
  And Cato, or a Cesar in their turn,
Or gentle Scipio, oft the people's choice,
  Whose spirits did with fearless ardor burn.

But vain would be the effort now to trace
  Thy beamings mighty o'er the soul of men,
For since the world hath known its power or place,
  Thyself hath wandered even now, as then,

Save more revealed in beauty every hour,
  While keeping passage with the march of time,
Letting thy glory, still incessant, lower
  In works and deeds with eloquence sublime.

What though the age of Plutarch now is past,
  When Roman authors spent their classic lore,
And orators of princely worth and caste—
  Have we not many—great as those before?

Greater than Dionysius or Polybius, sure,
  Or Ibid, and all others in their train,
Have rose to fame with laurels won secure,
  And thousands more her lofty heights shall gain.

While thou, fair Genius, prompts the froward mind
　To grand results, from youth to silvered age,
All arts, each science through thyself designed,
　Must roll advancing o'er life's fragile stage,—

Until the wreck of worlds proclaim the end
　Of all things here of sublunary reign,
When loud Jehovah's trump its warning sends,
　And calls this earth to chaos back again.

If not too void, at least a form be given
　Of holy origin and blissful joy,
Created into one unchanging heaven,
　Eternity itself cannot destroy.

HOPE.

What generous thoughts persuasive rise
　Upon the throne of feeling,
To throw soft light o'er reason's skies,
　The bliss of hope revealing!

E'en while misfortunes come apace,
　To shroud the soul in sadness,
When Hope unveils her smiling face,
　Our spirits drink in gladness.

The sunlight of her beauteous brow,
　All radiant with kindness,
Comes beaming o'er this vale of woe,
　To cheer our moral blindness.

For often gloomy passions sway
   Our better traits of reason,
Yet soon can Hope's delightful ray
   Dispel the cloudy season.

Thou art an angel surely sent
   To lift up hearts despairing,
Too oft with disappointments rent
   That come with visage daring.

Yes, crushing in some fatal hour
   Each trusting dream we cherished,
When thou, sweet Hope, with gentle power,
   Revives what nigh had perished.

And thus it is, thou nymph divine,
   When sorrow veils our nature,
If thy persuasive light but shine,
   Thou gladdenest every feature.

Then ever let thy anchor rest,
   With heavenly luster beaming,
Within my sad and stricken breast,
   While at thy altar kneeling.

And should stern disappointments fall
   Around life's moments given,
Do thou, 'mid time's rude changes all,
   Point me the path to heaven.

TO THE OCEAN.

Roll on, ye mighty billows, roll,
   Sublimely grand and free,
Subject alone to God's control
   And heaven's immensity!

What nameless wonders lie concealed
   Beneath your voiceless bed,
To lofty science unrevealed,
   Through countless ages fled!

Lo! down beneath your foaming waves,
   Rich groves of coral grow,
And mermaids sport through diamond caves
   With fair and beauteous brow.

And there doth august silence reign, ·
   Mid dreamless depths profound,
While onward rolls the raging main,
   With wild and boisterous sound.

Oh! that the mind, by magic spell,
   Could walk that hidden sphere,
What grand results it then might tell
   To wondering mortals here!

Perchance of music strangely sweet,
   Soft breaking on the ear,
While glad and answering echoes meet
   Mid crystal caverns there;

Or bands of naiads fair and bright,
    Swift dancing from their cells,
On pearly wings and tiptoe light,
    With wreaths and silver bells.

Is there a world so grand unseen
    Beneath old ocean's span,
That hath for countless ages been
    Still unrevealed to man?

'Tis even so.   Those scenes sublime
    Are closed from mortal view;
Yet picture we God's works divine
    With fancy pure and true.

And thus the mind is nobly taught:
    All grand creations prove
The whole are by Jehovah wrought
    In wisdom, power, and love.

Roll on then, mighty ocean, roll,
    Sublimely grand and free,
Subject alone to God's control
    And heaven's immensity!

5

A BALLAD.

I WISH I WERE A KNIGHT.

I WISH I were a valiant knight
In coat of burnished mail,
With brazen helmet shining bright,
And purse that would not fail!

And had a courser brave and good,
With trappings rich and gay;
He should be of Arabian blood,
And either black or gray.

I then would hurry to the wars,
And, by my bravery there,
Gain golden honors and applause,
To win some lady fair.

She should be beautiful as bright,
With spirit fond and free,
Just worthy such a valiant knight
As I would prove to be.

I'd lay my honors at her feet,
I'd kiss her snowy hand,
And then a thousand vows repeat,
Such as came at command.

I'd tell her she was passing fair,
And beautiful as true,
As bright as heaven's morning star
To my enraptured view.

And thus while bowing at her shrine
With eloquence and pain,
Would press the angel to be mine,
Nor let me sue in vain.

And if she gave one look of scorn,
I'd swear by earth's decree,
Or by my lofty helmet worn,
Revenged I'd surely be.

And calling romance to my aid,
Thus baffled in desire,
My gauntlet hand should not be stayed—
I'd quench the maddening fire.

At least I'd tell the pretty prude
Who bound me thus in chains,
If still I sadly, vainly sued,
I would blow out my brains.

And thus a deed of daring claim,
Knight-errant vows to keep,
Securing thus a valiant name,
And make the damsel weep.

But here my master comes, I see!
Avaunt with princely dreams—
I'm doomed a servant still to be,
Or yet his groom, it seems!

But when I see his lofty air,
His helmet plumed and bright,
His polished mail and armor glare,—
I wish I were a Knight!

THE MARINER.

THE mariner looks on the rolling wave
  With a bosom that's bounding and true,
And feels that many a sailor brave
  Lies hidden there—far from view.

Yes, down in those sea-girt caves below,
  There slumbers the ocean child
That struggled through many a hurricane blow
  When storms were raging wild.

His bones lie bleaching far beneath,
  Enshrouded in sea-weeds green,
And bind round his forehead the chaplet of death,
  As a tribute for what he had been.

The roar of the deep and the sea-bird's scream
  Is the dirge o'er the mariner's grave;
While the diamond and pearls on his shroud may gleam,
  'Tis worthy the true and the brave.

Sweet affection's kiss and the parting tear
  He shared, when he left his home,
And fancied a moment of meeting bliss
  Would fall to the sailor's doom.

But no! the solemn, the sad farewell,
  That hung on his faithful ear,
Proved but the deep, the withering knell,
  That he never again would appear.

That bark, which so often had battled the gale
    And weathered the howling storm,
Was wrecked, to make known the maddening tale,
    While the waves covered over his form.

No cowardly fear enthroned his breast
    When peril and danger were nigh;
He lived a hero, with true courage blest,
    Nor feared, like a hero, to die.

Thoughts waken'd, tis true, in his manly heart,
    Those forms he worshiped so well,
And he felt the gushing of warm tears start
    As he whispered his last farewell.

But what was the blessing that buoyed him up
    When the figure of death brooded o'er him?
It was the sweet treasure, the mariner's hope,
    That beamed in its beauty before him.

To God the eternal, the spirit adored,
    He looked with an eye of devotion,
And felt for their sakes his prayer would be heard,
    As he sank in the blue rolling ocean.

The mariner's hope! 'tis sweet to the soul,
    When the last ties of nature must sever;
He knows, though the mountain waves over him roll,
    His spirit will flourish forever!

And firm in his faith, he values it true,
    When the trump shall awaken the dead,
He will rise up, with countless millions in view,
    From his silent and watery bed.

5*

'Tis the hope of the Christian, on land or sea,
   That makes the soul fearless and brave,
While it points to a world, ever joyous and free,
   Beyond the dim bounds of the grave.

THE FIRST WRONG.

WHEN once the heart inclines to folly
   And shuns the voice of sacred truth,
How soon it leads to acts unholy,
   To cloud the paths of lovely youth!

The first sad step will often cling
   Around the portals of the mind,
And many a dark excuse will bring,
   That falsehood may a refuge find.

But veil a lie oft as you will,
   Another follows in its train;
To hide the first you lie on still,
   Which sinks the soul in deeper pain.

"To err is human," well we know;
   Yet brave are those, in age or youth,
Who proudly scorn to stoop so low
   As love a lie before the truth.

GOD'S NOBLEST WORK.

WHAT IS IT?

Is it the vast and roaring sea,
  With billows tossing mountains high,
Or like a mirror, smooth and free,
  Reflecting back the clear blue sky?

Is it creation, spreading wide,
  'Unfolding all her chaste designs,
Or hidden wealth on every side,
  Where many a mystic wonder reigns?

What treasures vast, supremely grand,
  Lie deep beneath earth's surface fair!
New glories rise on every hand,
  Which God's eternal impress bear.

Down, down, beneath the ocean waves,
  Far, far, concealed from human eye,
What coral groves, what diamond caves,
  And pearls in rich profusion lie!

Mid dark eternal silence there,
  What voiceless millions crowd the deep!
What wonders populate that sphere,
  And seeming in oblivion sleep!

Unfathomed mystery enshrines
  The unveiled grandeur of the main,
Lo! there, what golden luster shines
  Beyond the power of man to gain!

And is it in the rolling deep,
　Where countless finny millions move,
Where merry dolphins sport and leap,
　And mermaids unmolested rove,

That God's most noble work we trace,
　Mid depth and silence unrevealed?
Or through the wisdom of his grace,
　Is it o'er heaven's starry field,

Where roving worlds of beauty bright,
　In endless luster gem the sky,
Or in the sun's grand blaze of light,
　That mortals' sternest gaze defy?

Say, is it on this earthly sphere,
　Where mountain forests proudly grow,
And fertile vales in bloom appear,
　And fruits and flowers transcendent glow?

Or while we scan creation o'er,
　And see her beauties chaste unfold,
Whether along the pearl-strung shore
　Or in her treasured mines of gold,—

Can we God's noblest work descry
　In these creations, grandly true,
Where ceaseless wonders seem to vie
　In every charm that meets our view?

Nay, nay! 'Tis man He hath proclaimed
　The holiest of His great design;
'Tis man He in his wisdom named
　The mightiest here on earth to reign.

And all creation moves sublime,
  By God's all-wise revealed control,
Save man, who trifles with his time,
  And with his sadly erring soul.

The lovely seasons come in turn;
  They bloom and early pass away,
And day and night bid mortals learn
  They strict Jehovah's voice obey:

The tulip, from its dusty bed,
  All painted springs to human view,
Obedient to the voice that said—
  Bloom, beauteous floweret, and be true:

The tempests and the storms reveal
  His grandeur, strength, and power;
But to their bounds he sets His seal,
  That they no further lower:

The winds and hurricanes that blow
  Are subject to His sovereign nod;—
All earth obedient learns to know
  And fear, save stubborn man, his God!

ON THE CLOSE OF THE YEAR.

EXTEMPORE.

THE old year now is going out,
   The new one coming in,
And all things wear a change throughout
   This world of care and sin.

Yet while we look upon the past,
   And scan those moments gone,
Can conscience say we spent the last
   As Christians should have done?

Oh! what a solemn thought is this
   To wake the dreaming mind,
Since we the good so often miss
   And feel to err inclined!

What perils and what trials creep
   Across life's rugged way!
Some hearts through woe have waded deep,
   By folly led astray.

And some have seen the glad'ning star
   Of peace and plenty rise
O'er homes of love, and friends afar,
   And grown a year more wise.

And some have gone, and silent sleep
   Beneath the voiceless sod;
While loving friends are left to weep,
   They're harping praise to God.

And some—how horrible the thought!—
  Have left this mortal sphere
For worlds with endless sorrow fraught,
  To reign a demon there !

Oh! God of sweet eternal might,
  We own thy potent power ;
'Tis thou can set frail wanderers right,
  And bid them sin no more.

Where'er our human steps hath erred,
  Throughout this parting year,
Let now thy gentle voice be heard,
  And pardoning smile appear.

Receive our thanks for gifts bestowed
  By thy indulgent hand ;
We know all good from thee hath flow'd
  O'er our devoted land.

Then guard us through the coming year,
  And through all future time;
Our fate, let no misfortunes sear,
  Or stain our souls with crime.

Thus, when the final trump shall sound
  To wake the sleeping dead,
We may among the blest be found,
  With thou, our fountain head.

MY JESSAMINE VINE.

DULL winter has sped on its ice-covered wings,
    And spring draws apace, tho' young in her power,
And scarcely revealed are the offerings she brings
    In woodland or valley, or garden-trained bower.

Yet while in my chamber I musingly write
    An ode to her beauty, or magical shrine,'
My sense of devotion is cheered by the sight
    Of my clustering evergreen jessamine vine.

Ay, through the chill season of tempest and storm,
    When bleak came the winds from each northern hill,
Above me it reared its bright, beautiful form,
    And proudly flourished and blossomed on still.

Each day I have watched it with tenderest care,
    As sweet budding germs opened fresh to my view,
And now its rich blossoms, so golden and rare,
    Fall round me like spangles all burnished and new.

And many's the sheet from the spotless quire,
    Spread out neath its branches to favor my muse,
Or yet it may be my poetic desire
    Beneath it my sanctum of study to choose.

But down came the beautiful petals apace,
    Like snowflakes, though painted, upon my white page,
Or would gently hit me a tap in the face,
    To knock off a thought either witty or sage.

Ay, many's the nervous and timorous start
  I've given in moments of musing profound,
When naught of its presence swept over my heart,
  Till shaking its lovely blossoms around,

And then, like a poor little terrified hare—
  I own it with shame—though no coward I be,
Its touch hath nigh caused me to spring from my chair,
  And make a sad blot, ay, perhaps two or three.

Yet, ah! my sweet vine, thou art fair to behold;
  On every germ Heaven's finger I view:
It painted thy beautiful clusters of gold,
  And tells me that naught but the Author is true.

----*----

THE HORRORS OF WAR.

The loud din of battle was heard
    Booming over the plains of the West,
And many a patriot stirred
    With valor the truest and best.

At the sound of the tap of the drum
    And the clarion's echoing call
They rush, while each note bids them come
    To victory's triumph or fall.

With spirits exulting and brave,
    They rouse at the martial appeal,
Their country and freedom to save,
    And a soldier's privations to feel.

Ah, yes! while the war dogs afar
   Howl over the Mexican plains,
They fly to the dangers of war
   With the proudest of blood in their veins.

Shall we tell of the tears that were shed,
   Of the sighs that are painfully breathed
O'er the wounded, the lost, and the dead,
   By parents and kindred bereaved?

Oh, no! let us draw a dark veil
   Over ruins so mournfully sad;
Let us hide from the horrible tale,
   Lest pity and reason go mad.

Yet, no! 'tis best to be told,
   Tho' we shrink from the death booming knell,
Those hearts were the brave and the bold
   That soon on the battle-field fell.

How many through valor and zeal
   Left all that was dear to their life,
The direst anguish to feel,
   A mother, a sister, a wife;

A father, a brother, a friend,
   Or children so loving and pure,
Their country's call to attend,
   And the horrors of war to endure!

"To conquer or die" was their theme:
   They hung on the motto with pride;
Some lived through the terrible scene,
   Some breathed it and valiantly died.

And some were a desolate band ;
 No parents or kindred had they
To clasp them with love by the hand,
 Or friendship's devotions to pay.

Yet bravely they fought on the field
 Where carnage her horrors displayed,
And died too, before they would yield,
 Or suffer their honor to fade.

What though not a bosom survives,
 One tear of regret to bestow;
There's a Power above never dies,
 That will watch o'er His creatures below !

And those who have valiantly won
 The evergreen laurels of fame,
Whether father, a brother, or son,
 He will blazon with triumph their name.

A spot and a home for the dead
 Is reserved for the good and the true,
High over their gory-stained bed,
 With eternity's glories in view !

STANZAS.

EXTEMPORE.

COME, welcome, bright and rosy dream,
　That pencils fairy, laughing hours,
When joys fell o'er life's sunlit stream,
　To waken naught but gladdening powers.

Yea, moments past, forever gone,
　Yet left their lingering glow remain
In living hues, on memory drawn,
　To call their beauty back again.

Yes, phantoms flash before the mind
　To prompt the light, unconscious smile,
As dreamy thoughts admittance find,
　And venturous round our senses coil.

But then too soon the spell is broken,
　The happy vision fades away,
As though by some vile, envious token,
　To cloud in night our joyous day.

The ghost of saddened changes bring
　To mind a deep and painful gloom,
For mournful sorrows leave a sting
　Which oft attends us to the tomb.

ODE TO DAY.

THE orient blush of day behold,
Lit up with beauteous blue and gold,
　　Aurora mounts the skies:
High o'er imperial fields of space,
In all his majesty and grace,
　　Sol's golden chariot flies.

See! rolling clouds of silver meet
And gather round his glittering feet
　　And form a liquid throne;
Yet on he still directs his speed,
Until he runs his course decreed,
　　Or seeming scans earth's zone.

All hail, sweet day! thy cheering light
Throws off the dusky bars of night,
　　That shroud a dreamy world!
And grand art thou, and glorious too,
When thy bright robes of gold and blue
　　O'er nature is unfurled.

Dash on, thou august, beauteous mien,
While summer genial and serene
　　Now courts thy generous rays;
And other seasons, as they roll,
Must claim thy light from pole to pole,
　　Till time shall quench thy blaze.

6*

'TIS EVEN SO!

HAPPY, happy is the heart
    That knows no brooding ill,
That every moment acts its part
    By Heaven's approving will.

When every season as it flies
    Brings joy and inward peace,
Lifting us upward to the skies
    As righteous hours increase.

'Tis then that sweet creations wear
    A thousand glowing charms,
As onward rolls each fleeting year
    Bereft of sin's alarms.

But, ah! when mortals erring prove,
    To please the wayward mind,
They forfeit Heaven's eternal love,
    And sweet protection kind.

Yet ever pitying, loving, true,
    He guards each passing hour,
Where'er our wandering steps pursue,
    Exposed to Satan's power.

And oft mid danger and despair
    His precious arm is thrown
Around our thoughtless moments here,
    And saves us as His own.

Alás! that mortals should profane
   The trusting love of Heaven,
By sinning o'er and o'er again,
   Though countless times forgiven.

But thus the wayward spirit strives
   Against its lofty God;
It still in stern rebellion lives,
   Nor fears his chastening rod.

Forgive us, sweet Omnipotence,
   Nor hide thy angel face;
Let love enshrine our every sense,
   Renewed in every grace;

That when the dream of life is past,
   Our ransomed spirits, free,
May reach that heavenly bourn at last
   To live and dwell with Thee.

THE SLAVE'S COMPLAINT.

'TIS the voice of the slave, as he folds on his breast
   His hands, in devotion and prayer;
His eyes on the heavens now tearfully rest,
   And his visage is stamped with despair.

"How precious is freedom!" he mournfully cries;
   "Its pleasures unfettered and kind;
While no master the flesh-scourging lash e'er applied,
   And no galling chains fetter the mind.

" These manacles sadly ring on my ear,
    I shrink from their dull, clanging tones;
While the weight of these chains my poor body tear,
    And my feet burst and bleed on the stones.

"Alas! it was not always thus my sad fate,
    For once I was joyous and free;
With kindred and friends my bliss was replete,
    And my little ones sat on my knee.

" My loved Izabada, sweet wife of my heart,
    And three darling children were mine,
But the traffic man came and tore us apart,
    And doomed us in slavery to pine.

"But where is that wife, those children so dear?
    Oh God! they asunder are torn!
They are far, far away, no more to appear,
    And I live thus their loss still to mourn.

"Yes, loved Izabada! no more shall I see
    Thy soul-speaking smile, or hear thy sweet voice
That once was so joyous, so happy, and free,
    That thy own Zoriamba was prone to rejoice.

" Our dear little children, how smiling they grew!
    With what rapture their arms around me they flung!
'Twas then all my hours on glad pinions flew,
    Nor a pang of rude sorrow my poor bosom wrung.

"And oh! I remember our vine-bowered cot,
    Overhung by the mango and tall waving palm;
What bliss and contentment then sweetened our lot,
    While lovingly basking in sunshine and calm!

" But, alas ! for the changes that came o'er our fate
   When the blood-thirsty kidnapper tore us apart,
Set fire to our hut, when, through scourging and hate,
   We felt the thonged lash striking deep in our heart !

" But hushed was the wail of our piteous grief,
   For the gag pressed so painfully on our poor tongue
That death would have proved a most welcome relief,
   Had then our hearts bursted, so bleedingly wrung !

"Adieu, Izabada, adieu evermore !
   Farewell my sweet innocents, God be your friend !
Though you dwell far away on some foreign bound shore,
   May his mercy and blessings upon you descend.

" Though your fate is shut out from my agonized view,
   Perhaps you now writhe under torture and pain
From some hard-hearted master, whose voice and lash
     too,
   But serve you more cruel the more you complain.

" Oh, God ! give me patience my pangs to endure,
   For memory galls me e'en more than my chains,
And renders my wretchedness far more secure,
   While the proud blood of Africa flows in my veins !

" Yet here must I toil 'neath the hot, burning sun,
   Far out of the reach of humanity's voice ;
E'en when my laborious day's work is done,
   I have nothing but misery left to my choice.

" For if I could please but the lord of the soil,
   While the sweat drops of anguish start cold from my
     brow,
I would willingly suffer through torment and toil,
   If pleasure I could to my master bestow.

"But, oh! may that power which tempers the storm,
    Yet soften his bosom so callous, severe,
And the light of the Gospel reveal in its form,
    The duty we owe to humanity here.

"But see! there's a vessel approaching the shore,
    Her white snowy sails they flap in the air;
A female I see, with three children or more,
    And if I mistake not my master is there!

"'Tis strange, passing strange! my heart beats aloud!
    My brain, sure, is burning—ah! what do I see?
It is Izabada I view in the crowd,
    And my three darling children returning to me!"

They now spring on land with tear-streaming eyes,
    Led forth by the master once cruel and vain,
While the heart-piercing screams of their happy sur-
        prise
    Were sufficient to burst every bosom in twain.

"And now, Zoriamba, list, list! while I speak,"
    Said the soul-stricken master, and knocked off his
        chains,
While a tear of contrition hung on his brown cheek;
    " Thou art no more a slave here to toil on these plains.

" Thy prayer hath gone up where the angels reside,
    And often I've listened when thou wert alone,
Or thought that none other had heard thee beside,
    Yet thy pleadings hath softened this bosom of stone.

" Yes, Abraham's God hath taught me to feel
    The holding of creatures in bondage a crime,
And did by the light of the Gospel reveal
    The beauty of mercy and glory divine!

"I then, with exertions unceasing and true,
    Endeavored to find on a tropical coast
Your wife and your children, and bring them to you,
    When you thought in your soul they forever were lost.

"I traced them, and bought them with treasures of gold,
    And now I restore them with blessings sincere;
You may live many years, sunny joys to behold,
    And never have cause for a sigh or a tear.

"Yon hut that you see by the side of the hill,
    Fenced in by a garden of shrubs and sweet flowers,
I give you, as I have bequeathed in my will;
    Go there now and live while a lifetime is yours."

And who shall attempt now to picture the scene
    That followed this Christian devotion of soul?
Too seldom a sight of such greatness is seen,
    Where blessings were mingled with holy control!

And now do you think, dearest reader of mine,
    That all the bright treasures that glow on this earth
Would have purchased those feelings so sweetly divine,
    Which the thoughts of his merciful actions gave
        birth?

Ah, no! if the mines of Golconda had spread
    Before him the wealth of its diamonds so rare,
Or a crown had been offered to blazon his head,
    They could with these dearest of blessings compare.

Thus nothing on earth could afford the delight
    The kind-hearted master now felt in his breast;
He knew he had acted a part that was right,
    And God in his mercy his efforts had blest.

Around him they knelt, in a passion of joy,
　Each breathing a prayer of devotion and love;
'Twas a scene neither ages nor time can destroy,
　For angels recorded the moment above!

———❧———

THE INFANT QUERIST.

" DEAR father," said a beauteous boy,
Who was the parents' pride and joy,
　" You often have assured me
That all the wonders that abound
Above, below, and all around,
Are formed—no matter where they're found—
　By God, the Deity!

" You say from Him all blessings flow
To all his creatures here below;
　That He is good and kind,
And ever lends a pitying ear
To his afflicted children here:
If it is so, my father dear,
　Why is it you are blind?

" For often I have heard you pray,
When on our knees, both night and day,
　That He would give you light!
Nor let unceasing darkness rise
Before your weary, sightless eyes:
Can it be pitying, good, and wise
　To seal you thus in night?

"And mother too! is she not lame,
Who ever calls upon His name
    So lovingly and true?
It seems so very strange to me,
If God can all our sufferings see
And can relieve, how is it He
    Has thus afflicted you?"

" Hold, hold! my son!" the father said,
Patting him gently on the head,
    " The Lord is good and kind!
Thou art almost too young to know
What vast, what wond'rous blessings flow
Upon this thankless world of woe,—
    'Tis best that I am blind!

"And didst thou think, my precious child,"
And as he spoke he sweetly smiled,
    " I asked for earthly sight?
No, no, my son! thy father prayed,
To have his moral blindness stayed,
And be a perfect Christian made
    In all that's pure and right.

" Had not the Lord affliction sent
Upon my mind of discontent,
    To humble sinful pride;
Ere now my heart had stubborn grown,
Becoming far more hard than stone,
Profaning God's eternal throne,
    And unredeemed have died.

7

"And now, my boy, remember this,
That God can never act amiss
     In all afflictions given;
The burden of our trials here,
Though they may be indeed severe,
Are but intended to endear
     Our hearts to Him and heaven!"

———◦◦———

SPRING.

SPRING has opened with her flowers, in her mild and
     sweet array,
Decking woodland, hill, and bowers with her colors rich
     and gay;
And music sweet and swelling is borne upon the air,
All smiling nature telling—'tis a charming time of year.

The pretty birds are winging their way through wood
     and grove,
Their merry anthems singing of blissful joy and love;
The shepherd's pipe is sounding o'er mountain, vale, and
     hill,
While sporting lambs are bounding beside the murmur-
     ing rill.

Yes, joyous looks all nature in its robes of beauty rare
While every glowing feature shows the hand of God is
     there;
From the blossom in the bower to the tree of lofty pine,
We can see his heavenly power as in all things else di-
     vine!

Then welcome, lovely Spring, in thy rosy mild array,
Still thy budding treasures bring though they soon must
    pass away;
A moral in thy mien the noble heart can find,
For a lesson there is seen to improve the musing mind.

The spring of glowing youth, like the season, must de-
    part,
Then well it is, forsooth, if religion fills the heart,
That, like the fading flower of rich and sweet perfume,
We may triumph o'er death's power, and bloom beyond
    the tomb.

SUMMER.

The fervid beams of summer heat
    Oppressive fall around,
And herbage gay and flowerets sweet
    Lie drooping on the ground.

The cattle seek the cooling shade
    Beside the woody hill,
The sheep lie bleating in the glade
    Or by the murmuring rill.

The fields are ripe with golden grain,
    Abundance crowns the soil;
The farmer proudly views his gain,
    Sweet offerings for his toil.

He bears the burden of the day
    Through sultry hours and long,
And tosses up the new-mown hay
    With light, exulting song.

And when he marks the sinking sun .
　　Glide down the western dome,
He joyful views his labor done
　　And seeks his cottage home.

What happy smiles come circling round
　　To greet his weary breast!
'Tis bliss, he feels, to there be found
　　And e'er be thus caressed!

The rural joys of home, how sweet,
　　Mid sunny hills and dales,
Where hearts in glad contentment meet
　　And peace and love prevails!

AUTUMN.

THE autumn leaf, the dingy bough,
　　Proclaim the summer past;
And lonely flowers that linger now,
　　Their bloom is fading fast.

The woodland heights in gay attire
　　Show many a gorgeous hue
For moral fancy to admire,
　　And speak instruction too.

A gloom hangs o'er the pensive grove,
　　So late the scene of song,
Where birds attuned their hearts to love
　　In many a joyous throng.

No more the hedges, robed in green,
    Enriched with summer flowers,
Are round the smiling farmhouse seen,
    And stript are rosy bowers.

The tresseled vine, that proudly grew
    To shade the cottage door,
Or peep the humble lattice through,
    Is seen to bloom no more.

Yes, Autumn's chill and biting breath
    Hath fanned them near and far;
They wear the impress now of death,
    To mark the changing year.

A moral this for one and all:
    Life has its seasons too—
We like these vernal beauties fall,
    And fade from human view.

Like them, beneath God's heavenly sun
    Again expand and bloom,
When time shall tell our course is run,
    And points us to the tomb.

When basking in the Saviour's smile,
    With peace through faults forgiven,
He welcomes us through all our toil
    To live anew in heaven.

Blest immortality divine!
    The Christian's guiding ray;
What sweet, unfading joys are thine,
    Which ope to endless day!

7*

WINTER,

WINTER, winter! cold and drear!
Well we know when thou art here;
Yes, we know thy lonely wail,
Mid descending snow and hail;
Far from many a northern hill
We hear thy voice, bleak and shrill,
Rushing over wood and vale
In thy icy coat of mail,
While thy blighting, frigid breath,
Vernal beauties clasp in death!

Bound by many an icy chain
Is each lovely grove and plain;
Murmuring rills and fountains clear
Wear thy fetters far and near;
Mountain, forest, hill, and dale
Swept are now, by many a gale:
Nature owns thy potent sway,
Bearing thus its charms away.

Winter, winter! bleak and cold,
Thou art gloomy to behold!
Though in sparkling crystals drest,
Bright as gems on beauty's breast,
Still thy frigid breath and touch
Many creatures dreadeth much;
Yea, the wretched, lone, and poor
Fain would keep thee from their door.

While their shivering bosoms pant,
Pressed with hunger, pain, and want,
Vainly from thy breath they shrink,
Creeping through each crack and chink,
Sadly listening to thy wail,
Like some spirit's mournful tale,
Then in wild and boisterous strain;
Again they list, and yet again,
To thy solemn pæans loud,
Rushing from the stormy cloud.

Oh! what anguish fills each breast
Of the wretched and distressed,
When thy blighting presence brings
Want and trials on thy wings!
Well may then the needy pray
For thy reign to pass away,
Since it would be happy cheer
If summer lasted all the year.
Then speed thee, Winter, with thy train;
Hasten, lovely Spring, again!

———⁂———

LOVE DITTY.

CAN I love's rosy dreams forget,
  Those hours of hope and pleasure,
Where first my cottage youth I met,
  My bosom's only treasure?

But now he's gone far, far away,
  My brave and youthful ranger;
Sweet Heaven guide him back, I pray,
  And shield his heart from danger.

Still holy memory brings thee near,
  So kind, so open-hearted;
I see that smile and falling tear,
  As in the hour we parted.

And like soft music's plaintive knell,
  Its pathos sad revealing,
I think I hear thy sweet farewell
  Yet o'er my bosom stealing.

Thus shall affection fond and free,
  No power on earth can sever,
With many a blessing follow thee,
  My own true love, forever!

THE ROBBER.

A TALE OF TRUTH.

" THE moon, I see, is rising fast,
  She's peeping o'er the hill,
Yet not one traveling soul has past;
  The road seems calm and still!

"It must be near the midnight hour,
  And here I linger yet;
I've mused the deed of darkness o'er,
  But still no wanderer met.

"Oh, hunger! thou voracious worm,
    What guilt wilt thou not bring,
If thou but once the vitals storm
    And nature feels thy sting?

" How have I tried from day to day
    To gain a scanty store
Of bread, our hungry mouths to stay,
    And keep woe from our door?

" I never cared how hard the task,
    E'en 'neath a burning sun,
Nor never was too proud to ask
    For more when that was done.

" But though I toiled through snow and rain,
    Beat by the pelting blast,
Our humble daily bread to gain,
    They suffer want at last.

" It is not for myself I care,
    For little I deserve ;
But you, my wife, and children dear,
    I cannot see you starve.

" Here winter pours its northern breath
    Around our lonely cot ;
And now to see you starve to death,
    God knows that I cannot!

" Bread must be had, come as it will ;
    Your precious hearts shall live,
E'en though I stoop to rob and kill,
    Oh, God! forgive, forgive !

"Ah, hunger! thou poor meager worm,
　　Couldst thou not spare a heart
Who never done a creature harm
　　Or played a criminal part?

" But now, oppressed by grief and pain,
　　One effort more I make;
Food my poor children must obtain,
　　Though I some life should take.

" How shall I harden now my soul
　　To do so dark a deed?
I scorn an act so meanly foul—
　　To what will hunger lead!

" Then come some devil to my aid
　　And harden now my heart,
Nerve up my hand—it seems afraid
　　To act the robber's part!

" Ha! what's that? 'Tis but a leaf
　　Just twirling from the bough!
I start, alas! with nervous grief,
　　So fearful am I now!

" If but a squirrel leaves its lair,
　　I turn aside with fright;
And yet no coward's name I bear—
　　In courage I delight!

"And yet, a *coward*, here I stand,
　　With guilty, dark design;
If but some traveler was at hand,
　　His money should be mine!

"His life I do not wish to take—
　His gold is all I want—
And that for those dear beings' sake
　Who now in misery pant.

"But here I've waited many an hour,
　Starting with grief and fear ;
Dark clouds begin to threatening lower,
　Yet not one soul is near.

"Now while I muse upon the fate
　Of those I dearly love,
Who now my presence anxious wait,
　I almost savage prove.

"Then come some devil to my aid,
　Nerve up my heart and hand,
Let want and hunger now be stayed,
　The means I must command!

"Here comes a traveler, now, at last;
　He rides a noble steed ;
The time to question now is past,
　I hasten to the deed."

Now darting from the forest shade
　Into the open road,
Again one hasty spring he made,
　And by the traveler stood ;

He seized the reins with trembling hand,
　And, in a threatening voice,
Loud bid the lonely wanderer stand
　And give his gold of choice.

"Your money, sir, I now must have;
   Deliver it, I pray;
If now you wish your life to save,
   Refuse not to obey!"

He then the loaded pistol raised,
   And pointed to his breast
The muzzle, which the traveler seized,
   And thus the thief addressed:

"Be it for murder or for gold
   You thus my life would seek?
For both before you now behold:
   Speak quickly, robber, speak!

"If gold you want, and that alone,
   Here, take my purse, and go;
If for your guilt it would atone,
   It freely I'll bestow!

"Thou seemest, though, so over-bold—
   Why tremblest thus with fear?
Do I mistake if I behold
   One new in this career?

"I see thy pale and haggard cheek
   Looks touched with grief and care,
Yet out a night so cold and bleak—
   Say, what hath brought thee here?

"It cannot be my life to take—
   No enemy thou art;
And if my gold less want can make,
   Take it with all my heart!

"I'm traveling in this lonely wood
  To find a brother dear;
His cottage, I have understood,
  Cannot be far from here.

"I should have been there hours ago,
  But then I lost my way;
Besides, the road I do not know,
  Since through this wood it lay!

"The moon has hid her welcome light,
  And not one ray appears
To cheer the lonely wanderer's sight
  Or check his rising fears!

"But darkness hovers all around,
  Thick clouds o'erspread the sky;
The wind, too, moans with solemn sound—
  A storm is drawing nigh!

"Then tell me, stranger, who thou art,
  And lead me to thy home;
I will reward the kindly part:
  'Tis now too late to roam.

"Or point me to some friendly shed
  Where I may shelter gain,
And have myself and charger fed,
  Secure from wind and rain!

"Keep thou the gold thou hast in hand;
  To that I will add more,
If thou comply with my demand,
  And show some friendly door!"

8

"Alas! dear sir, you seem so kind,
　　So generous and so free,
Although to rob you I designed,
　　I pray you pardon me!

"'Twas want, yes, haggard want alone,
　　A starving family near,
That almost turned my heart to stone
　　And brought me madly here!

"I once was gentle, true, and brave,
　　Could honest virtues boast;
But fate a bitter wound hath gave,
　　And I am almost lost!

"The hand of penury and grief
　　Spread terror round my home;
I was resolved to find relief
　　And shun a fearful doom.

"My children dear, my angel wife,
　　Are starving day by day;
I love them better than my life,
　　So good, so kind are they!

"But thus to see them wanting bread
　　When I have none to give,
With haggard misery round them spread,
　　Nor can they longer live!

"I gladly toil from morn till night
　　When work I get to do,
And often, sir, till broad daylight
　　Breaks on my weary view!

"But, oh! my God! stern sickness came;
　For months my wife was ill:
Then my sweet children took the same,
　And all are feeble still.

"No work, dear stranger, far nor near,
　My willing hands could find;
Since winter hath set in severe,
　We're thus to woe consigned!

"But let the gods my witness prove,
　My first attempt you've seen;
'Twas naught but poverty that drove
　Me thus to act so mean!

"But, sir, your noble conduct now
　Hath plunged my soul in shame;
This money that you now bestow,
　I keep it in God's name.

"Few kindred, sir, I have on earth,
　I lonely here remain,
Save one dear brother, twin by birth,
　I ne'er may see again.

"Ten years ago he went away
　To some far distant land,
And often have I mourned the day
　We gave the parting hand!

"Dear youth! he was so noble, brave!
　Few hearts were like his own,
For what he had he freely gave
　Where poverty was known.

"And if he knew our solemn fate,
  And of this manless deed,
The miseries too that round us wait,
  His generous heart would bleed.

" But then 'tis well he should not learn;
  Some change I trust to see
In my poor fate ere his return,
  If that should ever be !

"But come, kind sir, I now will lead
  You to our humble cot,
Yet thou wilt find it poor indeed,
  Since misery is our lot !

" Though clean and neat, we can supply
  From this thy friendly gold
Those blessings money e'er can buy,
  Where'er they may be sold."

" Lead on, my friend ! point out the way;
  Thy tale hath pained my heart;
I'll soon thy suffering wants allay,
  And bless thee ere we part !

" Tis passing strange we thus have met !
  Veiled blessings oft descend;
Thy kindness I shall not forget,
  And thou hast found a friend !

"I have a brother somewhere near,
  As I have understood ;
We have not met for many a year;
  He lives beyond this wood !

"They say he leads a farmer's life,
 And owns a pleasant seat;
He has five children and a wife,
 With all things round complete.

"But this I heard long, long ago,
 Through means I can't define;
And yet from him, too well I know,
 I've ne'er received one line!

"When I forsook my native land
 To rove the ocean o'er,
I took a vessel in command
 And sailed from shore to shore.

"I settled in fair India's clime,
 And prospered in my toil;
Sweet pleasure crowned the march of time,
 And riches, too, the soil.

"Years flew apace; I married well,
 A damsel young and fair;
Her gentle heart none could excel—
 We lived a happy pair.

"But death approached with chilly hand
 And tore her from my view,
I then resolved to see the land
 Where my first breath I drew.

"I wrote—yes, o'er and o'er again—
 To him, my brother dear;
Yet all my efforts proved in vain,
 I could no tidings hear.

"At last a thousand doubts arose
　　Upon my troubled brain,
Such as the force of memory throws,
　　Lest we'd ne'er meet again.

" I fancied oft my brother dead,
　　Perhaps in want or woe,
And was resolved once more to tread
　　This land—to learn and know!

" Then, generous stranger, tell me where
　　His homestead I may find;
For even now I should be there
　　To calm my anxious mind!

"His name is Robert Emlin, sir—
　　Why start and turn so pale?
His rustic home, I should infer,
　　Is somewhere in this vale."

" Robert Emlin is my name;
　　Thou dost that brother see;
I am, oh, yes! I am the same—
　　A wretch behold in me!

" Oh! spurn me not! forgive, forgive!
　　I sought thy life to slay:
How can I think of this and live?
　　Forgive me, James, I pray!

" Tis far too painful to be told,
　　At thy return to me,
Thou should'st a robber thus behold
　　Who aimed to murder thee!"

"Hold! hold! dear brother, speak no more;
   'Twas misery urged the deed;
That painful venture now is o'er—
   Let want thy causes plead!

"Wert thou a stranger, rash and bold,
   And asked me to forgive,
Could I my pardoning voice withhold,
   Nor wish thee, blest, to live?

"Nay! nay! then come, my brother dear,
   To this my throbbing breast;
Let all our sadness disappear;
   Set now thy heart at rest.

"Thou art no robber! that vile name
   Thy fate shall never stain;
My soul relieves thee from all blame;
   Thou art thyself again!

"Thy kind, that penitent appeal,
   Hath more than all repaid;
My bosom would be more than steel
   If it could dare upbraid!

"No! no! that was no murderous hand
   Raised at my heart this night!
Why didst thou thus so trembling stand,
   If urged through guilt outright?

"Thy tender nature shrunk within,
   Thy face turned wan and pale;
'Tis haggard want must bear the sin;
   I saw thy courage fail!

"If I had e'en withheld my gold,
  And thou hadst gone to strife,
Thou couldst have never been so bold
  As then to take my life!

"Thy mad'ning rush, thy frenzied air,
  Told desperation's aid;
I saw that wild, unearthly stare;
  'Twas it my anger stayed!

"But something warned my hasty zeal,
  And bid me have no fear,
E'en when I saw the murderous steel
  Close to my breast appear.

"It was the shielding will of Heaven,
  To guard by its decree,
Or, as I hope to be forgiven,
  I should have murdered thee!

"For I was armed: my holsters bore
  Two pistols safely primed;
A dirk within my belt I wore,
  To use when thought well timed!

"So that thy life was at my will,
  If I but choose to slay,
For either had a right to kill
  In self-defense's way.

"But if my anger had now led
  To such a fatal scene,
I should have thought, while memory bled,
  Thy murderer I had been!

" So both have thus in peril stood,
　　Beneath God's shielding care ;
Neither hath seen his brother's blood,
　　Nor hath the sin to bear.

" Then come once more to my fond arms,
　　Thou brother lost so long ;
We'll think not of our wild alarms ;
　　Let rapture be our song !

" Lead on ! lead on to thy rude home ;
　　Why tarry here or stay ?
Thou little knowest the joys to come,
　　What blessings strew thy way.

" The pangs of poverty are o'er ;
　　My wealth is vast and great ;
Thy heart shall share my golden store,
　　With happiness complete !

" It was for this I sought thy cot,
　　In case that thou wert poor,
To bless, without delay, thy lot,
　　Bring gladness to thy door."

But who can now portray the scene
　　That night of bliss bestowed
Within that cottage, thatched and mean,
　　Of all the tears that flowed ?

Of all the blessings then that fell,
　　Or prayers that then went round ?
Not all the bards on earth can tell,
　　Or paint that rapture found.

And years, since then, have rolled away
    'Neath time's consuming urn;
Yet ever have they blessed the day
    That brother did return.

STANZAS.

How beauteous is the summer flower,
    Just opening to the day,
Still moistened by the gentle shower
    That hangs on every spray!

How chaste the early morning's beam,
    Just bursting o'er the sky,
When sunlight glory decks the scene
    With many a golden dye!

And lovely is the tuneful bird
    That chaunts its cheerful song,
When soft and clear its notes are heard
    The vernal bowers among.

And then 'tis sweet at eventide,
    When dusty shadows throw
Their lurid beauty far and wide
    O'er nature's vale below.

Yet sweeter, and more chaste by far,
    Is that devoted hour
When many a bright and beaming star
    The heavens bespangle o'er!

When soft and fair the crescent moon
    Throws out her silver light,
More beauteous than the blaze of noon,
    To crown the hours of night.

Yes, gentle empress, while I view
    Thee sailing far above
In that pure, hallowed vault of blue,
    It wakes my heart to love!

For something in thy visage seems
    So stainless and so true,
That memory turns to holy dreams
    I fain would oft renew.

Yea, thoughts that chasten; yet how kind
    They scan the spirit's throne,
And teach the soul to bear in mind
    The Lord is God alone!

THE BACHELOR'S LAMENT.

Now fifty years old! 'Tis horrid to think,
    A bachelor yet I remain!
And marriage, how often I've been on the brink,
    But as yet not a wife could I gain!

I've traveled the world, in my days, nearly round,
    Seen beauty in every clime;
But the girl of my bosom is yet to be found,
    If a wife is to ever be mine!

A fortune and more, yea, two, have I spent,
  To please all the treacherous fair ;
And as for obliging, the further I went,
  The more I was led in the snare !

So cautious and kind each beauty would seem
  When attentions polite I bestowed,
That life, for a season, passed on like a dream,
  While with it my money too flowed.

While staying in Paris, 'mid scenes of gay life,
  A pretty French damsel I met ;
I strove might and main to make her my wife—
  But the prude I shall never forget.

She feigned to return my ardor sincere,
  And promised to give me her hand,
Then away to the chapel we sought to repair,
  To join the connubial band.

As soon as we got to the door of the priest,
  She bid me a pleasant good-night,
And told me she only was joking the least,
  By the way of a little delight.

I felt rather mean, but rather more mad,
  And back to my chamber I flew,
Resolved not one moment to make myself sad,
  And to blot her from memory's view.

But somehow or other, the treacherous prude
  Had made a deep wound in my heart ;
For days and long nights her ghost would intrude,
  As I mused o'er her whimsical art.

And I thought in my soul what a Stoic I'd live
    From that most detestable hour,
That women so fickle I ne'er would forgive,
    And be caught in their meshes no more.

I ordered my baggage, got into a hack,
    My journey once more to pursue,
Determined that Paris should ne'er see me back,
    And bid merry France then adieu.

I hastened to Germany, thinking that there
    The changes of scenery and sight,
With being among that clime's blooming fair,
    Would bring me once more nearly right.

But, luckless forever! a beautiful maid,
    With eyes of celestial blue,
Once more my most holy affections betrayed,
    And strove my poor heart to undo!

But soon as I found how matters would be,
    For the prude had two strings to her bow;
If she could not get him, she thought to take me,
    And thus her sad cruelty show.

So I left them, and also brave Germany's coast,
    To travel the Indias o'er,
Well pleased while on the ocean rude tost,
    I could boast of my freedom once more.

And now I resolved, in the truth of my soul,
    Where'er I might tarry or stay,
A woman no more my heart should control,
    Though I lived to be fifty times gray.

9

But scarce had I touched that sunny lit soil,
  Than a lovely creature appeared,
The light of the harem; I saw but her smile,
  When my heart with her beauty was seared.

If ever perfection had fell from the skies,
  I thought it must surely be her;
Such features I never beheld with my eyes,
  So classic, so gentle they were.

'Twas over with me, for I plainly saw
  That my heart was already in chains,
For my eyes from her beauty I could not withdraw,
  And love ran like flame through my veins.

And now, through the system of plotting and scheme,
  I won the fair creature at last;
We were to elope, when fairly unseen,
  When Hymen would bind us more fast.

The time was appointed, some very dark night,
  Which would favor our happy design,
When the moon and the stars shut out their soft light,
  Was the season she wished to be mine.

Beneath the high wall of a garden I stood,
  When the hour of appointment drew near;
'Twas midnight, and dark as my grandmother's hood,
  Yet my angel did not yet appear.

But now, 'mid the silence, I thought I perceived
  Some damsel approaching the place—
Yes, a figure I saw, I was not deceived,
  Though I could not discern the sweet face.

Yet, presently, what should I fatally hear
    But the voice of a jealous old Turk,
Dressed up like a female, as such to appear,
    And gave me the point of his dirk.

I instant perceived the terrible snare
    That now so endangered my life,
For a husband enraged, in fact, I had there,
    Instead of his beautiful wife.

Now it happened this creature, so young and so fair,
    Had late been in marriage bestowed
Upon the old Turk, whom her heart could not bear,
    Though his coffers with riches o'erflowed.

And anxious she was those bonds to escape,
    And fly with a soul she could love;
This caused her a step in young romance to take,
    And willingly faithless to prove.

Thus led on benighted, I knew not the truth,
    That she was already a bride,
That the old rich bashaw was her husband forsooth,
    Though the creature she could not abide.

'Twas this that induced her to silent remain,
    Nor my innocent heart undeceive,
Lest knowing, our love would be severed in twain,
    And I very soon take my leave.

But her husband, somehow, suspicious had grown
    On account of her beauty and wit;
He followed her walks, and thus it was known,
    The plan we so fatally hit.

So here, once again, in sorrow I flew,
  With a wound or two more in my breast,
But the one which the point of the dirk gave, I knew
  Was not quite so deep as the rest.

But home I returned to my own native land,
  Resolving that Cupid no more
Should get me in bondage by will or command,
  While I linger on life's busy shore.

And still I am single, and must so remain,
  For to marry seems out of the way,
For, old maids or young, to court them is vain,
  Since they will not have me, or I they.

WRITTEN ON A CLOUDY DAY IN AUTUMN.

SEE the sky with clouds o'erhung!
  The wind is cold and shrill,
And seems to speak, with many a tongue,
  From many a northern hill!

The raindrops fall in lazy tone,
  'Mid shadows dark and drear,
And, mingling with the wind's low moan,
  Proclaim a tempest near.

The storm-bird shakes his heavy wing,
  And screams aloud on high,
While mountain clouds their shadows fling
  Across the frowning sky.

The dingy leaf twirls from the bough
　　That rocks amid the blast,
And hurled promiscuous are they now—
　　Are round earth's altars cast.

So late in vernal beauty clad,
　　Then robed in richest dye,
But now to earth forlorn and sad
　　They seared and scattered lie.

But when the hurricane's rude blast
　　Comes sweeping bleakly o'er,
And snow and sleet fall thick and fast,
　　They'll linger there no more.

And now, while heavy clouds appear
　　To shroud the beauteous sky,
The raindrops fall more fast and clear,
　　And winds more hoarsely sigh.

Yet dearly do I love the day
　　Or night with gloom o'erspread,
When not a sun nor lunar ray
　　Their cheerful luster shed.

It will the thoughtful soul incline
　　To scan life's rugged picture,
And view what storms and woes combine
　　To darken human nature.

But then the sun of joyous light
　　Breaks o'er the spirit's feeling,
Dispelling all the shades of night,
　　Bright hope and bliss revealing.
9*

Thus, like the lovely heavens veiled
  In gloom, a transient while,
If God's sweet presence be but hailed,
  All nature wears a smile.

———⚶———

THE VOICE OF WAR.

HARK! the distant martial strain
  Bursting on the desert air,
Wafted from the battle plain,
  Now it thunders on the ear!

Loud is heard the cry of war,
  Loud the noisy cannon's roar;
Dimmed is freedom's peaceful star,
  Now her banners stream in gore.

Loud the eagle's scream is heard
  From the storm-cloud, soaring high,
Misery writhing, vengeance stirred,
  Flashes from his fiery eye.

Hungry vultures snuff the air,
  Prowling o'er the helpless dead,
Ravenous, darting here and there,
  Ere the soldier's life hath fled.

Noble warriors scattered lie
  O'er the bloody, smoking field;
Valor beams in many an eye
  Ere to tyrant death they yield.

Many an aspiration brave,
　Unuttered in their dying breast,
Sinks into the Hero's grave,
　And with them in silence rest.

Perhaps a husband, father, son,
　Give the winds their parting breath,
Or a lover's course is run,
　Weeping out his blood in death.

Oh! what wishful thoughts arise
　In each anxious, aching heart,
Torn from all they dearly prize,
　Perchance 'neath foreign skies to part.

No pitying life, no gentle voice
　Is there to sooth the warrior's pain;
The battle-field, the soldier's choice,
　Receives the brave, the fallen slain.

Still upon the shrine of fame,
　While long years roll slowly on,
Will hallowed memory carve the name
　Of every noble patriot son!

Record his fate, his battle toils,
　His weariness and gloom,
And treasure up as noble spoils
　To live beyond the tomb.

Peace to their dust! where'er they rest,
　May nature's brightest foliage spread
Its richest bloom upon their breast,
　And deck each brave and dreamless head.

And if a halo bright be given
　　To span the noble hero's grave,
May one, the signal gift of Heaven,
　　Descend upon the gallant brave !

———— ❦ ————

BE CAREFUL WHOM THOU BLAMEST.

Dost thou a fault in others see
　　Of some condemning nature ?
Think well, before thou censure free,—
　　Art thou a sinless creature ?

Be not too hasty to contemn
　　Those minds to error prone;
Perchance the faults thou seest in them
　　May yet imbrue thine own.

Ne'er let the hated frown of scorn
　　Upon thy forehead venture,
To those who are more humbly born,
　　'Tis not a trait to censure.

Nor let the proud, the haughty sneer
　　Rest on the child of sorrow,
Whose lonely, sad, and dark career
　　Hath dimmed the joyous morrow.

Whose hopeless bosom feels o'erhung
　　With gloom and melancholy;
That heart should be no further wrung
　　Which suffers for its folly.

Hast thou more wit, more learning chaste,
  With charms of outward beauty?
Let not on them thy scorn be placed,
  'Tis not the Christian's duty.

For no deformity, I find,
  Is half so base, notorious,
As that well learned, yet haughty mind,
  That stoops to acts inglorious.

Then chide not others more unblest;
  The same hath God created,
Though not in all perfection drest,
  Should not by thee be hated.

No, no! for Heaven is all love,
  A sea of holy kindness;
And where we cold and heartless prove,
  His spirit mourns our blindness.

It is the sound of pity's voice,
  More sweet than music's strain,
Can make the lonely heart rejoice
  And soothe misfortune's pain.

We hear the blind, the halt, the lame,
  In ages past and gone,
Oft to the suffering Saviour came,
  Who did not them disown.

But, no! in meekest faith and love
  He blessed each pleading heart:
Then shall we less devoted prove,
  Nor act the Christian's part?

Nay, nay ! let love and pity e'er
　To sorrowing hearts be given ;
Then may we hope to prosper here,
　And share a home in heaven.

———❧———

HOPES FLATTER.

How oft in life's uncertain vale
Our brightest hopes and prospects fail,
And while we deem all sure and fair,
The flimsy bubble bursts in air !

The wayward fancy still pursues
Some object it may fondly choose ;
Yet seldom do we grasp the prize
Our vain ambition aims to seize.

Thus "Father Time," on rapid wing,
Will e'er some disappointment bring ;
Yet brave the heart, and brave the mind,
That meets opposing ills resigned.

THE BLIND MARINER.

THE ship rolled on the stormy deep,
   The snow-capt waves rose high,
And winds came o'er with howling sweep,
   Thick darkness veiled the sky.

The lightning flew among the shrouds
   That rocked amid the gale;
And sea birds circled in the clouds
   Pregnant with rain and hail.

High on the foaming waters rode
   Our gallant bark amid the storm;
The rain poured down a perfect flood,
   And mists curled round in horrid form.

The dancing hail slid o'er the deck
   Like balls of crystal to our view,
And nothing seemed our speed to check,
   So gallant o'er the waves we flew.

And thus we tugged against the gale,
   The mighty tempest raging wild,
Leaving behind a foaming trail
   Like froth in mimic mountains piled.

The rigging shook her tarry cords
   Amid the hoarsely howling blast,
And seemed to utter ominous words,
   While torrents poured more thick and fast.

Yes, every rope that hung aloft,
   As if by gamut so arranged,
Gave out its music, hard and soft,
   As though into a wind harp changed.

Oh! horrid blackness! still more dark
   The heavens appear, of inky hue;
And now our swift and noble bark
   The tempest scarce could struggle through.

Now diving 'neath the boisterous waves
   That rolled their billows mountain high,
Then opened, like vast yawning caves,
   To swallow up all that came nigh.

The gallant and unflinching crew
   Hold skillful duty at their post,
Yet while at each command they flew,
   Now felt a fear that all were lost.

The timbers soon began to creak;
   The storage rocked from side to side;
And now the ship had sprung a leak
   And bilged with more than rapid stride.

The lightning flashed, then streaming down
   The masts in searing liquid flame,
As though disaster's self to crown,
   Along the fearful deck it came.

Like fiery serpents flaming bright,
   As though it were in zigzag play,
But, oh! my God! that fearful sight
   Shut out from me the light of day!

Yes, yes! that horrid flash, behold,
  Hath stricken me forever blind;
Nor can my piteous fate be told,
  Since I must grope my way to find.

But, gentle stranger, oh! forgive
  My feeble heart to thus complain;
Yet while on earth I'm doomed to live,
  I have to mourn o'er greater pain.

Yes, memory gives a scathing pang
  Whene'er I turn to that sad hour,
When death from my poor bosom wrang
  An only son to now deplore.

Yes, yes! he was a noble youth,
  And firmly at the helm he stood,
For I had made him mate—forsooth
  He was a boy of bravest blood.

Ah! how he loved me! that dear boy
  Was more to me than life or health!
My pleasure was his only joy,
  'Twas more to him than India's wealth.

But when he heard the mighty crash,
  And saw me fall, he thought me dead;
He also saw the coming flash
  Descending on my hapless head.

I knew no more for many days;
  Deprived was I of sense and light:
Ah! how mysterious are God's ways!
  I came to life, but not to sight!

10

But, then, I heard a solemn tale,
  How my poor boy had mourned and raved
Loud, far above the tempest's wail,
  That he was sadly thus bereaved.

But, presently another crash
  Came booming from the bending skies ;
The vessel parted, then a splash,
  She sank—and never more to rise.

The long-boat had been launched to save
  The brave, the weary crew,
From that broad, yawning ocean grave,
  And I was with that few.

But, ah ! my boy ! that darling son
  Was lost in that sad hour,
Whose manhood bright had just begun—
  I've heard of him no more !

Some say he sprang into the main
  While frenzy wrecked his mind,
For when they fled they sought in vain
  My darling boy to find !

They looked around the sinking wreck,
  Fast fading from their view,
And when they sought the vessel's deck
  He was not there they knew.

Five other lives were lost beside—
  Oh ! God ! that fatal day
There's naught can from my memory hide,
  Though ages pass away.

For many days our boat was tossed
   Upon the ocean wide,
And each believed himself as lost,
   Exposed to wind and tide.

But that devoted God, who ne'er
   The friendless soul will slight,
Bid smiling land once more appear;
   It was a welcome sight!

Though my poor eyes could not behold
   The grand and fertile scene,
I felt my loneliness tenfold,
   At what I once had been.

But, thanks to God for all his care
   And kindness e'er to me,
He has preserved me many a year,
   While tossed on life's rude sea.

But weather-beaten now, and old,
   I'm worse the wear 'tis true,
But still the gospel helm I hold,
   And keep blessed heaven in view.

If to that friendly port I sail
   When my last voyage is o'er,
There my dear Tom I hope to hail,
   And part from him no more.

"God bless you, father!" cried a voice,
   And grasped the old man's hand;
"Your Tom's alive! come, come! rejoice!
   He does before you stand!

" Come, dearest father, to my heart ;
　　I stranger am no more;
With pain I've listened to the part
　　Thou hast recounted o'er.

"And now, let me my fate explain ;
　　'Tis not so sad as thine,
Since I my blessed sight retain,
　　Though lost, indeed, is thine.

"Yea, father dear, that fated time
　　That fortune bid us sever,
I thought the power of God divine
　　Had parted us forever—

"At least on this vain world below—
　　For sure I thought thee dead ;
And then so shocking was my woe
　　That every passion bled.

"And when I heard the second crash,
　　The ship she burst in twain,
I seized a plank, and with one dash
　　Plunged in the raging main.

" The billows rolled with mountain sweep
　　And bore me far away ;
I still my hold did firmly keep
　　To this, my flimsy stay.

"Thus buoyed up for many hours,
　　Tossed by the pelting gale,
When nearly gone were all my powers,
　　A vessel came in hail !

"As though the gods would have it so,
   The winds directly bore
Me 'neath the vessel's friendly bow,
   But then I knew no more.

"But they had seen, had heard my cry,
   And instant came to aid,
When every act they could apply
   For my relief was made.

"With joy and weakness overcome,
   I wept, that they should save
Me from so terrible a doom,
   (The ocean's depthless grave.)

"I fainted then; but soon again
   My feeble heart revived,
Yet only more to feel my pain,
   To find myself bereaved.

"And now the kindly ship was bound
   Far to some foreign shore;
And when myself on land I found,
   I was in slavery's power.

"To Barbary's coast the vessel steered,
   Where I was captive made,
By some decree that interfered,
   And since I there have stayed.

"Nor could I leave that hated clime
   Or from my bondage flee,
Until this blest propitious time
   That I return to thee.

10*

"And now, dear father, here am I,
    Thy faithful Tom, thy son,
Returned to thee to live, and die
    When life's last voyage is run."

Come to my arms, my noble boy!
    For I must call thee.so;
Thou hast come back to give me joy,
    Through this dark vale of woe.

May God be praised for all He's done,
    Although I cannot see,
Since he has thus preserved my son
    And brought him home to me.

————

THE SPIRIT OF WRATH.

THE spirit of wrath is the spirit of woe,
    Wherever the demon may find us;
As we travel these earthly courts below,
    He stalks in his speed behind us.

In palace, or cottage, or temple of state,
    He comes, with his fiery wand,
To touch human feelings with vengeance or hate,
    By the wave of his murderous hand.

To combat and war he beckons the way,
    With the promise of glory and fame
To those who are willing to slaughter and slay
    And in blood carve a valorous name.

In the brothel of crime, in the home of the vile,
  He stalks with imperious mien;
With the finger of death he will point with a smile
  To the features where beauty hath been.

Yet what but the lurkings of irony there,
  Or a smile that is doomed to deceive?
He will flourish his scepter regardless of fear,
  And a snare for their dreamy souls weave.

Over mountain or vale, or through caverns deep,
  He lurks with untiring skill,
And nerves up the hand of the robber to creep
  From his den for to plunder and kill.

And now from the courts of vile Bacchus he turns
  To escort the poor drunken sot home,
Whose heart with the spirit of fury now burns,
  To scatter some deadly doom.

Perhaps there's a wife, or a daughter most fair,
  The blast of the tempest must feel;
While their shrieks of despondency mount on the air,
  But touch not his bosom of steel.

The knife may glow with the purple blood,
  And drip from his fingers foul:
'Tis the spirit of wrath that renders him food
  To harden his guilty soul.

And now the lover, whose passionate mind
  Lets jealousy gnaw at his breast;
'Tis there the dark demon a subject will find
  As fatal and sure as the rest.

Perchance a young bosom he fancied most true
   Was fatally prone to deceive,
And naught but her life's blood revealed to his view,
   Could the deed of dishonor retrieve.

Avaunt! to thy shades! thou demon of guilt,
   Thou perilous spirit of ire!
We might float on the ocean of blood thou hast spilt
   Through the promptings of madd'ning desire.

Away! yes, away! to thy murky domains,
   Where demons of vengeance dance round thee;
'Tis there thou art worthy to rule and to reign,
   Since hell first ordained thee and crowned thee.

MY PET KITTEN.

My pretty pet kitten! a kitten thou art
Just after my mind, or the choice of my heart,
For thou art so merry, so frisky, and free,
I am sure there was never a kitten like thee.

But then thou art very mischievous I own,
And will not let things for a moment alone,
For all that thou carest about the whole day
Is to idle thy moments in frolic and play.

And then if thou canst, like a villanous pet,
Just privately into my work-basket get,
The tapes and the bobbins, and such things in store,
Are soon in a muss and strewed over the floor.

If into the garden thou takest a run,
By the way of a little amusement or fun,
Thou art sure to exert all thy meddlesome powers
In tearing and spoiling my beautiful flowers.

And if a young grasshopper ventures in sight,
Or a bug, or a spider should near thee alight,
Such bruising, such scratching, such teasing and that,
Was never performed by a barbarous cat!

But thou art a kitten, and it is thy nature
To be a contrary and mischievous creature:
But go, my poor puss! for I plainly see
That all reformation is foreign to thee!

THE BETRAYED AND THE PENITENT.

A TALE OF TRUTH.

Oh, yes! she was beautiful, chaste to behold,
  Her eyes of a liquid and heavenly blue,
Her hair hung in soft glossy ringlets of gold,
  And her figure was symmetry's self to the view!

Her voice was so gentle, so thrillingly sweet,
  It seemed like the breathing of music to hear,
When her accents of love she would playful repeat,
  And a smile on her bright cherry lips would appear.

Her step was as airy and swift as the fawn
  That darts o'er the prairie silvered with dew,
Or the pet lamb that sports o'er the green velvet lawn,
  And her love was by nature as gentle and true.

I saw her when bright as the rosy lit morn
    That breaks in its beauty o'er bower and grove,
Or fair as the snow-drop, or white budding thorn,
    She moved through the circles of friendship and love.

Her musical laugh was as clear as the shell
    The naiads allow with soft melody ring;
Her delicate graces they bound with a spell,
    As moments departed on life's sunny wing.

Yes, lovely Zorada, how charmingly fair,
    How beautiful thou in thy morning of youth,
With spirit and feelings as buoyant as air,
    And soul brightly beaming with virtue and truth!

But the spoiler, alas! with its terrible blight,
    Like a storm-cloud, fair girl, came over thy fate,
And sought to array all thy beauty in night;
    Thou saw his approach—when to shun was too late.

It was the voice, yea, of love! that came, gentle maid,
    Breathing eloquent meaning, and winning thy heart,
'Twas vows seeming constant thy nature betrayed,
    And left thee to writhe 'neath the terrible smart.

Young Edgar was handsome, was manly in form,
    Was gay and persuasive, with talent and wealth;
His mind seemed impervious to tumult or storm,
    And his visage shone bright with the glory of health.

A thousand attractions sat high on his brow,
    That looked but the index of greatness and worth,
And told of a spirit that never could bow
    To aught that was mean on the face of the earth.

So noble, so lofty did majesty sit
  On his visage and mien, that the daughters of grace,
Of favor, of love, of beauty and wit,
  All wished in his bosom to hold a fair place.

'Twas then that Zorada, so beauteous and young,
  Beheld him whose manners won constant applause,
Whose voice uttered melody soft from the tongue,
  And thus could not fail in the heart-pleading cause.

He whispered a tale deeply laden with love,
  And spoke of devotion unchanging and true,
Invoking the gods in high heaven to prove
  His honor unspotted, and constancy too.

And while in the fervor of rapture he knelt,
  To pour out his passionate vows at her feet,
No doubt in that moment he honestly felt
  Disposed to perform what he dared to repeat.

Alas, gentle girl! too confiding wert thou!
  'Tis the nature of woman too trustful to live;
And even when folly compels her to bow,
  How soon will she pity, how soon will she forgive!

Though proud indignation may flash from her eye
  For a moment, at what may give insult or pain,
If love rules the throne, and some kind words apply,
  'Tis over, and woman is trustful again.

And thus was it, fairest Zorada, with thee;
  Thy spirit revolted and fain wouldst thou chide;
But love promised still ever faithful to be,
  And make thee, poor injured one, early his bride.

But triumph is o'er, the victory is won,
 And Edgar's devotions began to decline ;
A cloud passes over thy morning's bright sun,
 For thou wert now left in neglect to repine.

With bosom nigh bleeding, though chastened and true,
 Didst thou shrink from the gaze of the world in thy
  shame,
Yet solitude brought his false image to view,
 And memory carved but too often his name.

And is it a wonder, when moments reveal
 That thou art a mother, dishonored so young,
While thy beautiful babe bears the impress and seal
 Of him who betrayed, and thy gentle heart wrung ?

Yet blessings, Zorada, had Heaven in store,
 'Mid trials and dangers that darkened thy day,
To save thee from falling from virtue yet lower,
 For friendship and sympathy hung in thy way.

And, like a proud daughter, we see thee arise
 In firmness and beauty, yet pensive and wan,
Resolving in future those moments to prize
 Which Heaven would suffer upon thee to dawn.

And thus it was well; God watched thee with care,
 Rewarding thy steady devotion and trust;
Though years had now past, thou wert destined to share
 The blessings He often reserves for the just.

And where is thy Edgar, the inconstant one?
 Hath joyous pleasure illumined his brow,
As a tribute for all the vile wrongs that he done,
 In leaving thee, fairest, a victim to woe ?

Ah, no ! there's an angel unslumbering and just,
  Whose eye wanders over creation's extent,
Regarding the souls God hath given in trust,
  Performing the mission for which she was sent.

That angel is Constancy ! and let us beware
  How we trifle with time and eternity here ;
She is constantly warning our hearts to prepare,
  And do all that is noble, just, right, and sincere.

And Edgar knew well this bright angel of grace,
  Who followed, and ceaseless breathed in his ear,
The time he would virtuous honor deface,
  And the sorrows he drove through that bosom once
    dear.

And thus, while the torment of sorrow oppressed,
  He grew like a shadow with sickness and pain,
For conscience resolved he should never have rest
  Till he made the poor injured one happy again.

But, alas ! he now finds himself nigh to the grave !
  Zorada still haunts him in vision and dream ;
He mourns o'er the heart-rending wounds that he gave,
  And found this too painful for life's closing scene.

Her beauty, her innocence rose to his view,
  As when she appeared in the world's giddy throng,
With her loving affections, so spotless and true,
  Which to him, and him only, did all then belong.

The physicians give o'er, their skill is in vain;
  He sends for a pious and noble divine,
And stated the cause of his sorrow and pain,
  And begged his advice at eternity's shrine.

11

The good man advised, while he brushed off a tear
    That fell on his furrowed and manly cheek,
And bid him the past solemn deed to repair,
    And peace in an action of nobleness seek.

"Alas! if I thought," said the penitent man,
    " She would love, and forgive my most pitiless slight,
I would make her my bride ere the night shadows wan,
    Or morning reveals her soft coming light.

" Five years now have passed; she surely must scorn
    A soul who could leave her so long in her woe;
But if she will pity a conscience thus torn,
    I will, instantly, kind reparation bestow."

'Twas enough! the fair girl was sought for, and came,
    And nursed by his pillow, as mother and wife;
She canceled the deed, and smothered the blame,
    And God, in his mercy, gave back health and life.

Now years have rolled on, and a happier pair
    There cannot be found in this promising land;
Five sweet little innocents bloom 'neath their care,
    And he blesses the hour he gave her his hand.

Ye skeptics, frown not, while this tale ye may scan;
    Deeds noble and brave are as victories given;
That penitent being in soul was a man—
    May his deeds and his name be recorded in heaven!

THE ELOPEMENT.

THE lovely moon, as bright as noon,
  Beamed o'er the silver water,
When Yambanoo, in his light canoe,
  Bore off the chieftain's daughter.

An Indian maid, in jewels arrayed,
  And painted in many a hue,
He thought her the pride of the wigwam; beside,
  He loved her most earnest and true.

Her father, the seer, would never give ear
  To their union, through motives unkind;
The cruel old sage always flew in a rage
  When he saw them for marriage inclined.

Though the youth, good and brave, not a cause ever
      gave
  For this stern indignation and ire,
Though his crime, to be sure, was just being too poor,
  And daring thus high to aspire;

Yet young Yambanoo loved faithful and true
  This beautiful gem of his heart,
And thus had designed, in his heroic mind,
  With the damsel he never would part.

And Winglet, she loved devoted as he,
  Though her father raved madly on,
And swore by his head, and the scalp of the dead,
  The youth he'd ne'er own for a son.

Thus ever the two, so loving and true,
  Were harassed by sorrow and pain,
When the wicked old chief, like a villainous thief,
  Declared they should ne'er meet again.

He then, on a day, tore his daughter away,
  And bid Yambanoo to depart,
And if he did not, he might look to his lot,
  For an arrow he'd send through his heart.

But the dauntless brave, though the chief would thus
      rave,
  Flinched not in his love or his duty,
But made up his mind, some way he would find
  To bear off his wilderness beauty.

The lovers they met, though with dangers beset,
  One night in a myrtle wood bower,
When with mutual consent on escape they were bent,
  To fly from dark tyranny's power.

"Dear Winglet, my dove," said our hero, "your love
  Is the dream and the hope of my life;
Though your father may curse, to make matters worse,
  To morrow I make you my wife!

"By my wampum I swear, and the war axe I bear,
  To guard and protect you or die!
Your own Yambanoo shall prove dauntless and true;
  Your hero, sweet dove, cannot lie."

The very next night, by the aid of moonlight,
  While the stars hung like gems in the sky,
Did the maiden repair to the trysting place, where
  She had promised her lover to fly.

THE HOME OF THE BLEST.

THERE'S a home for the weary, a home for the true,
In a land of perpetual flowers,
Where joys never-ending unfold to the view,
And summer make up the glad hours.

A holy dominion of bliss and repose,
Where glory unceasingly reigns,
Where rivers like crystal their beauty disclose,
And music steals over the plains.

Ay, music from lyres of gold,
And tuned by angelical hands,
While seraphs their pinions unfold,
And soar in celestial lands.

No sunlight is there to illume
Those regions of beauty and light,
Where life is eternal in bloom,
And glory entrances the sight.

A home where the weary may rove,
Exulting in triumph and grace,
And flashing wherever they move,
In the light of Jehovah's sweet face!

Then blest is the sanctified soul,
Redeemed by the blood of the Lamb;
Though ages eternal may roll,
They shall dwell with the holy "I AM."

11*

LITTLE NELLY DALE.

"WHAT is your name, my pretty child?"
   A lady said one day
Unto a little girl, that smiled
   And skipped along the way.

" You are a perfect fairy bird,
   So light, so gay, and free ;
Your dainty steps can scarce be heard,
   Although so near to me."

" They call me Little Nelly Dale,"
   The modest child replied,
Whose lovely cheek, though somewhat pale,
   Looked like a roseleaf dyed.

" I am my father's only pet;
   He has no child but me ;
But now, since I remember yet,
   Once sisters I had three.

" But sickness came with burning hand
   And caused each flower to die,
And now they, in a foreign land,
   Within the churchyard lie.

"And then our mother, too, must go,
   Who was so good and kind ;
I cannot see why it is so,
   I should be left behind!

"And dear papa, he tries to keep
　A gentle smile for me ;
Yet I can often see him weep,
　While sitting on his knee.

" And then he looks so very pale,
　His cheeks so wan appear,
That something, I am sure, must ail
　My loving papa dear.

"And oft he seems so sadly wild
　While o'er my bed he leans
And murmurs—'Ah ! my child, my child !'
　I wonder what it means ?

" It makes me feel so bad, I own
　I cannot help but cry,
I fear I shall be left alone—
　That dear papa will die !

" I wonder what will then become
　Of Little Nelly Dale,
Who then, perhaps, will have no home,
　Or friends to hear her tale ?

"Though I have heard my mother say
　She had a sister dear,
But she was far enough away,
　Yet often wished her here.

"For then, she said, if they should die,
　Their child a friend would have
To guard her, when they both should lie
　Deep slumbering in the grave.

" They said her name was Ellen Wain,
   A gentle heart had she,
And if they ne'er should meet again,
   They hoped she might find me."

"Ah!" said the lady, staring wild,
   And with a sudden start
She snatched the darling, prattling child,
   And pressed it to her heart.

" You are my little love !" said she,
   While tears fell thick and fast ;
" My sister's child ! and now, I see,
   I've found you out at last !

" Long I have weary searched to find
   Whither your parents fled,
And had made up my anxious mind
   You, one and all, were dead.

" But sacred joy ! How kind is Heaven !
   How marvelous its decree !
Since it has thus so strangely given
   My darling niece to me.

" Your mother called you by my name,
   Sweet treasure of my heart !
And now, while health and life remain,
   No more on earth we part.

" We'll now, sweet child, to home repair,
   And bless this sacred hour,
That Heaven so kindly joined us here
   Through its all-seeing power."

THE PIONEER OF THE WEST.

FAR, far o'er the mountains high,
 And into the valleys below,
The bold pioneer is seen to hie
 With his dog, his gun, and his bow.

At the early dawn of the morn,
 Ere the sun shows his glittering face,
The forests resound with his echoing horn,
 And his dogs bark aloud for the chase.

The bounding stag, and the prairie steed,
 The elk and the fleet chamois
He gallantly follows with vigor and speed,
 The hero of mountain boys.

On, on! like an arrow he speeds his way,
 Nor heeds his pleasure or toil,
Until he returns at the close of day
 Well weary and laden with spoil.

Then again up, up, at the dawn of light,
 And away over mountain and hill,
Like an eagle he takes his wandering flight,
 With a hearty and right good will.

Then ho! for the land of the west,
 Where the stag and the buffalo roam,
And the condor and proud eagle rest,
 Secure in their wild mountain home!

There the yeoman with brown sunny brow,
    And feelings exulting and free,
Follows after his oxen and plow,
    As happy as yeoman can be.

And there, too, the Indian's trail,
    The warrior's war path, is seen,
Through dark tangled woodland and vale,
    Where scarce yet the pale face hath been.

And there doth the pioneer dwell,
    Though well he remembers the day
The horrible tomahawk fell
    His dear ones to slaughter and slay.

And though he may drop the warm tear
    As a tribute to memory and love,
Yet still, all regardless of fear,
    Through those wilds he continues to rove.

Yet often the flash of his gun,
    Since the times have become more secure,
Has caused the bold savage to run
    From his aim, ever steady and sure.

Thus, now in the flourishing West
    Prosperity ladens the soil,
While the white man's proud labors are blest
    By his honest and ceaseless toil.

Far, far on the waters now glide
    Mighty ships with their snowy sails spread,
And steam vessels move in their pride
    Through haunts where the savage once sped.

And still though the barken canoe
   Of the red man may ply o'er the waves,
Their war deeds they seldom pursue,
   For soon they'd be hurled to their graves!

For the pioneers, sturdy and free,
   Are ever alert to defend
The cause of sweet famed liberty,
   And will fight, and fight on to the end.

Then ho! for the glorious West!
   Where cities now boldly rise,
Where the toil of the white man is blest
   'Neath freedom's own prosperous skies.

TO ZUMENIA.

I've seen the sun in beauty shed
   Its glory o'er the morning sky,
Or dancing on the waves that spread
   Their blue expanse both far and nigh;
Yet nothing in their charm I see,
Sweet love, that can compare to thee!

I've watched the evening stilly hour,
   When stars peeped from their deep domain,
And moonlight fell in dreamy power
   O'er mighty ocean, hill and plain—
Each object, love, was fair to see,
Yet dearer far art thou to me!

Where'er my spirit fain would stray
   'Mid glorious walks of nature's own,
Whether by night or noonlit day,
   Thou art my rising star alone;
For fancy still, by fate's decree,
Can find no joy but loving thee.

Though I may watch the billow's crest
   Receding from the sea-girt shore,
And skies in gold and purple drest,
   Or bright with moonbeams silvered o'er—
Still, 'mid all things sublime I see,
My thoughts are constant fixed on thee.

Though years have passed well steeped in pain
   From pangs of unrequited love,
I now behold thee once again,
   Thy earthly guardian friend to prove;
And may the gods, by blest decree,
Bid thou my chosen bride to be!

THE CREOLE BRIDE.

A SOUTHERN TALE FOUNDED ON FACT.

A WEALTHY seer of some renown,
   Though proud and wayward mind,
Lived in a far-off Southern town,
   In ease and wealth refined.

No wife had he, or daughter fair,
   Or son, so it appears,
To need his tender fostering care,
   Or bless his failing years.

Yet once he had all three, they say,
  And bliss around him shone,
But death soon bore them all away,
  And left him thus alone.

Yet like a Benedict of old,
  With morals firm and sure,
He would not have his mansion sold,
  But kept his home secure,—

Still thinking at some future time
  In this eventful life,
As he was yet in green old prime,
  He fain would seek a wife.

But then as years slid on apace,
  Although to wed inclined,
He could not meet, in time or place,
  With one to suit his mind.

Thus very oft a frown of care
  Was seen upon his brow,
Because upon no legal heir
  His wealth he could bestow.

Yet one thing he had fixed upon,
  Through freak of romance wild,
Since wife and children he had none,
  He would adopt some child:

One poor, and beautiful withal,
  Who might indulgent prove,
And, while obedient to his call,
  Share his paternal love:

12

One worthy to possess his name
   And all his glittering store,—
He thought if he could find the same
   On earth, he'd ask no more.

It would be charity, he knew,
   If such he could but find,
Who, as in older years she grew,
   Would treat him truly kind.

Long, long indeed, he looked in vain,
   For one to meet his choice,
Since perfect beauty he would gain
   In feature, form, and voice.

Now, be it known, this wealthy seer
   Who thus so liberal felt,
Was like some other great folks here—
   In Southern slaves he dealt.

Although a humane man in heart,
   Still custom ruled the day;
With them he often had to part
   And send them far away.

Yet he was very kind to those
   He held beneath his care,
Save in one instance, where he chose
   To act unkind, severe.

One day two female slaves were bought,
   A mother and her child,
And when into his presence brought,
   He looked surprised, and smiled.

The daughter was a creole born,
　Of light, clear olive hue,
With features beautiful as morn,
　And eyes of heavenly blue.

The mother was as black as jet,
　An African by birth;
No homelier slave was ever met
　On this delusive earth.

Quoth he: "Here is an ill-matched pair
　As mortals need behold;
The daughter is exceeding fair,
　The mother black and bold.

"A gentle spirit, sure, is here,
　In this young, beauteous child; ·
No doubt she has a heart sincere:
　Her looks are sweetly mild.

" Then I shall take her 'neath my care
　And treat her as my own;
The mother—you must send her where
　Her child shall ne'er be known.

" For, from this hour, nevermore,
　Although it gives me pain,
Must she remain upon this shore—
　They ne'er must meet again."

The mother wept; her heart was sad,
　To hear her master's will;
For, though so black, ah! yet she had
　A mother's feelings still.

But pleadings were of no avail;
　　They now were doomed to part:
She pressed the little trembler pale,
　　In anguish to her heart.

The child was only four years old,
　　And to its mother clung;
When of its infant fate 'twas told,
　　Its little heart seemed wrung.

But then the kind and wealthy seer
　　Used some persuasion mild,
By telling what his motives were
　　Toward her beauteous child.

He said—"She ne'er should be in want,
　　Or held in slavish chains,
Or under cruel usage pant
　　While life flowed in his veins.

"That if she in affection grew,
　　And truthful, pure, and kind,
She would in him, too well he knew,
　　A loving guardian find."

This sealed the test; the child she gave
　　Into her master's care,
Then soon was borne upon the wave
　　To some far distant sphere,—

With many a caution, strict and stern,
　　Well noted at the time,
That she must never more return
　　To that sweet Southern clime.

The mother gone—the child she grew
  In beauty and in years,
Endowed with every virtue true
  Which meek perfection wears.

Ere thirteen summers bright had fled,
  So charming had she grown,
So sweetly good, the seer was led
  To love her as his own.

Nor did the gentle creature know
  Much of that dreadful day,
When, 'mid a mother's bleeding woe,
  They tore her form away.

For all rose like an infant dream
  Upon her youthful view,
While gliding o'er life's happy stream,
  'Mid changes vast and new.

And though sometimes a darkening face
  Would peer o'er vision's throne,
She soon was taught in it to trace
  A murky nurse alone.

For often thus the worthy seer
  Would teach her infant heart,
Whene'er the child would sad appear,
  Or prompting teardrops start.

And thus each happy season past,
  Pale memory waned apace,
Until the beauteous child at last
  No gloomy hour could trace.

    12*

And all the lovely creature knew
   Was that her fate was blest;
She had an uncle kind and true,
   And of all men the best.

But now an era comes, to change
   The golden dream of life,
And every joyous scene derange
   To dismal woe and strife.

The aged seer had thought it right
   To send his pet from home,
That in some Eastern town she might
   A perfect star become.

In boarding school he had her placed
   Beneath the kindest care,
Where every art of learning graced
   Her heart, from year to year.

But in due time he sends to bring
   His peerless gem away;
And soon the beauteous Anzoming
   Had cause to rue the day.

And what were his paternal views,
   Although most kindly meant?
The charming girl soon hears the news—
   On marriage he is bent.

And there now stood a noble youth
   Of manly form and make,
And one, if we may speak the truth,
   She was not loth to take.

His beauteous mien, his flashing eye,
　Were grandeur's self to view;
And while she gazed, she knew not why,
　She felt she loved him too.

Besides, the aged sire had told
　Fair Anzoming that he
Would give her weight twice down in gold,
　If she his bride would be.

The youth he loved the maid at sight;
　He was a planter's son:
Thus all things seemed to omen right
　When they should be made one.

Both worthy seers were men of wealth,
　And both of some renown,
And thus they planned the thing by stealth,
　And knocked the matter down.

For many a confab there had been
　Between the worthy twain,
As each for mighty gold was keen,
　And lovers, both, of gain.

They wished their children nobly joined,
　And wealthy made outright,
And thus considered money coined,
　Two fortunes to unite.

The marriage knot was early tied;
　All things propitious seemed;
Blest were the merry groom and bride,
　Who naught of sorrow dreamed.

But, ah! the dark and horrid gloom
  Which early did prevail;
How soon was changed the lover's doom—
  But on this hangs a tale.

Three days had passed in nuptial joy,
  In music, dance, and song,
When fate their dream would fain destroy,
  And felt their bliss too long.

While music rang throughout the halls,
  And merry laugh went round,
A demon crept within those walls
  And changed the mirthful sound.

For soon was heard a piercing scream;
  The bride was seen to start,
And from appearance all would deem
  A knife had found her heart.

Ay, but no gory dagger stood
  In bold relief to view;
Yet there stood one of blackest blood,
  And near the maiden drew.

And while she gazed in fiendish pride
  Upon her beauteous face,
She hissed within her ear, and cried—
  "Hail! triumph and disgrace!

"So, so! bend down your pretty ear
  And hear what I shall say;
Behold your black born mother here,
  To take your bliss away!

" Your short-lived glory I have spoiled ;
  Your pride and pomp have fled !
Come to my arms, my darling child—
  Alas ! I think she's dead !"

No wonder, for the beauteous bride
  Had sank into a swoon,
And well were it had she then died ;
  Alas ! she woke too soon !

With horror all the guests looked round
  To see the demon dread,
Who uttered thus the dooming sound—
  But she, the wretch, had fled.

What terror and amazement thrilled
  The noble husband's brain !
Despair his very life-blood chilled ;
  His soul was crushed with pain.

He gazed upon her beauteous form,
  Appalled, and with disgust,
For now his heart, by frenzy torn,
  Was filled with vile distrust.

The wretched guardian stood confessed ;
  He owned the fraud he'd played ;
Yet horror filled his manly breast
  At being thus betrayed.

'Twas now, with feelings deep and sore,
  And accents sadly wild,
He owned the sacred love he bore
  Toward the creole child,—

Whom he had passed on son and seer
　With fraudulent intent,
That she amazing wealth might share,
　As one of French descent.

The husband listened, all amazed,
　To this most startling tale,
And while upon her form he gazed,
　His lips grew deadly pale.

He bore her, fainting, in his arms
　Unto her nuptial bed,
And while he viewed her youthful charms,
　All love and pity fled.

" Vile, beauteous siren !" he exclaimed,
　" The truth is now revealed ;
Although you should not thus be blamed,
　Still, still your doom is sealed !

"Your cruel guardian is the cause
　Of this appalling part ;
To earthly bliss there is a clause—
　This dagger finds thy heart !"

'Twas then one fearful plunge he gave,
　And drove it in her breast,
Believing that an early grave
　For his lost bride was best.

He then the guardian sought, and found
　Amid the wondering throng,
And soon he drove a mortal wound
　For solemn proffered wrong.

Then with a yell of wild despair
    He fled the fearful place,
To hide his shame—ah! God knows where—
    His steps no soul could trace.

Some said he fled to wilds unknown,
    In solitude to dwell,
And there his tragic fate bemoan—
    But who of this can tell?

———⁂———

GRANDPAPA'S WIG.

SAY, do you remember, dear Helen, the day,
    As we sat in the myrtle wood bower,
A messenger came in a hurry to say
    Our dear grandpapa was no more?
Ah, me! how we wept, that no more we should see
    His darling old face, meek and pale,
Sitting with us, beneath the large sycamore tree,
    Telling many a startling tale.
Alas! never more we shall run at his call,
To hang up his wig on the peg in the wall.

How sweet were the seasons when he would come down
    To stay at the cottage awhile!
His loving old brow never dimmed by a frown,
    And his lips always wreathed with a smile;
And then at the close of the long summer's day,
    While the sun rested over yon hill,
Would he take us, all merry and laughing, away
    To fish in the stream at the mill.

And then, after night, we would run, one and all,
To hang up his wig on the peg in the wall.

Ah, those were the times! yet I think I can see
　　Him just as he was when he sat
With dear little Nell climbing up on his knee
　　To play with his three-cornered hat.
His old honest face looked so gentle and kind,
　　And his laugh was so pleasing to hear,
While always some right merry joke he would find
　　To humor our juvenile ear ;
And then, at bedtime, we would run, one and all,
To hang up his wig on the peg in the wall.

Sweet treasured gone hours to memory dear,
　　How often I bring them to mind!
When he romped with us all in the cherry grove near,
　　Or played hide and seek—who will find ?
What rapture would beam in his loving gray eyes
　　When he peeped all around with such care,
Pretending to find us, as though by surprise,
　　Though he knew all the time we were there !
Ah, darling old man ! then at night he would call
Us to hang up his wig on the peg in the wall.　　　.

That beautiful wig I can never forget,
　　With its long silver curls all so trim ;
Then on his bald pate it would have such a set—
　　I am sure it would fit none like him !
And oft, as the night of the Sabbath declined,
　　Would he bid us assemble for prayer ;
'Twas then, as each one in his arms he entwined,
　　He would kiss us all round, with a tear ;
Then, bidding good night, we would run, one and all,
To hang up his wig on the peg in the wall.

OLD DOBBIN.

POOR DOBBIN is old! yet many's the time
 I have seen him go prancing gaily,
But that, to be sure, was when young and in prime,
 And he traveled in harness daily.

'Twas only to speak, and the beast he would go
 Most willing wherever you told him,
And that very often too, whether or no—
 Indeed, you could scarcely hold him.

'Twas then he was proud, and would cock up his ears,
 If he saw a vile thing in the road;
Some slanderers said it was naught but his fears,
 And wished to get rid of a load.

But that was a fib, for we know very well
 That a stake or a stump will not scare him,
For away he would go if he over it fell,
 But then from such freak we would spare him.

And scandal again, ever busy, would say—
 And we think it a shame to be spoken—
That the beast was a stumbling brute in his way,
 And they marveled our neck was not broken.

Poor Dobbin! if he only knew all was said,
 Although now in years he is growing,
Would never be able to hold up his head—
 However, of this there's no knowing.

13

The creature he never done wrong in his life—
   In this I can venture to clear him—
Save once, when he knocked over Katy, my wife—
   But then she'd no business near him.

True, once in my time, I did hear it said—
   Though I never would credit the story—
That he pulled a straw bonnet from some lady's head,
   And munched it all up, in his glory.

But some people have such a passion for fibs,
   They owe him a grudge, and I know it;
And if they but dare, they would pummel his ribs,
   Ay, kill him, perhaps, for they show it!

But, ah! never mind; each one has his day,
   And Dobbin is now in the stable,
Nor am I afraid of his running away
   If even the creature was able.

Though, true, he one day took a notion or two
   Just to peep from the old stable door,
When, shortly after, the first thing I knew,
   He was over in Gosling's store.

Yet this silly venture I never could blame,
   Though neighbors considered him mad,
For his oats were all out, and he knew whence they came,
   And he went where the thing could be had.

And this clearly proved him a brute of some sense,
   And I petted him up for his caper;
Thus feel it my duty, though years should glide hence,
   To hallow his name upon paper.

THE REPOSE OF THE DEAD.

How holy the spot, the home of the dead,
　Where rest the remains of the blest;
Those beings we honored, as life onward sped,
　And loved as the kindest and best!

'Tis pleasant to ramble in solitude there,
　And muse over days now no more,
And drop o'er the turf affection's warm tear
　As the tribute to those we adore.

For though now no longer we have them, yet we
　Can wander to where they are laid,
And in the fond mirror of memory see,
　And, seeming, speak with their shade.

And there we can muse on the future and past
　Of the world, with its changes and strife,
And feel what we all are to come to at last,
　When borne from this troublesome life.

For moral instruction is there to be found
　In every season and age,
And what is not heard in the death-dooming sound,
　Is seen on eternity's page.

Ah! then how important, in life's little hour,
　Our time to improve for the best,
That when our short journey on earth here is o'er,
　We may enter the home of the blest!

MY PET ROBIN.

SWEET warbler! ah! how I pity thy fate,
Thus kept in a prison—both early and late!
And though thou art fed on the daintiest fare,
It seems, to my heart, that thou shouldst not be there.

For what though thy beautiful cage is of gold,
With ornaments bright and rich to behold,
And chickweed in plenty, with sugar and paste,
Hung over thy bars to encourage thy taste,—

Still, still it appears, if thou only couldst speak,
Or a voice could come forth from thy delicate beak,
Thou wouldst soon to this fickle and wide world declare
Thou wouldst rather be out in the forests than there.

Sweet bird! how I wish I dare now let thee fly
And soar far away, ay, toward the blue sky;
How soon would I open thy golden cage door,
And let thee enjoy holy freedom once more!

But should I now let thee, in pity, depart,
Some huntsman, perchance, would soon aim at thy
                heart,
And at the report of the gun's fearful sound
I might see my dear pet falling dead to the ground.

Or if thou shouldst off to the tall forests fly,
Where thou art a stranger, and no kindred nigh,
A bevy of birds of most quarrelsome kind
Would soon the new home of my poor robin find,—

And then they would battle and treat thee unfair,
When soon thou wouldst wish thyself under my care ;
For all thy sad wailings could never be heard,
And nothing could save thee, my beautiful bird !

Then be thou content 'mid thy wires of gold,
For I know that my robin is safe in his fold,
And each new-born day he shall have the best fare
The hand of affection can for him prepare.

For soon frigid winter, with boisterous breath,
Will wrap up the forests in slumbering death ;
But thy cage shall be hung in my boudoir warm,
Secure from all danger and free from the storm.

But when balmy spring shall return once again,
And flowers enamel the woodlands and plain,
Then, robin, I'll open thy pretty cage door
And let thee go free—I can do nothing more.

So now my sweet pet must whistle and sing,
And at night tuck his head 'neath his beautiful wing ;
Then soon as the heavens are soft, blue, and clear,
Sweet freedom is thine, though it cost me a tear.

But when winter comes, with its breath bleak and chill,
Harping loud from each stormy and northern hill,
Then, robin, come tap on the clear window pane,
And soon will I welcome my pet home again.

OUR MOTHER'S GRAVE.

COME, sisters, let us seek the grave
    Of our own mother dear,
And there the lovely green turf lave
    With memory's holy tear.

Alas! no more her loving face
    Among our group is seen;
The grave is now her resting-place,
    Where father long has been.

Ah, yes! that meek and loving voice,
    That sweet and gentle mien,
Which made our hearts so oft rejoice,
    Is yet by memory seen.

For still affection calls to mind
    How late she did appear,
While all her soothing accents kind
    Fall gently on our ear.

But what though we are orphans, left
    To brave a world of woe;
That God, who has our hearts bereft,
    Will shield us well, I know.

He never, never will forsake
    The heart by sorrow torn,
But rather 'neath his pinions take
    And comfort those who mourn.

Then never let us fail to trust
    In his protecting care,
Who is so holy, wise, and just
    To all his children here.

He knows our every want and need,
    Our every grief and pain,
And will to earnest prayer take heed—
    None ever ask in vain.

Then let us look to Him above,
    The orphan's guide and friend,
Whose gentle nature is all love,—
    He'll shield us to the end.

AUTUMN IS HERE.

AUTUMN now is here, with its trees all in the sear,
    And many a blushing leaf hangs from the bough;
But it is a darling time, now the season's in its prime,
    And seldom 'tis as beautiful as now.

The hedges they are bright with colors dark and light,
    And the meadows they are dusky in their hue;
The waters they are clear as at any time of year,
    And the wild birds they are coming not a few.

The harvest now is o'er, and the reaper's song no more
    Is heard to echo gaily o'er the plains,
While the merry woodman sees 'tis time to cut his forest
        trees,
    And have the worth of labor for his pains.

We hear the sportsman's gun while the stag is on the
    run,
  And the hunted hare is hiding in the vale;
The village lass is seen coming o'er the mottled green,
  And the milk maid, too, is skipping with her pail.

'Tis a pleasant time of year, though faded scenes ap-
    pear,
  And the whistle of the robin lingers still;
While through the forests gay we hear the mournful lay
  Of the wild dove, and the lonely whip-poor-will.

Yet soon each gaudy hue that meets our roving view
  Will hurl their fading beauty to the blast,
While snow and frozen sleet will crash beneath our feet,
  And nothing will be seen of them at last.

For winter's chilly breath will soon wither them in
    death,
  And naught of lovely Autumn will appear;
Yet ever dear to me are the changes that I see,
  As they make up the full glory of the year.

THE HAPPY FISHERMAN.

Do you know of the cottage down by the sea side,
  Standing under the brow of the hill?
There honest old Robert was known to reside,
  And perhaps he is living there still.

His hut was of logs put together with clay,
 And not very large to be sure,
Yet was a snug cabin enough in its way,
 As it kept him from tempests secure.

There Robert resided, contented and free,
 With a wife suited well to his mind,
And sweet little children, perhaps two or three,
 As rosy as any you'd find.

And a blessing for him that his household was small,
 For Robert was humble and poor;
Yet he managed, somehow, to provide for them all,
 Keeping poverty out of the door.

Let me see—there were five! and Towser beside—
 A pretty good number indeed;
And then the pet cat with the turtle-shell hide,
 He had all by his labor to feed.

But never old Robert was heard to complain
 When things did not go as they might,
For he always believed, whether losses or gain,
 The matter was perfectly right.

But one thing with him was well understood,
 As he was a Christian for sure,
That sinners should take the bad with the good,
 And what they can't help, must endure.

A very good creed for the patient and strong,
 But seldom brought into effect,
For vile discontent to our natures belong—
 Thus the bright golden rule we neglect.

But not so with Robert; as moments would glide
    And things would oft take a wrong course,
He would always endeavor to view the bright side,
    Nor grieve to make matters grow worse.

And thus he trudged on through a lifetime of toil,
    Bearing with him a guileless breast;
Believing, though fate our best efforts may foil,
    All that happens is sure for the best.

He never was known to foam or to fret,
    Or torture or give creatures pain,
Save the poor little fishes he caught in his net,
    Or would sometimes run into the seine.

And that was his living, we very well know,
    For Robert ne'er thought it a crime,
Whenever his fortunate net he would throw,
    If hundreds he caught at a time.

'Twas then a sweet smile of happy content
    Would light up his good-humored face;
Believing the Lord all the fishes had sent
    Through his infinite mercy and grace.

It was pleasant to see, at the close of the day,
    When his toil and labor were o'er,
How snug he would stow all his tackle away,
    And moor his light craft to the shore.

Then home he would trudge with a heart light as air,
    And a spirit contented and free,
To see how all matters were going on there,
    And his children to take on his knee.

But then if some travelers chanced to pass by,
    And would wish him to ferry them o'er,
Though ever so weary, poor Robert would try
    To favor them all in his power.

No matter if winds blew high or blew low,
    He never was known to refuse,
But ever believed it his duty to go,
    Though in the long run he should lose.

Yet there is a saying, and one very true,
    As the feature is oft brought to light,
That a man will lose nothing by trying to do
    What is worthy as well as polite.

And here in one case we will truly admit
    The motto was brought to a test;
Where honest old Robert he lost not a whit,
    By acting his kindest and best.

One night, if the time we can rightly remember,
    'Mid terrible snow, sleet, and rain,
A traveler called—it was late in November—
    The fisherman's service to gain.

The hurricane winds blew fearful and drear,
    And surges beat wild on the shore;
So honest old Robert was heard to declare
    Such a time he had scarce seen before.

But then he was never a coward, and fear
    Was unknown to his weather-worn breast;
Yet he told the lone stranger that danger was near,
    But he'd do all he could for the best.

"I must go," said the guest, "though the storm rages
  wild;
I am neither much loath or afraid;
On yon island I've got a dear sick wife and child,—
  Your labor shall be nobly paid."

Ah, that was enough! the humane appeal
  Struck deep to his heart, ay, his life;
For Robert, indeed, knew too well how to feel,
  Himself having children and wife.

Off, off was the boat soon got from the shore,
  And bounding across the mad waves;
Amid the bleak storm and the surges' wild roar
  You'd have thought they must soon find their graves.

But Heaven was kind! they succeeded at last;
  The vessel got safe to the land;
When the stranger, as soon as the boat was made fast,
  Rewarded with liberal hand.

Withdrawing a purse from his pocket, he said—
  "You have acted most nobly and kind!
Take this, but I do not consider you paid—
  In me a sure friend you will find.

"Whenever in sickness or in distress,
  Or if ever in want you should be,
I will always endeavor to make your woes less—
  Be sure then to call upon me."

With thanks, honest Robert prepared to depart
  Once more 'mid the tempest and storm,
With a tear on his cheek, for his faithful old heart
  Felt now with deep gratitude warm.

Soon, soon he was plowing the billows once more,
  While the winds harped with ominous sound;
But soon he was plodding his own happy shore,
  And safe in his cottage was found.

And what do you think, when the purse he undrew,
  After kissing all round with delight?
Dear reader, he found there a hundred or two
  Of gold ducats, to bless his old sight!

And never were hearts more supremely glad,
  While tears filled with rapture all eyes;
You'd have thought in your soul they would all have gone
    mad
  At this blessing bestowed in disguise.

Though Robert declared he knew, for a sign,
  That something was brewing that way,—
That a number of kinks had got into his line,
  And his hand had been itching all day.

However, we know there was joy and delight,
  Such as seldom to mortals is sent,
On that stormy, blustering Saturday night,
  In this cottage of happy content.

THE SUICIDE.

'Twas midnight—and appalling gloom
  Was o'er the city spread;
All seemed as silent as the tomb
  Where lie the slumbering dead.

14

The world seemed locked in dreamy sleep,
  The air was dank and foul;
Yet on the mournful silence deep
  Was heard the watch-dog's howl.

Or, ever and anon, a sound
  Came up upon the ear,
As some lone sentinel took his round
  'Mid shadows dark and drear.

Such solemn stillness and such gloom
  Was seldom ever known;
One would have thought the night of doom
  Was round creation thrown.

The heavens were black as ebon hue;
  Thick darkness fell around;
And not one single star in view
  Relieved the gloom profound.

Yet, while this midnight silence hung
  Around the city fair,
There was one wretched soul among
  The wakeful sons of care.

For there are some who cannot sleep,
  When conscience rends the mind,
Though gladly they in slumber deep
  Repose would sweetly find.

But misery, with its demon power,
  Will on the vitals gnaw,
And at the noiseless midnight hour
  Will oft the life's blood draw.

And such a one we offer here,
   Whose life seems but a shade,
Whose soul is wrecked with woe and care
   Through some most faithless maid.

Alone he sat, in solemn mood,
   Within his chamber walls,
Plotting a scene of crime and blood
   Which now the heart appalls.

His features were most pale and grim,
   His soul was seared and sad ;
Ay, any one to look at him
   Could but pronounce him mad !

Such fearful and unearthly light
   Flashed from his sockets bold,
That while it pierced the gloom of night,
   'Twere awful to behold !

And then those muttered words, that fell
   With deep and guttural tone
Through his clenched teeth, could sadly tell
   Some deed was to be done.

"Base world !" he cried, with frenzied air,
   " How have ye wrung my soul !
Your dreams of bliss are false as fair ;
   Accurst is love's control !

"A demon 'neath an angel's guise
   Lured my fond heart astray :
False Julia, thy Menander dies—
   Love's perjured vows to pay !

"Foul phantom! come not near my brain,
  This death accurst will be;
A thousand lives of endless pain
  Will now devolve on me!

"But fate is fixed! my doom is sealed!
  Why should I pause in dread?
Why fear the future unrevealed,
  Or wish to shun the dead?

"Why linger thus with paltry fear—
  The deed it must be done—
Though countless damning ghosts appear
  To claim their victim won?"

And now, with frenzied look, he raised
  A dagger that was near,
Then on the fatal blade he gazed,
  And dropped one burning tear.

But then that tear was only one
  From memory's inmost core;
He gave one thrust—the deed was done—
  Menander was no more.

THE BLIND CHILD.

PRETTY child, with flaxen hair,
Light-blue eyes and features fair,
Dimpled cheek and polished brow,
What a darling pet art thou!

But say, whither dost thou fly?
Why thus rudely hurry by?
Canst thou not one moment stay,
Nimbly passing on thy way?
Little stranger, pause awhile;
Let me see thy rosy smile,
Hear thee gently speak thy name,
Tell me too from whence thou came;
For thou art a darling pet
I cannot very soon forget!

"Lady, lady, it is true
That my eyes are azure blue,
And that ringlets soft and fair
Float around my shoulders bare;
And of dimples, which you speak,
Playing on my rosy cheek:
All are blessings sweet and kind—
But, dear lady, I am blind!

"Ah, you start in deep surprise!
Look once more into my eyes;
Though they seem both blue and bright,
They are sealed in endless night.
Yes, dear lady! and I'd give
A hundred ages, could I live,
But to drive the mist away
And behold the light of day,
Which so beauteous must appear
Throughout the glad and rolling year.
But 'tis vain to wish; I find
I must live forever blind.

14*

"Yet how often have I smiled,
Though I'm but a little child,
When from others I can hear
How fair and bright all things appear:
The earth with all its fruits and flowers,
Its forests gay, and garden bowers,
Its sunny skies with planets bright,
That look like spangles in the night;
How holy all must be to view!
But, ah! this joy I never knew,
For dear mamma, in accents kind,
Oft told me I was always blind.

"Yet, lady, still I think I hear
Her sweet and loving voice near,
Painting on my sightless view
All nature perfect, grand, and true,
Until I almost thought I saw
The very picture she would draw;
Yet, still, she taught my heart to pray,
And thank my Saviour, day by day,
For all his mercies free and kind,
And love him dearly, though I'm blind.

"But now I am an orphan lone,
For mother she is dead and gone,
And father he is far away—
If he is living to this day;
But many think he is no more,
And died upon a foreign shore;
Yet, of this, I cannot learn,
And often pray for his return,
Still hoping Heaven kindly may
Bring back my dear papa some day:

Although his face I cannot see,
Still I can hear him speak to me
In loving accents, sweet and kind;
Then I'll be happy, though I'm blind!"

"Dear little prattler! go thy way;
May Heaven guard thee day by day,
And all thy steps from danger keep!
Thy painful story makes me weep:
Think not those eyes, now sealed in night,
Are closed forever from the light;
Ah, no! those sightless orbs shall see
The glories of eternity!"

THE VILLAGE GREEN.

LOOK, upon the village green,
What a merry troup is seen,
A happier set hath never been
　　In all creation fair!
Just watch each lovely smiling face,
And if contentment you would trace,
As well as purity and grace,
　　You'll surely find it there.

And yonder is old Parson Gray—
He always tries to come this way
On every merry gala day;
　　He loves the little clan!

And, if I don't mistake my view,
There is the honest piper too,
With bagpipes, though by no means new,—
    Dear clever-hearted man!

And there is Ned, the miller's son,
A worthy lad he is for one,
But loves a little rural fun—
    For 'tis his very nature;
Yet folks, who will talk matters o'er,
Say that young Ned loves something more—
A lass within yon cottage door,
    With smiling face and feature.

Yet while they speculate so free,
The whole may village scandal be—
Such matters have been known to me—
    However, let it pass!
For, say, what right have we to know
Who has or who has not a beau?
It is no harm, I tell you so,
    To love a pretty lass!

Hark! now the music has begun!
Behold the frolic and the fun!
They now in every figure run
    And dance with garlands gay;
Or some in merry circles meet,
With airy forms and nimble feet,
Their songs of welcome to repeat,
    For 'tis the first of May.

And see! with what delight they bring,
Each one, their posey offering
To crown the lovely nymph of Spring
    With gaily painted flowers;

Ah, yes! of all the charming year
No moments are so sweetly dear,
Or half so glad or bright appear,
    As these fond rosy hours.

And ever welcome is the day
Of lovely, smiling, first of May,
When troups of lads and lasses gay
    All hasten to the scene;
Most neatly, if not gaudily, drest
Up in their tidy, Sunday best,
To sport away a day of rest
    Upon the village green.

———❧❧———

WHAT IS LOVE?

WHAT is Love? It is a flame
That does not only live in name;
A tender passion, toying, teasing,
Sometimes warm and sometimes freezing;
A feeling smothered up with sighs,
And almost killing to the eyes;
Something much beyond control,
A perfect tempest in the soul;
Bringing often tears and sadness,
With fits of melancholy madness;
Dooming, tearing mind and reason,
Duly in and out of season;
Crushing every joy in view,
Causing pistols oft for two!

Dismal source of pain and pleasure,
Often horror without measure,—
Then avaunt! thou prudish ranger,
Demon oft of death and danger!
Since thy presence torture brings,
Reason ought to clip thy wings.
Away, avaunt! I'll none of thee,
Thou little rogue of destiny!
To bother with an imp so blue
I would not for all famed Peru;
For what would be its mines of gold
If I myself to torment sold?
I know thee well! I've seen thy hoaxing,
Sometimes threatening, sometimes coaxing,
Flattering, fawning, laughing, fooling,
Almost half creation ruling;
While thy votaries, over-kind,
Call thee a little god that's blind.
Ha! a pretty thing to tell!
Vain rogue! thou seest but too well!
Sure Argus never had more eyes!
Though thou art but a babe in size,
Yet ever into mischief creeping,
In every hole and corner peeping;
Until we find, without a doubt,
The heart is riddled inside out;
And all would seem a question whether
The wounded parts would hang together.
Then get thee hence! thou pigmy thing,
Fluttering round on gauzy wing!
Shoulder thy quiver and silver bow,
And away to thy goddess mother go!
For if the truth were known, no doubt,
She knows not, rogue, that thou art out.

THE MOSS-COVERED SEAT.

How often fond memory loves to retrace
   Those hours of childhood now gone,
When innocent rapture lit up our young face
   As time glided swiftly on !
How well I remember the dark, shady wood,
   And the spring and the running brook too,
Where often I wandered in right merry mood
   To cull the sweet violets blue !
Yet dearer to me was it ever to rove
To the charming old moss-covered seat in the grove.

Ah ! many's the time, in the warm summer hours,
   We sought out its beautiful shade,
After running to gather our basket of flowers—
   And there our sweet garlands we made
To give, as a tribute of holy esteem,
   To juvenile friends that were dear !
And great was the joy and delight that would beam
   From many an eye bright and clear ;
Then away we would scamper, with hearts full of love,
To the darling old moss-covered seat in the grove.

But now, like a dream has all faded away ;
   Dark changes have come o'er the scene ;
Yet memory, faithful, still turns to the day
   When pleasure and hope shone serene ;
Yea, fond recollection, in coloring true,
   Can paint those bright halcyon hours
When the morning of life was unclouded to view,
   And visions of purity ours.

But gone are those seasons of childhood and love,
When I sat on the moss-covered seat in the grove.

How many sweet friends have departed and gone
   To the shadows of death and the grave,
While I am still left to plod onward alone,
   And the storms of misfortune to brave!
Ah! who would have thought that so dreary a change
   Would have clouded the day-dream of life,
And every hope of enjoyment estrange
   Into scenes of confusion and strife?
Yet so it hath proved, nor more can I rove
To the charming old moss-covered seat in the grove.

Yet what though afar from the scenes of my youth,
   From the fields where I sportively played,
Or see nevermore the bright woodlands forsooth,
   Or the clear running brook in the glade!
Yet memory still, with its holiest power,
   Shall treasure those scenes of repose,
And muse on each glowing and sweet sunny hour,
   Till life and its changes shall close;
Ay, still will affection and memory rove
To the charming old moss-covered seat in the grove!

THE PARTING.

Don't weep, don't weep! life of my heart!
   It wrings my soul to see that tear!
Though cruel fate now bids us part,
   We'll meet again, ah! do not fear!

What though the rolling waves shall bear
    Me o'er their bosom, far away!
Thy own loved image, true and dear,
    Shall never, never from me stray!

No matter, dearest, where I roam:
    Though raging seas our hearts divide,
Affection still will wander home,
    And find me ever at thy side.

Ay, every loving look and tone,
    That from thy gentle lips now flow,
Shall seem to me, when I am gone,
    The same as now—that well I know!

Think not that absence e'er can break
    Affection's sweet, devoted chain;
Ah, no! it only serves to make
    The bosom prone to greater pain!

Ay, pain that rankles deep and keen
    Within the true and faithful breast,
And prompts to many a tear unseen,
    While loving memory has no rest.

For such is true and holy love!
    Such gushing purity shall be—
No matter, dearest, where I rove,
    Devoted fondly still to thee.

And many a fervent, silent prayer,
    As weary moments may depart,
Shall be that Heaven will land me where
    I soon may fold thee to my heart.

15

And then, what nameless joy will bless
　　Our bosoms reft so long in twain !
What rapture hail the parting kiss—
　　Ay, meet, nor part till death again!

———✻———

THE MISER.

Look, look ! say, do you not behold
Yon miser with his bags of gold ?
See how he clutches, counts his spoil
With wakeful eye and ceaseless toil !

Ay, what of holy sleep knows he?
A very wretch he seems to be !
He fears the drowsy god to feel,
Lest rogues his hoarded wealth may steal ;
And if he falls in drowsy mood,
His mind still o'er his treasures brood,
Counting his gold for pleasure's sake—
The same asleep as when awake—
And with the same insatiate eye,
As though he ne'er was born to die.

Poor sordid wretch ! what demon foul
Hath took possession of thy soul ?
He sees not, in his thirst for gain,
The penalty of guilt and pain ;
He fears no dread of curse or doom
Beyond the precincts of the tomb.

What cares he for gospel sound ?
He ne'er within its reach is found !

It is to him a letter dead,
Of which he bothers not his head;
But gold! ah, gold! that is the theme
Which ever proves his wakeful dream;
Of it alone his soul can think—
It is to him both meat and drink.
A crust, or penny roll, each day
Will keep him in his meager way,
With but his shining hoard in view,
Good bread and water, it will do.

Count, count! ay, count it o'er;
Perchance he's added to his store?
Or if there is no further gain,
He finds his counting is not vain;
For pleasure sparkles in his eyes
To see the heaps before him rise,
Though not one jot or tittle more
Is present than there was before.

Ha! how he clutches in his grip
Each weighty bag, lest it may slip
Or tumble from his bony hand
And make a jingle on the stand,
Or yet upon the dusty floor,
Which might be heard outside the door,
And thus attract some robber bold
To come and steal his hidden gold!

Alas! what looks of fear and doubt
His eyes are seen to cast about!
A mortal dread runs though his veins
Lest he may lose some of his gains;

And e'en at night, when toil is o'er,
And penny rushlight burns no more,
When all is safely placed away
To count again another day,
The sordid wretch his arms will fold
Around his darling chest of gold;
And there he dreams the long night through:
He has the glittering hoard in view,
Nor cares for devils, grinning, prancing,
Or fiery tongues around him dancing,
Or demons hissing in his ear
"Beware, O miser! ah, beware!"
He heeds them not, still lightly deeming
He only had been foully dreaming.
Thus he plods the whole night through
Without one future joy in view,
Waiting with mind benighted, steady,
Until the time Old Nick is ready
To bear him off from all his pelf,
Unknown, unbidden by himself.
When he must hear the dooming sound—
"Go! thou among the lost art found;
Thy homage was to Mammon given;
Thy earthly gain has lost thee heaven!"

CLOSE NOT THINE EAR.

Shun not the voice of counsel good and true,
    When given with a motive pure and kind;
It may a generous warning prove to you,
    And saye from dangers that enthral the mind.

For when we scorn reproof that's mild, sincere,
 And cling to sin, regardless of our fate,
We'll find that judgments follow our career,
 And deeply mourn our rashness when too late!

'Tis wise to listen, ignorance to scorn
 Sweet counsel given by a friendly voice,
When it is meant our stubborn hearts to warn
 And save us from some dark misguided choice.

None are so firm but what the best may err,
 And none so good but they may slip or fall;
Though God's displeasure we may oft incur,
 There's mercy offered still for one and all.

Ay, mercy! if the heart will turn and live,
 Nor too long trifle with eternal might;
For there's an hour God ceases to forgive,
 And mournful takes his everlasting flight.

THE VOICE OF NATURE.

I HEAR it in the rushing tide
 That sweeps against the shore,
Or when along the mountain's side
 The ocean sends its roar.

I hear it in the tempest shrill
 That shakes the earth and sky,
Or when the air is calm and still
 In every zephyr's sigh.

15*

I hear it in the woodlands gay,
   When Spring's soft beauties reign;
In every warbling tenant's lay
   That hail their shades again.

I hear it in the murmuring rill
   That rippling steals along,
While countless busy insects fill
   The desert air with song.

I hear it in each beauteous note
   Of pipe or shepherd's horn,
That o'er the distant mountains float
   When còmes the blushing morn.

Each wild, uncultivated strain,
   Through self-instruction given,
Is nature's music o'er again,
   Just echoed back from heaven.

'Mid caves of solitude is heard
   The mutterings of its voice;
The rocks, though mute, proclaim the word
   That nature's works rejoice.

In storm or calm, in every hour,
   Is ceaseless wisdom shown;
The stars, the planets, speak with power,
   And make God's glory known!

Each plant or flower that mutely blooms
   Retains a voice to tell
That nature's God the whole assumes,
   And in the midst doth dwell.

And, louder still, more firm than all,
    Is that meek voice within,
Which o'er the spirit's feelings fall
    To chide the heart for sin.

And do we see thus nature speak
    In all, o'er all, still on,
And yet refuse that wisdom meek
    Which Heaven smiles upon?

The earth, the sea, the holy sky,
    All have their speaking claim,
That tells, in vast immensity,
    Jehovah is the same!

THE REUNION;

OR,

THE WINTER'S FIRESIDE TALE.

" HARK, mother! how the pelting storm
    Howls round our humble cot!
Though we are here secure and warm,
    And share a kindly lot;

"Although we have a cheerful blaze
    To throw its light around,
And peaceful nights and happy days
    Are in our cottage found,—

" How many beings, lone and poor,
    Are wandering far and wide,
Across the bleak and frozen moor,
    Or by the mountain's side!

" Perchance no friend or bosom dear
   To bid them welcome home,
Nor bright nor sunny thoughts, to cheer
   Them as they onward roam.

" Momentous gloom hangs o'er the vale ;
   Loud groans the dismal blast ;
The clouds pour down both rain and hail—
   I'll make the shutters fast !

" Now, mother, I will sit by thee
   Before the cheerful hearth,
And pray that thou wilt tell to me
   A tale of woe or mirth.

" For thou hast, many a night like this—
   Perchance not so severe—
Told me of tales once fraught with bliss,
   That pleased my heart to hear."

MOTHER'S REPLY.

" 'Tis true, my child," the dame replied,
   "I many a tale have told ;
But one that memory fain would hide
   I will this night unfold.

" Thy tender years hath long forbid
   My feelings to impart
What now shall be no longer hid
   From thy inquiring heart.

" Yea, dear one, start not with surprise !
   Come, seat thyself by me;
For soon, perhaps, these aged eyes
   May gaze no more on thee !

"Thou thinkest, 'cause thy heart is gay,
  And sadness never knew,
And thornless flowers strew thy way,
  That mine is joyous too!

"But, ah! thou knowest not the storm,
  And far more drear than this,
That robbed my once gay, happy form
  Of every earthly bliss!

"But, hark! the tempest fury bears
  Its spirit on the blast;
I have not known, for many years,
  The sleet to fall so fast!

"Just such a night of threatening gloom,
  Some eighteen years ago,
Bring swift to mind my early doom,
  A sight of weal and woe!

"'Tis true this cottage then was new,
  With merry woodbines crowned,
And flowers around fantastic grew
  As from enchanted ground.

"The old oak tree before the door,
  Now rocking in the gale,
Once threw its laughing branches o'er
  The subject of my tale.

"A dear companion shared my bliss,
  The partner of my fate,
And when he stole the wedding kiss,
  We thought our joys replete.

" The rolling seasons passed away
    On bright and sunny wing,
And every cheering new-born day
    Its sure delights would bring.

"I thought those dreams of joy could ne'er
    Depart from holy view,
But demon Fate came brooding here—
    In all its horror too!

"Autumn had fled; the tall trees now
    Heaved out their wintry moan,
While snow-wreaths hung from every bough
    Like gems from beauty's throne!

" With dear Fitzgerald at my side—
    He was thy father, child!—
I thought myself, in truth, a bride
    On whom kind Heaven had smiled.

"'Twas night—just such a night forsooth,
    Now eighteen years or more—
When, sudden, a mysterious youth
    Rushed in the cottage door!

"A furious band in strange attire
    Now met our frighted view;
We were the victims of their ire,
    And merciless vengeance too!

" The tempest howled; loud was the blast;
    Oh! dark, tremendous night!
The heavens, with blackness overcast,
    Gave not one ray of light.

" Descending snow and heavy sleet
  Beat round our cottage walls;
And thus, to make my woe replete,
  Fitzgerald lifeless falls.

" The wretches seized me as I hung
  Upon his fainting heart;
The cruel accents of their tongue
  Soon told a treacherous part.

"A band of robbers, threatening, bold,
  With visage fierce and wild,
Soon tore him from my sacred hold,
  But took not thee, my child.

" Swift, swift they bore him from my sight;
  And since that fearful hour,
No charms afford my heart delight,
  And hope revives no more !

" Where'er they led him, I could ne'er
  By every effort learn;
But live, I have, a victim here,
  His murdered fate to mourn.

" Yet I must tell, and tell again,
  I was the cause of all !
Which maddens feelings into pain
  Of dear Fitzgerald's fall !

"A rival lover, child, was he,
  My soul's adored, I own !
And when I vowed his bride to be,
  Rugald's heart turned to stone.

" He swore, by every stern decree,
That vongeance was his aim,
And should his darling motto be,
If me he could not claim.

"Thus when he threw his mask aside
I saw his fearful mien ;
Said he, ' Thou hast a robber tried,
In Rugald thou hast seen.

" ' No more shall human pleasures bring
Their fairy dreams of rest,
For thou hast placed a lasting sting
Within my tortured breast.

" ' The civil ranks of men no more
Shall have me in their throng ;
The voice of mirth I now abhor,
And all where joys belong.

" 'A bandit's life I woo with pride ;
Its gloomy toils are mine ;
Since now thou art Fitzgerald's bride,
My misery shall be thine !

" 'Torn from him ever thou shalt be,
Though kill thee I will not,
But learn thou shalt, to feel like me,
No parting pain's forgot.

" ' Then fare thee well ! pursuit is vain ;
Stir not from here this night !
For if I meet with thee again,
There's danger in the flight !'

"Thus spoke the savage youth, and fled
  Amid the howling storm;
While on the heartless bandits led
  Thy father's captive form.

"God only knows whate'er they done,
  For search were all in vain;
For horsemen, on the morning's dawn,
  No sight of him could gain.

"From that tremendous night, my child,
  No tidings could I learn,
And sorrow round my heart hath coiled
  To find him ne'er return.

"And thus I would not pain thy heart,
  Or quote the saddening tale,
And oft assumed a cheerful part
  Lest thy young hopes might fail.

"I told thee he was dead, my dear!
  For that it might be true
I think I had much cause to fear,
  Since naught of him I know.

"Be he a captive, dead or not,
  The world I'd give to know;
Nor can I from my memory blot
  That night of weal and woe.

"And thus I thought it time to tell
  Thy lovely virgin heart
The sorrow which my fate befell
  Ere thou couldst feel the smart.

16

" No terrors o'er thy infant head
    Were numbered as thou slept,
Nor knew thou how the bosom bled
    That o'er thy cradle wept.

"I've gazed upon thy slumbering brow,
    And kissed thee o'er and o'er ;
And many a prayer, as well as now,
    Hath smoothed the midnight hour."

DAUGHTER.

" Dear mother! thou hast burst a chain
    My feelings long hath worn,
In silence, o'er and o'er again,
    That thou did'st ne'er discern;

" I mean suspense, that long hath clung,
    Around my spirit's throne,
And whispered some strange mystery hung
    O'er future fate unknown.

"And, mother ! odd as it may seem,
    Last night thy only child
Did revel in a curious dream ;
    'Twas e'en romantic, wild !

" I thought the moon was shining bright,
    The heavens were blue and clear,
And countless stars threw down their light
    The evening hours to cheer.

" The summer's sweetly soothing breeze
    Blew round our vine-clad cot ;
The night birds warbled in the trees,
    And flowers adorned the spot.

"And soft a strain of music stole
  Upon the balmy air,
While every note entranced the soul
  As if from angels near.

"At length a stillness seemed to reign
  Around the sacred place;
I looked and listened—looked again,
  But could no being trace.

"Just then a whisper met my ear
  More sweet than music's sound;
I thought I heard a father's prayer—
  His blessing I had found.

"But hark, dear mother! don't you hear?
  The watchdog gives alarm!
Some traveler surely must be near—
  I hope they mean no harm!

"For since thou hast revealed to me
  This deep and saddening tale,
Each object that I hear or see
  Alarms me that I quail.

"The sighing of the tempest, too,
  Breaks mournful o'er my soul,
And causes feelings strange and new
  Beyond my heart's control.

"The mighty boughs wreak out their moan
  In accents sadly wild;
And, mother, here we are alone,
  Thyself and orphan child.

"But God, who rules the tempest, still
  Our sovereign friend will be;
And thus, I trust, he surely will
  Defend both thee and me!

"But listen! footsteps near the door—
  I hear them in the snow!
Perhaps some soul would aid implore,
  Or wish the way to know!

" Then courage, mother! surely none
  Could harm thee in thy years,
But reverence, when they look upon
  Thy visage steeped in tears!

"But list! the hand is on the door!
  My bosom quails with fear;
Sweet Heaven send thy shielding power
  If danger now is near!"

ENTER STRANGER.

" Dear ladies, fly not! fear not one
  Bewildered, strange, yet kind;
For as the shades of night came on
  No shelter could I find.

"I've come o'er many a woody height,
  Through many a frozen vale,
Till heaven shut out its friendly light
  By clouds of rain and hail.

"And night in all its hideous form
  Came on to clothe the scene;
For many a year not such a storm
  My exiled soul hath seen.

"While distant far, a glimmering flame
  I from your casement viewed ;
Thus cold and lost, you will not blame
  That I should thus intrude !

"A stranger, I, in truth appear,
  Yet would most humbly pray
That you will let me tarry here
  Until the break of day,—

" When I must leave you purse in hand
  For what you now bestow,
And other blessings at command
  When more of me you know.

" 'Tis many years since I have trod
  This well-remembered soil ;
But fate had marked out my abode
  For misery and for guile.

" It must be sure not far from here
  Where once in peace I moved
With one to every feeling dear—
  A wife I fondly loved.

"My own Zuphelia, chaste and true,
  In all her lovely charms—"
The cottagers now screamed, and flew
  Into the stranger's arms !

It was the exiled father, who
  For years had been away ;
But then with time such changes grew
  That altered much were they.

16*

And scarcely could they now believe
 Years could such ravage bring;
And thus each other's looks deceive
 Where love's devotions cling.

But nature's own affections e'er
 A leading trait will prove,
To call us to those scenes most dear,
 And those we truly love.

For lengthened years can never blot
 From memory's holy view
Those objects, not to be forgot,
 With all their changes too.

Fitzgerald now caressed by turns
 His wife and daughter dear ;
While every thought with rapture burns
 To swell the melting tear.

And now did he each scene explain
 That had his fate befell,
With scarce a hope that e'er again
 He would among them dwell.

He said, " When Rugald's fiendly hand
 Had dealt the treacherous blow,
He ordered his tyrannic band
 No freedom to bestow,—

" But lead me to the nearest shore,
 Where then in waiting stood
A vessel which too quickly bore
 Me on the rolling flood,—

"Intending, when far off from land,
  To give me to the waves;
But other advents were at hand,
  And your Fitzgerald saves!

"Feeling his rival in his power,
  He most imperious grew,
And told me I should never more
  My home or country view.

"Thou hast exulted in thy claim,
  And blighted all my joy;
Yet though Zuphelia bears thy name,
  Your bliss I will destroy!

"Never each other shall ye greet
  If my best strength prevail;
Thou art destined for fishes' meat—
  The hungry shark and whale.

"How did the tempest drive along
  Our flimsy, leaky boat!
The ocean's wild and roaring song
  Did horrid tales denote!

"But hardened in their foul design,
  He and his hellish crew
Laughed but to scorn the plot of crime
  And raging tempest too.

"Morning brought still its lowering gloom,
  Though rushing storm had ceased;
I looked upon the waves' broad tomb
  Designed for me at least.

"Some whisperings now of meanings kind
    Their plotting lips expressed,
That plainly told my troubled mind
    I soon would be at rest.

"But now a flag in view appears
    Just through the misty light;
And swift a boat toward us nears—
    'Twas pirates then in sight.

"Escape was vain, too well they knew;
    Our little vessel they
Did gallantly, in truth, pursue,
    And claimed before broad day.

"Then no reluctance did I feel,
    For doomed I seemed to be;
I thought it needless to appeal
    For life or to be free.

"But when I told to them my case,
    Although they pirates were,
They did to confidence give place,
    And thus my life did spare;

"But did the others instant slay,
    And robbed them of their store;
Their golden pelf they took away—
    They could not well do more!

"They bore me to a distant isle,
    There sold me for a slave,
Where years of anxious pain and toil
    I for my freedom gave.

"And when redeemed, I instant sought
   Some ship to bear me o'er
To that sweet home affection taught
   Was on my native shore.

" But oh! what thoughts my soul oppressed,
   Lest I should find you dead!
How oft have I God's throne addressed
   While every feeling bled!

"I knew not what befell your fate,
   No chance had I to learn,
Yet feared that wretched Rugald's hate
   Did vilely on you turn.

" It were more terrible than death
   Had he dishonored thee;
But then I knew, with life and breath,
   Thy soul was constancy.

" But all is passed! It is a dream
   O'er memory to preside!
Deem it, my love, a little theme
   Adventure hath supplied.

" Here, here we are, all safe and sound,
   With blessings yet in store;
The exile hath his loved home found,
   And those he loves still more.

" Here, in this sweet pastoral spot,
   Devoted we will live;
Joy shall again attend our lot,
   While praise to God we give.

"Our beauteous daughter, chaste and true,
    Will bless our future life ;
Thus joys unceasing will pursue
    The father, child, and wife."

Years now have fled; but legend still
    Holds out the tale to view,
And many a roving minstrel will
    The exile's fate renew.

------- ⋰⋱ -------

THE APOSTATE DAUGHTER.

AN OVER-TRUE TALE.

LEDELLA was a beauteous child,
    Exceeding fair and kind;
'Twas holy sweetness when she smiled—
    And lovely was her mind.

Her eyes were heaven's purest blue,
    Her hair of auburn bright;
Her figure, fairy-like to view,
    Was buoyant, chaste, and light.

A thousand graces sweetly played
    Around her perfect form,
As though by sacred nature made
    To fascinate and charm.

Her parents, they were proud and vain,
    And as in years she grew,
They strove her feelings to restrain
    From subjects pure and true.

Religion they received with scorn ;
    They doubted Heaven's power ;
And thus they sought their child to warn
    In many an evil hour.

"Beware !" said they, " of all you hear,
    Dear daughter, for we own,
If you to serious thoughts give ear
    Our hearts are turned to stone !

" 'Tis folly, madness, when they tell
    Of future worlds of bliss ;
'Tis but to bind your heart by spell
    With doctrines such as this.

" See, you are placed on pleasure's ground,
    With friends and kindred dear,
And if true joys are to be found
    They surely must be here !

" Trust not to what those teachers say
    Who in the pulpit stand ;
They'll take your happiness away,—
    There is no other land !

" They'll tell you angels crowd the throne
    Where great Jehovah reigns ;
That all whoe'er his laws disown
    Are doomed to hell and pains.

"Then listen not ! you know we love
    You more than all on earth !
Then do not disobedient prove,
    But join the ranks of mirth.

" See pleasure while you can, my child !
  For this your life was given ;
On you hath wealth and virtue smiled,—
  There is no other heaven !"

But holy thoughts were brooding o'er
  This daughter meek and fair,
Although her parents sought to pour
  Temptation in her ear.

To church, unknown to them, she went
  To hear the gospel sound ;
And there the Lord his angel sent—
  His spirit there was found.

But soon the parents saw the change ;
  Her spirits gay were fled ;
They now began to think it strange,
  And thus the father said :—

" This will not do ! our child will die—
  How pale she looks and sad !
What is the cause ? I know not why !
  A doctor must be had !"

A famed physician now was brought,
  Who valued Heaven's laws ;
And soon the anxious parents taught—
  Religion was the cause.

" It shall not be !" the father said ;
  " 'Tis but a phantom dream ;
I'd sooner see my daughter dead
  Than harbor such a theme !"

And now he gives a brilliant ball
  To lure her pensive mind ;
And far and near invited all
  His friends of gaudy kind.

A glittering dress, all spangled o'er,
  He forced his child to wear ;
While diamonds bright as beauty's power
  Were woven in her hair.

And thus with tears the parents won
  Upon her youthful heart ;
And when the mazy ball begun,
  Ledella danced her part.

Adored, caressed by flattering friends,
  All gloom was thrown aside ;
But Heaven its own chastisement sends
  To quell the force of pride.

The change of dress, the heated room,
  With force of thoughts combined,
All sealed the fair Ledella's doom
  From that sad night, we find !

Borne to her chamber, there she lay
  With burning heart and brow ;
Her parents, with what anguish they
  Look on their daughter now !

Each day they view, with painful grief,
  The sinking, wasting frame ;
No power on earth could give relief—
  For Heaven had willed the same.

17

One day, her parents weeping near,
   She called them to her side
And said, " My honored parents dear,
   How vain is earthly pride !

" Go bring, I pray, my spangled robe,
   And diamonds for my hair ;
Ere life's best pulses cease to throb
   I wish to see them here."

They started back in deep surprise
   At such a strange request;
But still she wished before her eyes
   What in she once was drest.

And now the gaudy sight they placed
   Before her ghastly view ;
Then on her parents loved she cast
   A look to pierce them through.

" Dear parents, see ! the time is past !
   I once to grace was given !
Till this bright robe was o'er me cast
   To steal my heart from Heaven.

" I once upon my Saviour's breast
   Had felt disposed to lean,
Till in this robe you had me drest
   To join the ball-room scene.

" Oh ! look upon my ghostly form
   And see the end of pride,—
A creature for the earth and worm,
   Perhaps for hell beside!

"'Tis now too late, my doom's revealed,
  My soul is clothed in night!
Dear father, mother, you have sealed
  Your child from glory's light!

"Dark demons round my pillow wait
  To bear my soul away;
Oh! how I wish, when now too late,
  For time to weep and pray!

"Dear parents! then give up your creed
  Of which you vainly boast;
There is a holy God, indeed,—
  Turn, turn, or you are lost!"

Then on their trembling knees they fell
  And clasped her dying hand;
Conviction bound them as by spell—
  'Twas Heaven's supreme command!

They gazed upon her marble brow
  With solemn, deep despair,
And plainly could they feel it now,
  The cause that placed her there.

And now a sacred vow they give,
  In one united bre ath,
The holy Lord's to daily live,
  And claim him after death!

CONSCIENCE.

IF e'er I do wrong by heart, deed, or tongue,
    And friends would write caution below it,
'Tis then I would say, without much delay,
    " Don't tell me, for surely I know it!"

If day after day I throw time away,
    When God is so kind to bestow it,
No one need to tell that I fail to do well,
    'Tis certain I feel it and know it.

If ever the poor should call at my door,
    And meanness, I ventured to show it,
None need then to warn if I treat them with scorn,
    My heart, if so wicked, must know it!

If e'er it should be I must treachery see,
    And make no attempt to o'erthrow it,
But league in with art to act a base part,
    I sin, and most truly must know it.

If anger should e'er before me appear,
    And I to a flame would dare blow it,
'Tis then I would feel what truth must reveal—
    That I had done wrong, and must know it.

But if I do well, my conscience will tell,
    For feelings of pleasure o'erflow it;
For when I do right in Heaven's broad sight,
    Don't tell me, for quickly I know it!

THE GOBLIN, OR REFORMED COWARD.

A TALE.

THE night was dark, the winds blew hoarse
  Along the mountain side,
And not a star in nature's course
  With light the gloom supplied,—

When Horace, on his stubborn steed,
  Was weary homeward bound;
He spurred, he coaxed, yet still indeed
  The brute crawled o'er the ground.

And now a horrid storm arose;
  The lightnings flashed severe;
The rain in mighty torrents flows;
  Yet home was nowhere near.

The thunder rolled along the sky,
  The trees heaved out their moan;
In everything that met his eye
  Some phantom grim was shown.

But what made matters worse was this—
  It was a haunted wood!
Nor could he ugly thoughts dismiss
  That nearly froze his blood.

It was the village talk.—'Twas said,
  On certain nights was seen
A man to walk without his head,
  Who murdered there had been.

17*

But Horace thought, to be afraid
  Would manly not appear,
And thus he now quite loudly said—
  " I am no slave to fear !

" Who cares for village paltry chat?
  Of goblins or of ghost?
'Tis some old woman's tale, all that,
  To scare one, at the most!

" Come, Dobbin, get yourself along !
  You are a lazy brute !
I vow I'll sell you for a song,
  For me you do not suit !

"You hear the thunder rolling round,
  And see the lightning's glare;
So that they shake the very ground
  And almost raise my hair !

" Yet here you go, just half asleep,
  While I am drenched with rain ; ·
Ay, in one crawling pace you keep—
  A fool you be, that's plain !

" But as to fear, it's all a fudge !
  No ghost that e'er could be
Would cause me from this spot to budge—
  What ! scare a man like me ?

" Why, if a regiment were here
  Of goblins pale and grim,
I'd show some sparring, that is clear,
  In every bone and limb !"

Thus thought young Horace, as again
   He spurred his stubborn beast ;
To get him in a trot were vain,
   Or hurry him the least.

" Gee up, Dobbin ! gee up ! gee ho !
   The animal's possessed !
For thumping will not make him go
   Out of a creep at best !"

And now a sudden freak he took,
   Nor would he move at all;
And Horace felt that he must look
   As whitened as the wall.

No wonder ! just at such a time,
   And in just such a place !
Besides, his every guilt and crime
   Now stared him in the face.

Bewitched he thought the horse must be—
   He now began to stare,
And fancied he could plainly see
   Winged spirits in the air !

The lightnings still most glaring flew
   Before his wondering eyes ;
The thunders rolled, the winds they blew
   Enough to shake the skies !

And now before him seemed to stand
   A tall and ghostly mien,
That pointed with its meager hand
   Tow'rd something yet unseen.

And noises strange came booming round,
  And thundered in his ears;
The lightnings roll along the ground,
  And Dobbin snorts and rears.

"Ye gods, defend me!" Horace cried;
  "Your aid, in pity lend!"
As there he stood, mouth open wide,
  And every hair on end!

Then down he fell upon his knees
  Into the soaking grass,
And begged the Lord that he would please
  To let him onward pass!

"For here, Lord, I am weather-bound,
  By imps and ghosts beset,
And stunned to death by many a sound,
  While dripping cold and wet.

"Do let a trembling wretch go on!
  I don't know how to pray;
But Dobbin he has crazy grown,
  And here intends to stay.

"What ails the beast I cannot tell;
  He's but a sorry tool;
The varmint sure is bound by spell,
  Or else he's turning fool!

"Then help, O Lord! dispel the charm,
  And get me through this wood—!"
Just then he thought he felt an arm,
  And some one near him stood.

Ready to die with fear or fright
 He gave one groan and fell,
When some one lifted him upright,
 And broke the horrid spell.

" Why, Horace ! are you really crazed?
 What are you, man, about ?
My very soul you have amazed,
 Till I must laugh right out !

" Why can't you find a fitter place
 Than this, dear boy, to pray ?
Why, if you had all Heaven's grace,
 Need you exposed here stay ?

" I was toward the village bound,
 The storm did me o'ertake ;
When near this spot I heard a sound
 Most strange, and no mistake !

" Thus drawing near, I list awhile ;
 The voice I thought I knew,
Nor could I help, dear man, but smile
 When you so frightened grew.

"What scared you man ? I pray you tell;
 I vow you look most dead !
Hath sudden illness you befell,
 Or has your senses fled?"

" Good God ! dear George ! oh, what a storm !
 What is that yonder stands ?
It looks like some great ghastly form
 With outstretched arms and hands !

" Heaven ! my senses are most gone,
    And Dobbin is scared to death !
I could not make the beast go on—
    He's panting now for breath !"

"And you are too," said George, " I see !
    Why for one moment hark !
That is an aged, a blighted tree,
    Stripped clean of all its bark !

" Years hath the thing been standing there,
    But not as you see now ;
It is enough your horse to scare,
    But then not you, I vow !

" This morning, very early, I
    Was passing through this wood,
When this dead tree I did descry
    Which here so long hath stood.

" Thinks I, this poor old timber sure
    Has weathered many a gale,
And many more it may endure
    Should its old trunk not fail !

"And being in a private road,
    And in this forest drear,
I thought it yet might do some good
    As friendly way-mark here.

" So as the lightning long ago
    Its bark had loosened quite,
I just set to, my skill to show,
    And stripped it ; thus 'tis white !

" One lower limb I left to stand,
   Perhaps five feet in length,
Just as a kind of pointing hand,
   But won't insure its strength.

" So now, my boy, when this I done,
   But as a kindly deed,
I thought I had no risk to run—
   And no one else, indeed !

" Thus if my plans so dangerous prove,
   I shall without delay,
To-morrow this sad ghost remove
   Out of the traveler's way.".

" Well, well !" said Horace, "I am beat !
   Is this the phantom ghost ?
The thing that knocked me off my feet—
   An old dead tree and post ?

"And now I tell you what, my friend,
   I honestly admit
I thought my days were at an end—
   To die I was not fit !

" The many tales of goblin kind
   The village folks relate
Made me of superstitious mind,
   The very thing I hate !

"And thus you know this wood hath been
   A dread to neighbors round,
For ghosts, they say, are often seen
   To walk this haunted ground.

" To this I always gave the laugh,
     I ne'er would it believe;
It was a tale too gross by half,
     And framed but to deceive.

" But passing through the goblin bounds
     Just as the night drew near,
Amid the storm I thought that sounds
     Unearthly met mine ear.

" Each story I had ever heard
     About the haunted place,
Did coward fear their every word
     On burning memory trace.

" The storm so hideous coming on
     Amid this forest gloom,
Each thing I set my eyes upon
     Would spectral forms assume.

"And Dobbin, he must too turn fool,
     Amid perplexing fears;
'Twould serve him right if in some pool
     I'd plunge him neck and ears.

"And now, dear George, the secret hold;
     Expose me not, I pray!
In future I will prove more bold
     If passing by this way.

"When goblin tales again I hear
     In all their haunting form,
This comic-tragic night will rear,
     (A picture in a storm.")

And now the travelers onward speed,
For home and shelter's sake,
But laughing all the way, indeed,
As if their hearts would break.

———⁂———

THE TRUMPET OF WAR.

LOUD, loud sounds the trumpet of war
From the ramparts of glory afar!
Come, soldiers, for battle in majesty rise,
And exultingly send your brave shouts to the skies.
"Come, soldiers, arise!" is the chieftain's loud cry;
"Let it be our bright motto to conquer or die!
Our foes are surrounding, and nobly we
Will fight for our country, fall, or be free!

"The trumpet of war! sound, sound it aloud,
Let its echo ascend on the smoke-teeming cloud;
Scorn, scorn the mean trammels of cowardly fear,
And high on the ramparts of glory appear!
Fight, fight on, ye heroes, ye brave sons of war,
Our banners shall float 'neath a conquering star!
In martial array we will now to the field,
And valiant the sword and the battle-axe wield.
The trumpet of war! sound, sound it again!
Let it ring from the shore to the trackless main,
Our foes they shall never, in triumph, repeat,
We are vanquished and grovel as slaves at their feet;
Our mothers, our wives, our daughters shall ne'er
Have a blush on their lovely cheeks to appear,

18

Or thoughts of confusion, or sorrow, or shame,
That a cowardly blot is thrown over our name.

"Then arise, sons of battle! the trumpet of war,
Let it ring from the hills to the wave-beaten shore;
Spread, spread our gold banners aloft in the air,
Their stars and their stripes shall our victory declare:
Columbia's sons, let your proud motto be—
In battle we die, or live and be free!"

TO MY MOTHER.

WHEN all the world hath left me,
And fortune hath bereft me,
And grief hath nearly swept me
    From frail existence here;
Thy gentle love endearing,
Hath still been kind and cheering,
'Mid every sorrow searing,
    My angel mother dear!

Thy bosom, ever trusting,
Each wrong of mine adjusting
When my poor heart was bursting
    With pain and misery;
Who, while the tear was stealing,
And fate its pangs revealing,
Did blend with every feeling?
    Sweet mother, it was thee!

Thy pure and gentle brow
Was grieved, I scarce know how,
But yet can feel it now,
    And still I mourn it;
For all my cares were thine,
Each pang thou felt of mine,
And none but love like thine,
    My mother, could have borne it!

———⚹———

THE FATAL REQUEST.

A HISTORICAL TALE OF TRUTH AND ROMANCE.

A PROUD usurper of a distant realm,
  Whose haughty soul of vengeance well was known,
For he, as tyrant, could a place o'erwhelm
  With shame, as easy as to rule a throne.

A libertine he was, of artful will,
  Destroying virtue, beauty, everywhere
As far as laid within his demon skill;
  None, none were safe among the lovely fair.

The country round for many leagues had felt
  The loss of some fair daughter through his guile;
Beauty was of its early charms bereft,
  And virtue wrecked on dissipation's isle.

Many fathers felt the fatal scourge
  Of ruin found to stain their hapless name;
When innocence fell o'er the fearful verge
  That blots forever woman's lovely fame.

If parents had a fair and beauteous child,
    A daughter whom they proudly loved too dear,
A thousand apprehensions, vague and wild,
    Would fill their hearts with constant dread and fear.

For this proud monarch, where he cast his eye,
    And peerless beauty met his ardent gaze,
That creature was his victim, by and by,
    And in his palace honor's forfeit pays.

Should parents chance to be most lone and poor,
    He often would through bribes their daughter win;
Resolved that plenty should combine with power
    And act as cover to seducing sin.

But where those parents dwelt of virtuous mind,
    Who scorned his flimsy gold or proffered pelf,
Whose holy love hung round their daughter kind,
    'Twas then they lost in her all fear for self;

Ay, felt as though they fain would rather die
    Than see the ruin of that being dear;
Yet knew not where they could for safety fly,
    Since he, the wretch, had spies both far and near.

And when the object could not well be won,
    Or he perceived his offers held at naught,
'Twas then he ordered deeds perfidious done,
    To have her instant to his presence brought.

And many a sorrowing, bleeding parent's heart
    Hath been compelled to yield the tender prize,
And see in anguish that poor child depart
    To feast and glut a hateful monarch's eyes.

And oft the destined lovely object clings
  To those dear forms by every filial tie;
With what despair a mother's heart she wrings
  When with the merciless vassals doomed to fly!

'Twas on a deep occasion such as this
  That forms the present subject of my muse,
When this vile tyrant sought to mar the bliss
  Of child and father, as his fancy choose.

One evening, as he with his vassals rode
  A distance to inhale the balmy air,
He passed a humble cottager's abode
  And had a glimpse of his loved daughter fair.

The sun had sunk on rolling clouds of gold
  Behind the broad blue fields of western light,
A sight most pure and glorious to behold,
  And lingered o'er the soft approach of night.

The monarch paused to gaze upon the scene,
  And marked the glowing beauty of the skies,
As evening shadows gathered fast, serene,
  O'er painted hills that did in distance rise.

Then, turning to a favorite minion, said,
  "How grand is nature in her wooing power!
Yon purple skies, how rich with gold inlaid,
  Dropping their luster o'er the evening hour!

"But mark, Regaliüs! See'st thou yon hut
  Whose latticed window bears the merry vine?
There lives a beauty most excelling—but
  I must obtain her, she must now be mine.

18*

" This is a scene, Regalius," said the haughty king,
　" To waken dreams of love and fond desire;
I would that thou to me this damsel bring
　Before the hour of midnight shall expire !

" Her father is a man discreet and chaste,
　Noble in purpose, bold in every vein;
Therefore your precious time you need not waste
　To ask this sire his daughter to resign.

" He loves her with a more than doating mind;
　She is the very idol of his soul !
And she is perfect as her heart is kind;
　No fairer beauty could man's wish control.

" But I am stricken with her peerless charms,—
　A very angel lives she in my view;
To think of her the bliss of sleep disarms,—
　I must possess her, and that quickly too!

" 'Twas yester night, I wandered there alone,
　Just as the evening twilight spread around;
I wore a slight disguise, yet of mine own,
　And soon myself within the cottage found.

" Yet I could see some terror shade the brow
　Of that old man, and then the modest maid
Looked trembling as she did before me bow,
　For they perceived a regal visit paid !

" When undisguised, I lavished words of praise
　Upon the lovely damsel as she knelt;
And as her angel form I stooped to raise
　I felt as never soul of passion felt.

" I from my finger drew a diamond ring,
  And fain would place it on her snowy hand,
But she refused, and said, My gracious king,
  I am your slave, I own you can command:

" But I would rather not the gem accept;
  It suits not one so low in birth and state:
Then, leaning on her father's arm, she wept,
  As though she felt some dark, approaching fate.

"A sense of pity did with rapture blend,
  She looked so beauteous in her modest tears;
But then the maid would not her hand extend
  To take the ring your noble monarch wears."

" The saucy minx !" the vile Regalius cried;
  " She should have proudly pressed it to her heart;
But these low plebeians have a hateful pride,—
  It were but right for this to make her smart!

" Pruning, sometimes, will help a pretty vine,
  And bring it into majesty and shape;
And we can cause the sapling to incline
  The way we wish the stubborn thing to take.

" Then what are your commands, my noble liege ?
  You know us ever ready to obey;
Shall we the mud-walled hut this night besiege
  And bear the lovely maid by force away ?"

" Well, ye have ever proved my sturdy friends !
  And now this fair and sweet retiring flower
I would possess; then on ye all depends
  This night to bring the damsel in my power!

" I know that gold and praise can never win
　　This darling to my now enamored breast ;
The father would revolt at lawless sin :
　　Therefore 'tis strength alone can do it best.

" Now I propose that ye shall patient wait
　　Till midnight sends abroad her solemn peal,
For it were better it should be thus late
　　Ere ye attempt the lovely maid to steal.

" Thus, when all nature round is calm and still,
　　Go ye, and there the precious flower demand ;
Tell him, the father, that it is my will,
　　But use no cruel, weighty, ruffian hand.

" I charge you well, my friends, to hurt them not,
　　But tell the worthy, yet unwilling sire,
His charming child is not to be forgot,
　　Who did so late her monarch's love inspire.

"And that I do request the beauteous maid
　　To not oppose my royal mood of mind.;
And if in points respectfully obeyed,
　　She shall be treated by myself most kind !

" Then, if reluctant, they will not comply,
　　Use force, without a movement too severe,
And bring her to me, when my heart shall try
　　To win her favor or excite her fear !"

Thus was the message promptly conveyed,
　　As soon as night the favoring hour brought ;
They soon to the rustic habitation strayed,
　　And soon the frightened, harmless inmates sought.

How were their hearts now roused to deep alarm!
　　The father knew 'twere vain once to deny;
Therefore, to save his lovely child from harm,
　　He thought it best dissemblance to try.

The daughter stood with wild distracted air,
　　The very picture of Niobe's ghost;
While on her shoulders hung her raven hair,
　　Looking a victim to all reason lost!

" Stay!" said the father, with dissembling voice,
　　" This is an honor I did not expect;
I feel most flattered by his views and choice;
　　I could not such a grand request reject!

"My daughter labors under great surprise!
　　If ye withdraw I will these views explain:
She never yet my counsel did despise;
　　I think I can her willing answer gain.

"Return and bear my answer to the king;
　　Tell him, if he but till the morning wait,
I will to him my child in person bring,
　　In garments suited to her virgin state.

" You see her robe is for the night's repose;
　　Nor did we dream of this, your visit kind;
But from her wardrobe she will truly choose
　　Such garniture as we appropriate find.

" Believe me, on the honor of a man,
　　To-morrow I will to the king repair;
Ere morning half its usual limits span
　　My daughter and myself will sure be there."

When thus assured, they hurried from the spot;
   And to the king the faithful message bore;
While those chaste beings in the humble cot
   Were planning movements that importance wore.

"What!" said the king, "I did not once suppose
   He calmly would the lovely prize resign;
But now, perchance, he condescension shows
   To gain some favor which to give is mine!

"Surprised I am, but this doth please me well;
   His great submission shows a prudent mind,
And I, to-morrow, will this father tell
   He may in me a generous sovereign find.

"He knows I can transform his low estate,
   And help him up the lofty hill of fame;
'Tis I can make the lowly peasant great,
   And put a luster on the humblest name!"

Thus ran the monarch's thoughts till soothing sleep
   Shut out all views of present and the past;
While dreams of future bliss hung long and deep
   Upon his mind, till morning came at last.

When high he sat on his imperial throne,
   With guards in waiting, and his vassals gay,
Much splendor was on this occasion shown:
   He was resolved to grace the happy day.

It was not long before the honored guests
   Appeared and drew toward the royal seat;
A thousand charms upon the maiden rests
   That would the pencil's skillful power defeat.

The monarch thought such beauty ne'er before
　　Had met his ardent and voluptuous gaze ;
Her every grace a sweet enchantment wore
　　That called forth accents of admiring praise.

Robed in a simple tunic white as snow,
　　While round her temples fair a blossomed wreath
Of natal flowers reposed upon her brow,
　　And mingled their perfume with her sweet breath.

A velvet zone embraced her peerless waist,
　　Adorned in front with one rich crescent pearl ;
While o'er her shoulders brilliant, white, and chaste,
　　Hung many a raven and luxuriant curl.

Leaning upon her aged father's arm,
　　With gentle steps they neared the royal throng,
While greetings, most respectful, kind, and warm,
　　Were offered as they slowly moved along.

Rich swelling music now rose grand and soft
　　Along the high arched roof of gothic pride,
Sending its echoes in sweet strains aloft,
　　Then on the ear in plaintive murmurs died.

Now hushed as they recline before the throne,
　　The hoary sire essayed to humbly speak ;
Said he, "Most noble liege! we come to own
　　Our grateful joy, and your kind blessing seek.

" Here is my daughter, idol of my soul!
　　That you have honored by your regal choice ;
I give her now, my liege, to your control :
　　She gives consent with due submissive voice.

"She is a treasure of the holiest kind,
  Which angels cherish and will e'er protect!
To yield her is a struggle great, I find;
  But 'tis my king, and I cannot reject!"

"Take her, my liege! now to thy proffered hand
  Do I commit this pure and heavenly child;
And may the gods, that hear and understand,
  To future *points* and *deeds* be reconciled."

"I own thou art most just," the king replied;
  "A man of honor and of word direct!
Thy promise is fulfilled: I shall provide
  A good return through my profound respect."

Now with a conquering smile and grateful air,
  That seemed to speak exulting things within,
He slow descended from his regal chair
  To reach the hand he would ignoble win.

Down the short flight of marble steps he came,
  In gorgeous dress, well decked with diamonds bright,
And costly pearls, now much too vast to name,
  And music struck up anthems of delight.

When, just as he leaned forth with royal grace
  To take the hand the aged father held
In humble attitude in his to place,
  He to the earth the merciless monarch felled.

The hoary sire a dagger had concealed
  Beneath his robe, and was resolved to give
The deadly blow, for fate his heart had steeled;
  He would not have his child a harlot live.

And now, while o'er the fallen king they stood,
  Said he: "This is the point of which I named
That Heaven would sanction, steeped in his own blood,
  Rather than see my lovely child defamed."

And as he held aloft the dagger's point,
  Still wreaking in the guilty tyrant's blood,
Who can the scene that followed duly paint,
  As now the group amazed and wondering stood?

The king expired without a single groan;
  But did his guards or vassals deign to weep?
Did they the fallen monarch's death bemoan,
  Or lead the father to some dungeon deep?

No, no! they were rejoiced to see his end!
  Oft had they wished to see the fatal hour
That some most noble parent would befriend
  His injured child from his seducing power.

But fear had ever marred the effort bold,
  Until our time-worn hero done the deed;
He was not to be won by threats or gold,
  And thus resolved the tyrant's heart should bleed.

Now from the throng he bore his child away,
  While deaf'ning shouts rang through the stately hall;
Not one avenger sought their steps to stay,
  But gloried all to see the monarch fall.

19

ODE TO SUMMER.

THE morning breaks in beauty bright,
   The sun ascends the sky,
And countless glorious charms delight
   And feast the wondering eye!

The fields are blest with summer flowers,
   The forests wave in green,
And playful zephyrs fan the bowers,
   While blossoms peep between.

The sweetest strains of music rest
   Upon the wakeful ear,
From many a warbling tuneful guest
   That hails the pleasing year.

Summer its cheering beauties bring;
   The lark is sporting by,
She shakes the dew-drops from her wing,
   And mounts toward the sky.

The merry insect, too, is gay,
   And kiss the laughing flowers;
The bee bears honeyed sweets away
   To gladden winter hours.

Oh! joyous nature! could my heart
   In unison appear,
My soul would bless the holy part,
   And dry the gushing tear.

But, dearest Hope, impart one ray
    To heal the bosom riven;
Come, banish darksome thoughts away,
    And point from earth to heaven!

———🙚🙛———

THE STRAWBERRY GIRL.

HERE are strawberries ripe, here are strawberries fresh,
    From yon dear little garden just under the hill;
I must hasten to market and sell them for cash,
    For buy them I'm sure that somebody will!

My dear little brothers and sisters at home
    Are waiting, in fond expectation, to see
Me trip o'er the fields, when to meet me they come,
    And fold their arms round me with heart-loving glee.

Sweet darlings! I love them and pity them too!
    No mother or father we have to be sure,
But all that I can for to bless them I do,
    * And keep them from want and from hunger secure.

Ah! how I delight, while the soft soothing breeze
    Of summer steals over the landscape around,
And kiss in their triumph the sweet nodding trees,
    Those broad spreading oaks which our cottage sur-
        round!—

To rise with the peep of the new-coming morn,
    While dew-drops enamel the buds and the flowers,
And the lark's merry note from the sweet-scented thorn
    Is heard to the memory of night's closing hours!

Then still while my fingers are wet with the dew,
   And my bonnet is moistened with many a shower,
I hasten my basket with fruit to renew,
   And am home ere the sun gilds our cottage or bower.

The beauty of Summer, how soon it is past!
   Yet Autumn returns still to furnish the plain;
But seasons still bring me some blessings at last,
   And fill up my basket again and again.

But Winter arrives, with its dreary domain,
   And blossoms and fruit they are plenty no more,
But cold hollow winds, with sleet and with rain,
   Drift round our frail cottage and into the door.

'Tis then, only then, that I mourn o'er our fate,
   For though I am oldest, I find it severe
To provide for us all, though early and late
   We toil to make up this sad breach in the year.

My dear little brothers and sisters they knit,
   I flourish the wheel as our mother had taught;
And while all around in a circle we sit,
   I teach them as far as my knowledge is fraught.

And many's the hour and many's the day
   That we live in sweet union of heart and desire,
And all that we wish for, and all that we pray,
   Is that God will e'er bless us and lift our minds higher.

And this He will do, in my heart I am sure;
   We trust in His love through the gift of His son;
He knows we are friendless, He knows we are poor,
   And still will provide as He ever has done!

Then let dreary Winter in turn have its reign,
  From his hills in the north he may flourish awhile ;
But soon gentle Spring, with its mild breath, again
  Will bid fettered nature in beauty to smile.

Then, if I survive, with what merry delight
  Will I trip o'er the fields to yon favoring hill,
And while the blue sky scarce unfolds its soft light,
  I will be there my strawberry basket to fill!

MIDNIGHT VIEW.

Behold, by myriad splendid orbs empearled,
  The unveiled moon in all her beauty rise !
Now soft her beams illume the weary world
  As slow she skims the sable vaulted skies.

The distant plains are bathed in crystal dew,
  While o'er she throws her silvery floods of light;
A thousand glories wake the soul anew
  To themes of wonder and profound delight !

The voice of nature now is hushed in sleep,
  The busy hum of tumult now is o'er,
And musing nymphs their midnight vigils keep,
  And wander noiseless through the silent hour.

Now is the time for sweet prevailing thought
  To spread her wings and soar thro' mystic space,
To grasp some view, through venturous vision sought,
  On memory's page to hold a lasting place.

19*

Far through those starry, glorious courts of light,
    Where angels walk in grand, harmonious awe,
Would vision love to take her airy flight
    And some blest scene from heavenly impulse draw.

What but a God can bid those planets roll
    In mighty order through yon boundless sphere,
The thunder's voice, the lightning's flash control,
    While heaven's deep portals quake with seeming fear?

What but a God can hush the raging storm
    When angry billows form the roaring deep,
And caverns, dark as midnight's direst form,
    Moan out a dirge o'er many a mariner's sleep?

What but a God can bid the seasons change,
    And fading charms of nature bloom anew?
What but a God can every plant arrange,
    And ceaseless wonders still hold out to view?

What but a God can plan the human mind,
    With every conduit perfect to the frame,
Each organ, passion, structure, all combined
    To speak the greatness of the Author's name?

Yes, thou art all in all, unchanging God!
    Thy boundless scepter sways from pole to pole;
United worlds must tremble at thy nod,
    And every creature own thy vast control!

Let infidels in murky caverns dwell
    Of blackest darkness, far from human view!
They're but a cipher that remains to tell
    That wisdom, truth, and God they never knew.

THE PEARL OF GREAT PRICE.

DIAMONDS they are bright to view,
Gold is precious, silver too;
Yet these never can compare
With the charms of virtue rare.

Not Golconda's mines can boast,
Nor the richest golden coast,
Half the value of the mind
To holy purity inclined.

Not the shining stars above,
Beaming from the courts of love,
Can such beauty e'er impart
As the spotless, perfect heart.

But this treasure, bright and fair,
Sacred pearl beyond compare,
Is but seldom to be found
On Earth's vain, delusive ground.

But there is a future sphere
Where we can the treasure wear,
If the soul to grace be given,
And secures a home in heaven!

THE HUMMING-BIRD.

LITTLE creature ! gayly sporting
　　Through yon beds of gaudy flowers,
Now and then the sweetest courting,
　　Ranging to beguile the hours.

Gold and purple, green and blue,
　　Is thy plumage to the eye;
Sure, to paint thy every hue
　　Vainly would the pencil try.

Thou seemest like some spirit fairy,
　　Dancing from their mossy cells;
Thy figure is so light and airy,
　　Music with thee constant dwells.

And in many a honied cup
　　Dippest thou thy buzzing wing;
Drinking all the nectar up
　　Summer's gentle showers bring.

And I wonder, little creature !
　　Kissing every flower in view,
In thy giddy rounds of nature,
　　Thou dost not sip poison too ?

But thy pin-like bill is cautious
　　In thy ramblings, there's no doubt,
Shunning wisely all the nauseous,
　　Choosing all the fairest out !

A lesson to the moral mind
   Thy merry rovings may impart ;
In good or evil which to find
   The sweetest solace for the heart.

THE SNOW-STORM.

A TALE.

COLD, cold and dreary was the night,
   And sleet was falling fast ;
The moon and stars shut out their light,
   And piercing was the blast !

Around the lofty mountain's brow
   The snow in clusters hung,
While through the forest vales below
   The tempest loudly rung.

There, there a weary traveler stood
   Benighted in the storm,
While chilling horrors froze the blood
   Of his bewildered form !

Long, long he called for help in vain ;
   No kindly aid was near ;
And felt the joys of home again
   He never more would share.

He thought of those dear beings who
   Were waiting his return,
And well his dying feelings knew
   The tale they soon must learn.

"Oh, God!" he said, while deep despair
   Hung o'er his frantic mind;
"Be thou a guardian angel fair
   O'er those I leave behind!

"No more will my Addella bless
   My loving, anxious sight,
Or darling children e'er caress
   Their father with delight."

Now fainting with fatigue and fear,
   He yielded to the blast
And sank to earth; but God was near,
   His arms were round him cast!

Just then a woodman and his son
   Were onward, homeward bound,
Their faithful labors being done,—
   They here the traveler found.

"Ah, George, my son! look here!" he cries;
   "A traveler in the snow!
Come, bear him home—quick—ere he dies!
   Kind help we must bestow!"

Then to the cottage swift they bore
   Their now quite senseless guest,
While warm and healing draughts they pour
   Upon his senseless breast.

Blest hour of safety! soon they see
   His manly form revive;
Yet more surprised by far was he
   To find himself alive!

" Come here, my faithful friends," he said ;
   " For this your kindly care,
You have reaped blessings on my head,
   And shall my fortune share !

"A wife and children home I have !
   Through Heaven's protecting power
You did a dying creature save,
   And shall be poor no more !

" The lordly heights of Glenvill stand
   Not many miles from here ;
If some conveyance be at hand,
   Ere long we can be there."

" What !" said the woodman, with surprise,
   " Have we Lord Glenvill saved ?
I would for him 'neath winter skies
   Ten thousand storms have braved !

" Thy noble soul, some years ago,
   A kindness done for me ;
When bound in captive chains I know
   'Twas thou that set me free !

" Blest Heaven ! how I value this
   Defending, sacred hour !"
Said Maurice, as he stooped to kiss
   His bosom o'er and o'er.

" Hold !" said Glenvill; "thou must not!
   This homage I deny !
Let one thing never be forgot,
   'Twas God saved thou and I !"

Now onward to the castle they,
　　Through pelting storm of snow and rain,
With grateful hearts soon bend their way,
　　And soon its cheering threshold gain.

Yet scarce the portal bell had rung,
　　When wide the hall doors open flew;
And meeting hearts with rapture flung
　　Their arms around the neck they knew.

The husband, father, now is blest
　　Among his own domestic joys;
While Maurice proves a daily guest
　　Among a band of charming boys.

His lonely cottage on the moor
　　Is now a smiling, pleasant seat;
He feels himself no longer poor,
　　And loves his story to repeat.

And travelers, as they pass along,
　　Or in his mansion rest awhile,
May hear him chant his grateful song
　　With many a gladdening tear and smile.

And well he may adore the hour
　　The sinking traveler crossed his way,
Since through Lord Glenvill's favoring power,
　　Successive pleasures crown each day.

And now, when wintry storms hang o'er
　　Their stately home and forests round,
They venture o'er the frozen moor
　　To see if wanderers may be found.

And often strangers there are led
   To share their kind and generous care;
While blessings fall on Glenvill's head
   Who placed the friendly mansion there.

———✳✳———

THE ORPHAN GIRL.

COME, stranger, and pity a child of distress;
   'Tis painful to ask you I own,
But the least that you give will my aching heart bless,—
   An orphan I am and alone!

My parents and friends, they, alas! are all dead,
   A poor little stranger I be;
There are none to watch o'er my defenseless head,
   And neglected I am, you may see!

I am willing to labor from morning till night,
   And do all I can in my way;
I strive for to please and do all that is right,
   And love, if I can, to look gay!

I never encourage a frown on my brow,
   Or suffer my heart to feel sad,
When I really can help it, but now
   I have nothing to make me look glad.

If I had a mother, as others have got,
   How blest would my spirit appear!
Though ever so poor, I am sure I would not
   Give a murmur throughout the whole year.

How proud and how cheerful each day would I be,
　　And grateful to Heaven above,
That had granted a blessing so great and so free,
　　As a mother's protection and love!

A mother, whose eloquent voice would impart
　　A knowledge of Heaven and truth
As minutes rolled on, to teach my young heart
　　Immortal perfection in youth.

My once-loving parents were Christians, but they
　　Have gone to the shades of the grave!
And how can I ever look merry or gay
　　Since left a cold world thus to brave?

We lived in a mansion most richly attired,
　　And fortune propitiously smiled;
Yet little they thought, when caressed and admired,
　　Of the fate of their now orphan child.

A faithless guardian, of reckless heart,
　　In mask had my parents deceived;
He promised to act a most fatherly part
　　When of them my young soul was bereaved.

"Our child! oh our child! I pray you protect!"
　　Was the language they breathed ere they fled;
"Be father, be guardian, ah! never neglect
　　Our orphan when we are both dead!"

The promise was pledged; but how vain
　　Are the boasting affections of man!
Scarce in the cold tomb were the twain,
　　When my ruin of fortune began!

He early contrived to involve the estate
   My kind-hearted parents had left ;
The depth of his fraud was discovered too late,—
   Of my fortune I soon was bereft !

And thus on the cold-hearted world I am cast,
   A poor little child of despair ;
Yet hope that my trials will not always last,
   For they truly are too much to bear !

And if God in his mercy will bow down his ear
   To an orphan so feeble and lone,
I pray my vile guardian e'en yet may appear
   And be sorry for all he hath done.

And I'm sure if his merciless heart should relent,
   When he comes to our own native shore,
I will bless in my soul the prophetic event,
   And pardon him though I am poor.

GIVE THE HAND.

Say, dost thou see yon haggard form,
   With hollow eye and pallid cheek ?
That is a soul by sorrow torn,
   As doth his every look bespeak !
Misfortune hath beset his fate
   Here in a strange and foreign land,—
Then shall we not his woes abate,
   And take him kindly by the hand ?

Say, dost thou see yon wretched soul
    With bloated visage, swollen eye,
Whose heart drinks in potations foul
    As though he ne'er were born to die?
Say, shall we pass his palsied frame
    Or let it o'er perdition stand,
Nor breathe to him the Saviour's name,
    Or take that brother by the hand?

And what is that breaks on our ear
    In murmurs low and sadly wild?
List, list! it is the lonely prayer
    Of yonder trembling orphan child!
Then shall we with a bosom cold,
    Regardless or unfeeling stand,
While we their suffering wants behold?
    Ah, no! go take them by the hand!

And yonder, see, a stricken heart,
    A creature of abandoned fame,
Who, through vain man's beguiling art,
    Is bowed in sorrow and in shame! .
Then shall we not, for pity's sake,
    Here in a fair and Christian land,
This poor deluded sister take
    In loving kindness by the hand?

How solemn that a world so fair,
    So grandly beautiful and true,
Should such unfeeling spirits bear
    As sometimes fall before our view!
But vanity and self-conceit
    Soon gives the heart to understand
Why we the poor so seldom greet
    Or take the suffering by the hand!

Alas! that we should e'er forget
　Those holy virtues once displayed,
Or that sweet, bright example set
　By Him who rich and poor hath made!
But frail and fickle is the mind
　In every nation, every land;
Pride makes the human heart unkind
　And closes up the generous hand.

Away, then, with these mincing traits—
　A delicacy false as foul!
A thing the Holy Spirit hates,
　Who bids us try and save the soul!
No matter how depraved or lost,
　How poor or mean, when calls demand,
It is our duty at the most
　To offer them the Christian hand!

TRY AGAIN!

DEAR reader, will you from a friend
　A moral caution take?
When common ills of life descend
　Your pleasant dreams to break,
And spoil your airy castles vain,
Don't pause to grieve, but try again!

Do not despair when things go wrong,
　Nor come up to the letter,
For should you grieve for hours long
　It makes the thing no better;
20*

But up, and shake the morbid brain,—
'Tis wise, I say, to try again!

Don't ever pause to pheese or fret
   O'er trials that beset you;
'Tis moral courage not to let
   Provoking matters fret you;
But when your hopes are burst in twain,
Rouse up and try your scheme again!

If still appalling ills arise,
   Your views through life undoing,
Sail patient under cloudy skies,
   We knew not what is brewing;
For blessings yet may fall like rain,—
Then up, and bravely try again!

There was a worthy man of old,
   And Job they call his name,
Did ever crushing fate unfold
   More ills to mortal frame?
Yet did these troubles fall in vain?
No, no, my friend: then try again!

———⁂———

THE MARINER'S BRIDE.

To the waves! to the waves! the bark, love, is waiting!
   Yes waiting, my dearest, for thee!
The stars from their chambers of glory are waking,
   And music steals over the sea!

How sweet and how chaste is this evening hour,
　Now laden with richest perfume!
The nightingale's note is heard in the bower,
　Which moonbeams in beauty illume.

And now on the voiceless bosom of night
　Doth wearied nature repose;
And this is the time, dearest love, for our flight,—
　'Tis a moment to win or to lose!

Then away! yes, away! to the barge we must fly,
　And paddle across the soft sea,
While the stars hang like beautiful lamps in the sky,
　Their holy light shedding on thee.

Thy father, my love, will early pursue
　His fugitive daughter; then come
And lean on this bosom that's faithful and true,
　'Tis thy refuge, thy shelter, thy home!

But soon o'er the voiceless, trembling deep,
　Silvered now by the moon's gentle light,
Our barge, love, shall swiftly, merrily sweep
　To a land of unfolding delight!

A land of sweet fruits and fair flowers,
　Enchantingly rich to behold,
Where birds gayly sing through the bowers,
　In plumage of purple and gold.

There, there on the zephyrs of night,
　Sweetest strains of soft music arise
To ravish the soul with delight,
　As their echo rolls back from the skies!

Then away! then away to the lake!
  To the barge that is waiting for thee!
We must fly, ere the morning beams break,
  Far, far o'er the silver-lit sea!

THE LOCK OF HAIR.

'TIS nothing but a lock of hair
    Of gray or silver hue
Yet that one tress I would not spare
    For all far-famed Peru!

Ah, yes! and how I guard the prize,
    With what devoted care,
Lest it might vanish from my eyes—
    That little lock of hair!

And such associations, too,
    Come crowding o'er the mind!
It brings a darling face to view,
    Once sweetly true and kind.

A visage that will fondly be,
    In coloring deep and fast,
Impressed on holy memory
    While time and life shall last.

Ah, yes! I see in vision clear,
    As in those moments gone,
That tender, loving bosom dear
    I once could lean upon!

And if oppressed with pain or care,
   Her lips would then impart
A sweetly kind and soothing prayer
   While leaning near her heart.

And then how often could I see
   Upon her angel cheek
The tear of silent agony
   When I of woe would speak !

Then is it any wonder, pray,
   That I should guard with care
This little lock of silver gray ?
   It is my mother's hair !

THE WAY TO BE HAPPY.

WOULD you wish to be happy and never grow sad,
   For glooom is a terrible pest?
I'll tell you the manner the thing can be had,
   And leave you to manage the rest.

Encourage a heart of devotion and love ;
   Live meekly, humble, and plain ;
Have an eye to the pure and truthful above ;
   Nor sigh after things that are vain.

Never turn from the voice of the poor in distress,
   Even though you have little to spare ;
The mite you bestow may make suffering less,
   For the action is more than the share.

If the child of misfortune should fall in thy way,
    And call for protection and aid,
Let thy voice in a spirit of love be a stay,
    And lead back the soul that hath strayed.

Never fly from affliction or heart-rending woe,
    'Tis wicked as well as unkind ;
If we can but a word of affection bestow
    It proves a relief to the mind.

Be honest and truthful, discourage vain pride,
    Keep conscience unsullied and clear ;
Let the mind be with holy reflections supplied,
    And banish all cowardly fear.

But why thould I offer to hint this or that ?
    'Tis folly perhaps while I try !
Yet what moral conscience should aim to be at—
    " Is to do as we would be done by."

A sermon is taught in this one little line,
    Which if we would heed and obey,
We seldom would find real cause to complain,
    And life would glide happy away.

Yea, if we could practice this one golden rule—
    That is, do all the good that we can—
We then could live cheerful in nature's broad school,
    And sweetly lengthen life's span.

For what is it harrows and troubles the mind
    But a conscience most illy at rest ?
The truthfully good and the poor we e'er find
    Carry with them a cloudless breast.

THE FATAL RING,

OR

THE RESCUED BRIDE.

A HISTORICAL TALE.

In Switzerland there lived a prince
Of mighty wealth and power ;
Greater were none before nor since—
So says the page of yore.

For many slumbering years ago
This tale of truth occurred,
Though many minds may curious grow
And doubt my sacred word.

But as from history I will touch,
Whose inference seems plain,
I would not have some doubt too much,
Or deem my efforts vain.

I say in Switzerland there dwelt
A prince of great estate,
Whose passions were most keenly felt,
Whether of love or hate.

Most bold was he, intrepid, brave,
When on the plains of war ;
In peace he was sedate and grave ;
A smile he seldom wore.

Yet not a "Bluebeard" quite was he,
  Perchance not so severe,
That many wives should murdered be.
  Through jealousy or fear.

Still jealousy, that demon trait,
  Was half his nature's own;
Although so wealthy, proud, and great,
  Few friends to him were known.

His courtiers were a flattering train,
  Whose sycophantic skill
Filled up his mind with notions vain,
  And humored much his will.

Grandeur and pomp have their own charms,
  And cover much that's vile;
Ay, half the demon spell disarms,
  For gold can win the smile.

Crowds filled his halls; the lovely fair
  His banquets did surround,
And many a noble lady there
  Gay entertainment found.

And one, at last, most beauteous came,
  She won his royal mind;
Zuona was her gentle name,
  A being chaste and kind.

Lovely in all her perfect grace,
  With spirit mild and meek,
An angel smile lit up her face,
  And health glowed on her cheek.

He loved her with heroic zeal,
   And gained her willing hand';
None would have thought his heart of steel
   Such love could e'er command.

The nuptials past, the feasting o'er,
   Weeks, months, they flew away,
While his devotion seemed the more
   Increased each new-born day.

But ere a single year had fled
   Fate figured in the scene;
Connubial joys and hopes were dead,
   Nor days rolled on serene.

A beauteous page of winning form,
   And modest talents rare,
Now caused a matrimonial storm
   And did its horrors share.

He was the princess' favored page,
   And most attractive proved,
As now he grew to manhood's age,
   And in her presence moved.

He loved with feelings virtuous, true,
   His noble lady fair;
When wanted, swift on wings he flew
   As light as desert air.

Obedient, ever at command,
   Her kind esteem he won,
And presents from her generous hand
   Adorned this humble son.

21

The prince did not yet disapprove
  Of presents thus bestowed,
For he himself the page did love,
  Who such obedience show'd.

Yet oft he thought a partial smile
  And well-approving eye
Would rest upon the youth the while
  He stood in waiting by.

But then this dream would hurry past,
  When her endearing arms
Would round his lordly neck be cast,—
  Then love renewed its charms.

Now when Zuone became a bride
  The prince a present made;
A wedding-ring, with gems supplied,
  For which vast sums were paid.

The diamonds were of richest kind,
  Excelling, chaste, and bright,
Such as few mortals seldom find;
  They shone like stars of night.

Yet many rings the princess wore
  Of rare and costly kind,
But this, of course, was valued more
  Than all the rest combined.

As it had been the wedding gift,
  She guarded it with care,
Would seldom from the casket lift
  This precious gem to wear.

Nor could we wonder much at this,
  So rich and bright a token,
Lest she the costly gift might miss,
  Or have it rudely broken.

One day she laid the valued gem
  Upon her toilet gay
With other pearls, intending them
  Soon to be put away.

But fate doth many changes bring,
  And so it happened then,
For gone was now the wedding-ring,
  And how unknown, or when.

Alarmed at this most strange event,
  The prince she feared to tell;
Then for her trusty maid she sent,
  One whom she knew full well.

"Bartenia, I am in distress,
  And much I need thy aid;
If thou wilt strive my hopes to bless,
  Thou nobly shalt be paid!

"My wedding-ring is gone! and I
  Cannot tell how or where;
I laid it on yon toilet, by
  Those other jewels there.

"It is mysterious! ne'er a thief
  Could here an entrance gain;
And if they did, why let the chief
  Of jewels here remain?

" One would in common wit suppose
　　The whole had been their prize,
Nor would this valued necklace lose
　　So glittering to the eyes.

" Bartenia, I am nearly crazed !
　　The prince will madly rave
If he should learn the gem is seized,
　　Since he the token gave !

"And then his mandate when he placed
　　It on my proffered hand,
His own, before, it long had graced,
　　And this was his command:

" ' Regard this ring, love, as thy life !
　　It is of princely worth !
A regal gem, none but a wife,
　　And one most loved on earth,

" ' Should wear a treasure thus so dear
　　And high in my esteem ;
Its loss, by all the powers, I fear
　　With sad events would teem !'

" So now, Bartenia, canst thou plan
　　Some way for my relief?
Find out, dear girl, if that thou can,
　　The mystery or the thief.

" But do not breathe a word aloud ;
　　Use caution, gentle maid ;
The sad affair at present shroud
　　Till further plans be laid.

"Yet watch the vassals, one and all;
　　Take notice of their ways,
For oft a word or look may fall
　　That certain guilt betrays.

"And should the least impression make
　　The guilty creature known,
I would, for virgin mercy's sake,
　　Have sweet compassion shown.

"So I can only gain the ring,
　　I would forgive the deed;
But if 'tis brought before the king,
　　Their fate will surely bleed!

"Now who could in my chamber come,
　　And nothing take beside?
Bartenia, ah! it must be some
　　One in these walls supplied!

"I feel most sorry to accuse,
　　But must my ring obtain,
And will not one exertion lose
　　To have it once again!

"The gem is of mysterious make,
　　Its value too so great,
It would suspicion soon awake
　　When out of regal state!

"Therefore, Bartenia, strive, I pray,
　　To find out who could feel
So thoughtless as to take away
　　What would their ruin seal!

21*

" I trust some of my maids have thought
   The trinket I could spare,
Nor knew with what events 'twere fraught,
   And claimed it for their share.

" Knowing how many brilliants shine
   Within my wardrobe gay,
Have thought it were a gem, in fine,
   Not much to take away.

" But now be still a little while ;
   Perhaps some hours may throw
Light on this solemn trick of guile,
   And us the robber show !"

" Perchance, my noble lady fair,
   The prince hath in his play
The ring, thy lovely self to scare,
   In jest removed away !"

"Ah, no ! my own Bartenia, no !
   He doth no mischief court ;
He would not plunge my heart in woe
   Through mean or wanton sport.

" He knows how much the gem I prize,
   And were it out of sight,
Its very absence would surprise
   And fill my soul with fright.

"Therefore the prince hath never took
   The treasure, that I know !
He would not to gross trifling brook,
   Or fruitless pain bestow.

" So now, Bartenia, mind me well,
And act a searching part ;
That ring doth with some maiden dwell,
I fear, of treacherous heart !"

Some days rolled on ; no tidings met
The anxious lady's ear,
And not one ray of light as yet
Fell on the dark affair.

One evening, while the sun's last ray
Hung o'er the western tower,
And summer zephyrs sweetly they
Were borne upon the hour,—

The princess on the terrace strayed
To hail the lovely scene ;
Nature, in glowing charms arrayed,
Was beauteous and serene !

When suddenly her lord drew nigh
With strange, mysterious air ;
With passion gleamed his jealous eye,
His visage spoke despair.

" Zuona, I have much to say,
And that to thee alone ;
A certain circumstance to-day
Hath turned my heart to stone !

" Where is thy ring—the wedding-ring
I proudly gave to thee ?
Go thou the regal gem and bring,
I wish the gift to see !"

And while he spoke, a savage smile
  He did upon her raise,
That made her gentle heart recoil
  And shrink before his gaze!

"Ha, ha!" said he; "thy guilt is plain!
  Why tremblest thou, and weep?
Would I a siren heart retain
  Or in possession keep?

"Did I not charge thee, when the band
  Of Hymen made us one,
And placed that ring upon thy hand,—
  Such as but monarchs own,—

"To guard it with thy very life?
  And did I not believe
Thee worthy, as my regal wife,
  The token to receive?

"But thou art false! I long have strove
  To hide my doubts and fears;
I find our page secures thy love,
  And he the tribute wears!

"Not yet hath passed one lingering hour
  Since he before me came,
And by all holy virgin power,
  His finger bore the same!

"I feigned the treasure to admire,
  While I retained his hand;
And sickened while I did inquire
  How he did it command.

"A paltry, vile excuse he made,
  And said he found the gem ;
That it beneath the branches laid
  Of yonder towering elm:

" That while beneath its wooing shade
  He on the turf reclined,
The ring its brilliant form displayed
  Where flowers were thick entwined :

" That he had seized it, and did place
  It on his willing hand,
Until the owner he could trace,
  Who might the gem demand.

" Now this is sure a likely tale
  To place before my view,—
A very theme that could not fail
  To jealous pangs renew !

"Are wedding-rings so plenty they
  Among the posies grow,
Or scattered o'er the turf they lay
  And in the sunbeams glow ?

" However, I have fixed the point ;
  He on the rack shall go !
I'll tear him every limb from joint
  But what the truth I'll know !

" What ! thinkest thou I am so blind
  And ignorant, forsooth,
As not to mark thee over-kind
  To that poor plebeian youth ?

"Yea, I have watched thy sunny smile
    And sly prevailing look ;
But thou didst cloak a heart of guile
    As snugly as a book !

"Presents of lordly value thou
    Hast given to the page ;
The meaning I ne'er knew, till now
    The ring comes on the stage!

"Yet would these favors not suffice
    Thy young and amorous mind ?
Thy love must be too over-nice
    And generously inclined !

"When regal rings of honor shine
    Upon a page's paw,
That should alone grace proudly thine—
    What import must I draw ?"

"Oh, prince ! thy angry passion stay !
    The ring some mystery veils !
It was e'en lost or borne away ;
    But fate the subject seals !

"I know not, cannot tell, my lord !"
    The trembling princess cried ;
While anguish choked her every word
    And flowed the weeping tide.

"That token of united love,
    With other jewels rare,
I from my casket did remove
    Intending them to wear.

" But absent for a transient space,
　When I returned again,
The ring was taken from the place
　While all the rest remain.

" I was alarmed and called my maid
　Bartenia; when she came
I told her where the pearls I laid,—
　She knew naught of the same.

" Her virtuous, kind, and honest heart
　Hath vainly strove to learn
Some clew to this mysterious part;
　But none could yet discern.

"I feared to let your highness know,
　Lest you might wrathful be,
And say the accident did flow
　Through carelessness in me.

"And trusting still from day to day,
　That chance would soon reveal
The thief who bore the prize away,
　I did the secret seal.

" But, oh! prophetic saints! I ne'er
　Had thought a jealous pang
Did in your noble breast appear,
　Or o'er your memory hang!"

"Avaunt! seal up thy lying lips!
　They drop but venom foul,
Such as alone the devil sips,—
　Thou mad'nest my soul!

" Dost thou suppose a sly-born thief
   Would wear a trophy gay,
Before his mighty prince and chief,
   In open, glaring day ?

" Would he not hide his glittering prize
   From general human view,
Nor come before the owner's eyes
   With marked presumption too ?

" It ne'er was stolen ! if it were
   How came it in the turf—
And he alone should find it there ?
   This tale affords me mirth !"

Now in the tower he led her on :
   Said he, " Now follow me !
The page will love to look upon
   Thy marriage destiny !"

And soon he to the chamber led
   His trembling, weeping bride,
Whose soul with every horror bled :
   She there the page espied,—

Whose face was pictured in despair ;
   His bloodless visage threw
One glance upon his lady fair,
   Then at their feet he flew,

Craving to know for what or why
   He there was captive made,
Or why 'neath tortures doomed to die
   For wrongs against him laid.

"Have I not," said the noble youth,
  " In constancy and love
Filled up my part with spotless truth
  And e'er obedient prove ?

" What wrong is it that I have done?
  I cannot call to mind
One single instance—no, not one—
  Where I have dealt unkind."

" That very love hath been too deep,"
  The scornful prince replied,
"Since gems upon thy fingers creep,
  Bestowed by this, my bride !"

Too much for innocence was this ;
  The youth he fainting fell ;
He felt the blight of earthly bliss
  Through some demonic spell.

And now the prince, whose iron mind
  All sympathy defied,
Constructions of the vilest kind
  Placed on his beauteous bride.

Thinking the page had sunk through guilt
  At being now betrayed,
He little cared what blood he spilt,
  And thus his wrath displayed.

Soon as the fainting youth revived,
  And sense again returned,
He with demonic skill contrived
  To prove a plot discerned.

Said he, " I have by well-planned art
   Found out your lecherous schemes,
For which you both shall feel the smart ;
   My soul with vengeance teems !

" You to the painful, torturing rack
   Shall there your crimes confess ;
While you, Zuone, the air shall track
   To make your sufferings less !

" Down from this tower window, know,
   You'll instantly be thrown
Into the rolling flood below ;
   No mercy shall be shown !"

Now with a fiendly grasp he seized
   Her by the waist, and threw
Her o'er the window sash he raised
   From his demonic view.

Then turned he to the speechless page,
   Who horror-struck now stood,
With eyes wild flashing fire and rage
   That froze the poor youth's blood.

" Mind ! soon thy lonely doom is sealed,
   So give thyself to prayer,
For ere the midnight hour hath pealed
   Thou must for death prepare !"

Then drawing firm each bolt and bar,
   He swiftly fled away,
Intending 'neath the evening star
   This injured youth to slay.

He to his private chamber flew
  And closed himself within,
His deeds of dark revenge to view,
  Of murder's foulest sin.

But not an hour had passed away,
  When at the portal gate
A hermit stood, both aged and gray,
  Who on the prince would wait.

He was a favorite, but they said
  The prince no one would see;
The hermit cried, " I must be led
  To him immediately!"

Then soon they showed him to their lord,
  When, bending to the earth,
Said he, "I bring your highness word
  That will to joy give birth!

" Your noble mind has been a prey
  To very serious grief;
From sad events within a day,
  I hope I bring relief?

" I heard a valued ring was lost,
  And with your page was found,
A trinket of amazing cost,
  E'en many a thousand pound.

" Now, prince, this morning while I sat
  Beneath my humble vine,
I in my window placed my hat
  While I should calmly dine.

"A silver buckle that I wear,
   And glistens at its side,
Did lure a thieving magpie there,—
   The trinket he espied.

" Now pecking, trying hard to gain
   The buckle, mad he grew
Because he could not it obtain,
   Then swift away he flew.

" I now untied the band, and let
   The buckle loose and free,
When soon returned the craving pet
   And bore it to a tree.

" Then up I mounted, though I'm old ;
   I felt some strange belief
That made me more than over-bold,
   To watch this feathered thief.

" Then farther on I strove to rise,
   At last the summit gained ;
When scarce could I believe my eyes
   At what his nest contained.

" Now, noble prince, I did not touch
   An object that was there,
But wish for you to see it much,—
   The sight will make you stare !"

" How ?" said the prince ; " 'tis strange indeed !
   I'll to the lofty tree,
And have it brought away with speed !
   Come, hermit, thou with me !

"Some mighty feelings crowd my soul!
    Can this discovery mean
Most strange results to now unroll?
    I almost dread the scene!"

Swift to the topmost waving bough
    A speedy hand was sent,
While he impatient stood below
    To watch the strange event.

Soon down the twiggy storehouse came,
    They held it to his view,
But his surprise no pen can name,
    His deep confusion too!

'Twas evident this was the sly
    And busy thief at play,
Who did the wedding-ring descry
    And bore the prize away.

For jewels of most costly kind
    Now lined this roguish nest,
While there the prince made out to find
    A pearl he long had missed.

He also found a valued seal
    He lost a year before,
With gems, the artful rogue did steal,
    The maids of honor wore.

Now what confirmed the whole affair,
    'Twas on this very ground
The page did solemnly declare
    The diamond ring he found.

22*

The feathered thief had let it fall
   Near by the page's feet,
Nor could again the gem recall
   To bear to his retreat.

Now was the prince inured to shame,
   His brain with anguish riven;
How did he now his fury blame
   And pardon ask of Heaven!

He to the gentle hermit told
   His horrid, murderous tale,
That jealousy had made him bold
   And now his doom would seal.

He cried, "Oh! had this come to light
   Ere this dark, fatal hour,
My fair Zuone, my heart's delight,
   I should not now deplore!

"Gods! what a wretch do I appear!
   My conscience swims in blood;
Oh! could I from my vision tear
   The sight I have withstood!

"Henceforth I'll from the palace fly,
   And, penitent, repair
To some kind shielding convent nigh
   And live in ceaseless prayer.

"Forever will the murdered ghost
   Of my Zuona dwell
O'er wretched memory, tempest tost,
   And form a perfect hell!

"But now to poor Albaddin's fate,
My humble, trusty page,—
A thousand years were now too late
His injuries to assuage!"

Soon was the noble youth reprieved;
The prince hung on his breast
And wept aloud, for much he grieved
For every error past.

"Grieve not," the brave Albaddin said,
"My noble, princely lord!
Had I have died I should have prayed
For you with life's last word.

" I know that passion did oppose
Your reason and your soul,
That every misery round us rose
From jealousy most foul!

"And deep in prayer my spirit dwelt;
I felt resigned to die,
All the reluctance that I felt
Was that I knew not why.

"I was to sudden slaughter doomed,
When I had ever strove
To fill the office I assumed,
With gratitude and love.

" I know I did not merit death
Through any guilty deed,
Yet was resolved my dying breath
For thee should intercede,—

"Before the high and holy throne
  Where kings and princes reign,
That when death's triumph should be known
  We then might meet again."

"Ah! noble, brave Albaddin, thou
  Art great in soul, I own!
A demon I have been, but now
  That spirit fiend hath flown!

"Like Saul of Tarsus, now I feel
  The lion in me slain;
Like him my soul was hard as steel,
  Nor pity could contain.

"But oh, Zuone! my poor Zuone!
  Albaddin, this is more
Than I can ever for atone,—
  I did her heart adore!

"Till jealousy and hatred rose,
  Like blackened ghosts of hell,
To break my spirit's best repose
  While they o'er vision fell!

"But to the convent I will fly,
  And in repentance seek
That comfort Heaven can supply
  And renders to the meek.

No more a page thou now shalt be,
  But my own bosom friend!
A title I will give to thee,
  And riches at command.

" Had I have torn thy tender limbs
 On that accurst machine,-
In one of my relentless whims,
 Still worse my fate had been !

" Take thou my palace in thy care,
 With all my princely train,
While I to other climes repair :
 I cannot here remain !

"A little while abroad I'll go
 To take one parting view
Of this unhappy world of woe,
 Whose cares hath pierced me through !

" I shall most speedily return,
 Then in a convent find
What Christian hearts alone can learn,
 A peaceful, holy mind,—

" That is, if Heaven will wipe away
 Each murderous dream from view,
And turn my darkness into day,
 With life and hopes anew.

" Yea, when I shall return, I will
 To holy cloisters hie,
There my most godly vow fulfill,
 And learn to live and die !

" So now, Albaddin, thou wilt take
 Good charge of all I have,
Thyself at home in order make,
 Nor at my absence grieve !

" When I return to my estate,
    Though brief the moment be,
Thou shalt be rendered wealthy, great,—
    I hope that day to see !

" Then fare thee well ! but, ah ! how lone
    And lost my spirit seems !
My murdered, oh ! my poor Zuone !
    Thou wilt attend my dreams !"

The prince he turned away and wept ;
    His heart was wrung with pain,
For every earthly bliss was swept
    From life, he felt it plain.

Albaddin seized his hand and prest
    It to his throbbing heart,
And thus his grateful views expressed
    Ere he should now depart :

" Most noble prince ! I cannot bear
    Thy absence, and desire
To be thy page, thy travels share,
    I ask no station higher.

" Let me but be thy humble guide,
    And bear thy company still,
I'd rather be thus near thy side
    Than heir a monarch's will !

" Thou art my only guardian left ;
    How lonely would I be
When of my honored lord bereft !
    Then let me follow thee.

" Through good or evil I desire
    Thy fortune still to share;
Deny not then, my worthy sire,
    Thy page's humble prayer."

"Noble Albaddin ! e'er my own,
    My best, my bravest friend !
Though now is gone my poor Zuone,
    Thou shalt my life attend !

" Had I united kingdoms now,
    Them all I'd freely give
To gaze on my Zuona's brow
    As when she late did live!

" That being, in her beauteous pride,
    An angel was to me,
Till jealousy set me beside
    Myself, to aim at thee !

"All thy attentive kindness to
    Us both, thy willing air,
Brought demon hateful thoughts to view
    That drove me to despair !

" Thy strict obedience to her will,
    Her generous acts to thee,
Did but the fount of envy fill
    To doom my misery !

" She proudly lavished in thy praise,
    (And thou wert worthy such,)
Which did my jealous passions raise
    And every heart-string touch.

" Each look that was but kindly meant,
　When thou didst on her wait,
An arrow to my bosom sent
　Of anger and of hate !

" Blinded I was, and could not see
　Thy perfect worth as now ;
Although thou wert so kind to me,
　Still envy touched my brow.

" Ere this I had a love for thee,
　Of deep, surpassing kind,
And felt that thou wert dear to me
　By every power refined.

" But as each winning charm of thine
　Unfolded to the view,
I thought Zuone, that angel mine,
　Did more than love thee too.

" Thus night and day would vision's ghost
　My tortured feelings haunt,
Till now to every feeling lost
　I did for vengeance pant.

"And when the fatal ring appeared,
　I more than frenzied grew,
For envy had her bulwark reared—
　I deemed your tales untrue.

" I could not, dear Albaddin, see
　How thou shouldst it obtain ;
'Twas then a mystery to me,
　Though now it is too plain !

" How thou shouldst on thy finger wear
   My royal ring was strange ;
Before me too with it appear,
   It did my soul derange !

" I fancied thou hadst freedom used,
   And in an ardent hour
Had slyly from her finger loosed
   The gem you proudly wore,

" Without a knowledge of the deep
   Portentous charge it held,
Or thou wouldst not in favor keep
   What fear would have expelled.

" But now the fearful dream is o'er !
   Life's eloquence reveals,
That happy I shall be no more
   Till death my misery seals !

" Unless God in his mercy deign
   To wash away my guilt ;
'Tis he alone can blunt the pain
   For blood that I have spilt.

" But since thou dost so ardent crave
   To blend thy fate with mine,
With me life's lowering tempest brave,—
   I yield my will to thine.

" Yes, brave Albaddin ! ever true
   And constant thou hast been ;
And when my treachery stands in view
   How galling is the scene !
23

" Come to my arms, my noble friend!
    Thy virtues chaste shall be
A guiding star while life shall lend
    Her destinies to me !"

" Thanks, to my lord ! he doth in this
    My spirit joy afford !"
Albaddin cried, " it were a bliss
    O'er every feeling poured !

" Think not of solemn changes past
    Which hath thy bosom riven,
For though this word should be my last,
    My lord, thou art forgiven !"

Now after some arrangements, they
    Set out upon a tour,
Yet not intending long to stay,
    But Italy explore.

Then, after his return, the prince
    Designed to spend his life
Within a convent, not far hence,
    To mourn his sins and wife.

Now on a day, while autumn threw
    Her golden sunbeams o'er
A portion of creation's view
    That every beauty wore ;

In groves the clustering vineyards lay,
    Hung rich with melting fruit,
A scene where fancy fain would stray
    And would the muses suit ;

All nature in her fairest smiles
   This morning seemed to be ;
Glory lit up the distant isles
   And gilded o'er the sea,—

Our travelers they embarked to range
   Perennial, distant shores,
Trusting, among new beauties strange,
   To heal up memory's pores.

Their journey prosperous, brought them soon
   Among those templed shrines,
Where ruin stalks as broad as noon,
   And ivy rank entwines.

Those crumbling halls, all green and dark,
   Whose sculptured ruins lay
A living, though a mournful mark,
   Of greatness passed away.

Some weeks they spent in wandering o'er
   This fair and beauteous clime;
Each tropic scene they did explore
   Though grief kept pace with time.

Enchanting were the changing scenes
   That met their saddened view;
But now a subject intervenes
   As strange as it is true.

To Switzerland they now repaired ;
   All vernal charms had fled :
The wood, the vale, the bowers were seared,
   For winter round them spread

Her gloomy visage, keen and bleak;
　The wind moaned loud and wild;
They now a warming shelter seek
　Where comfort seeming smiled.

A favored hospice—here they gained
　Admittance for the night,
And were most kindly entertained,
　Or welcomed with delight.

Now seated at a frugal meal
　Of biscuit, bread, and wine,
For luxuries they did not feel
　Disposed to once repine.

The flask renewed, a monk drew near,
　Whose locks were silvered o'er
With snows of many a gone-by year;
　His cheeks deep furrows wore.

He joined in converse to amuse
　Each weary stranger guest,
But did a solemn subject choose,
　And thus the group addressed:

" The monastery where I reside
　Is but a mile from here,
It is with holy hearts supplied
　And many a daughter fair.

" For fifty years its cloisters have
　My pilgrim form retained;
I young in life to Heaven gave
　The homage I maintained.

"And peaceful have my seasons flown,
　Save sometimes an event
Would be across my pathway thrown
　As though by Heaven sent.

" Five months have passed since on a night
　Of deep and threatening gloom,
The planets all shut out their light—
　'Twas dark as murder's doom—

" Save now and then the lightning's glare
　Flashed o'er the traveler's way ;
The thunder rolled upon the air
　Where blackened vapors lay.

" 'Twas midnight; loud the portal rang,
　I to the summons flew,
Wondering what mystery could hang
　O'er this alarm so new.

" Soon was thrown back the portal gate,
　Two strangers to admit,
Thus wandering all benighted, late,
　For mercy sanctioned it.

" When, muffled in an ample cloak
　And hood of sable kind,
The loveliest fair that ever spoke
　Roused my astonished mind.

"'Admit a wanderer, father, do,
　Within your friendly walls,
For kindly shelter here we flew,—
　'Tis bleeding mercy calls !'

"I led them to a chamber, where
  Dry garments were prepared,
And what we had of comfort there
  Their wearied spirits shared.

" I gazed upon the lovely cheek
  Of this sweet angel form ;
Its paleness did more woe bespeak
  Than mere fatigue from storm."

The monk now paused—said he, " I fear
  My story pains your mind ;
If so, I will my theme forbear,
  For 'tis of tragic kind."

" Go on ! go on !" the prince replied,
  "I have a woman's heart ;
And mournful changes too, beside,
  Some gloomy thoughts impart !"

" Well, sires, the hermit with her then
  Revealed a murderous tale,
About a prince, the worst of men,
  That made my spirit quail !

"This lady was his beauteous love,
  Most innocent and fair,
But he did of her jealous prove,
  Yet had no cause whate'er.

"Yet from a lofty tower he
  Threw this, his lovely bride,
In one sad fit of jealousy,
  Into the rolling tide !"

" Hold, hold ! for God's sake, hold !"
    The frenzied prince exclaimed—
" I am that wretched murderer bold,
    You have so fitly named !

" Yes, yes ! I was 'the worst of men !'
    Thy lips hath rightly said ;
But, friend, I am not now as then—
    I have atonement made !

" Gods ! can it be ? what fate is this
    Hangs o'er my palsied soul ?
Say, does she live ? oh ! pray dismiss
    These doubts which round me roll !

" Speak, speak ! does my Zuona live,
    My life, my love, my all ?
The world's dominions would I give
    Now at her feet to fall !

"There in my soul's deep anguish plead
    For her forgiving love ;
Yea, there my heart would burst and bleed,
    Its contrite will to prove !

" Speak ! tell me, holy father, where
    Doth this, my angel live ?
If she's on earth, let me repair
    To instant comfort give !"

"She lives ! she lives !" the father cried ;
    " Calm now thy frenzied heart !
She in the convent doth reside
    And lives the Christian's part."

" Blest Heaven's most unforeseen decree,
    Is this eventful night !
Blessings disguised hath followed me
    And on my soul alight !

"But, holy father, lead me on
    To my own injured bride,
Then gratitude shall smile upon
    Thy heart, and wealth beside !"

How did Albaddin's bosom beat
    At every word that passed !
He clasped in joy the prince's feet;
    His tears fell warm and fast.

Said he, "My lord, come let us kneel
    To bending Heaven now,
Whose love hath set its sovereign seal
    Upon thy contrite vow.

" How passing strange is each event
    That o'er existence reign !   ·
Who could have thought decree had sent
    Thy bride to thee again ?

" Oh ! sweet exulting hour of bliss !
    That I should live to see
On earth a day of joy like this,—
    'Tis nigh too much for me !"

The prince the kind Albaddin seized
    And pressed him to his breast ;
In transport sorrowing, and yet pleased,
    He thus the youth addressed:

"Albaddin, my most cherished friend,
  Some doubts my soul pervade;
My rapture yet may have an end,
  My hopes be prostrate laid!

"That cruel, murderous design
  My loved Zuone may ne'er
Forgive, or yet consent again
  Before me to appear.

"Prophetic Gods! should this be true
  I'm lost—I'm lost—undone!
Death would be welcome to my view
  As morning's rising sun!

"Ay, if her sacred lips declare
  Me as a loathsome fiend,
Where shall I fly? ah! tell me where
  Shall I my misery end?

"Could I in earth's remotest sphere
  My bleeding sorrows hide?
Ah, no! the ghost of black despair
  O'er memory would preside!

"It were a kind, a sweet relief,
  If at her feet I lie,
There pardon ask, there vent my grief,
  There bless her, and to die!

"Rather than forever be
  Protruded from her sight,
A slave to living misery
  Shut up in sorrow's night!"

" Hark !" said the holy father now,
  " I would in turn just speak ;
I well that lovely angel know,
  And will her instant seek !

"A life devoted she has led
  Since in those walls she came ;
A very saint whose heart hath bled
  O'er thy unhappy name.

" How often, in the midnight hour,
  She in her lonely cell,
When soothing sleep denied its power
  Nor would her eyelids seal,

" Be on her knees in fervent prayer
  To Him, our lofty God,
Who bends in love his sovereign ear
  To every saint's abode.

" In deep, adoring spirit, her
  Chaste orisons would rise,
Pleading to Heaven, noble sire,
  For thee. ' O God !' she cries,

"' Wilt thou spread out thy shielding wing
  O'er him, my prince, my lord,
His soul to just repentance bring ?
  Oh ! speak the pardoning word !

"' Oh ! could I through some venture learn
  He mourns his horrid plot ;
And poor Albaddin's fate discern,—
  If murdered or if not !

"'I trust the potent loving arm
    That kindly rescued me,
Hath saved this guileless youth from harm,
    And guards his destiny!

"'For visible by every view
    Is thy prevailing power,
That bore my struggling spirit through
    That dark, tremendous hour.

"'Then, God immutable, I give
    My prince into thy care,
That he a holy life may live
    Of penitence and prayer.'

"And thus, while weary hours rolled,
    This saint would plead for thee;
Then if by heavenly love controlled
    Could she revengeful be?

"Could she, who thus for thee would plead
    From hour to hour, disdain
To look on thee? ah! no indeed!
    Nor love thee once again.

"It cannot be! her holy mind
    Still lingers o'er thy form;
Affection of the purest kind
    Her noble feelings warm.

"She loves thee! ay, she loves thee still,
    Though grief pervades her soul!
Forgive thee she most surely will
    For all thy treatment foul!

"And how will her angelic heart
　　Throb with new-born delight
When I the truth to her impart
　　Of this eventful night!

" So, mighty prince, thy feelings calm,
　　For all will yet be well ;
For every wound there is a balm
　　In holy Gilead still!"

"I will! I will!" the prince replied ;
　　"Her perfect heart will ne'er
Reject my prayers, or yet deride
　　The burning, contrite tear.

" So bring her, holy father, to
　　My longing arms I pray,
That I my loved Zuone may view
　　Before the break of day."

Now taking leave, the monk with speed
　　Soon gained the convent gate,
Did to Zuona's cell proceed,
　　For yet it was not late.

When, tapping gently at the door,
　　Admittance begged to gain,
As he had weighty news in store
　　To instantly explain ;

Suspecting something strange indeed,
　　Zuona quickly flew,
With heart well-nigh to burst and bleed,
　　And soon the bolts undrew.

A hundred vague ideas rose
  Across her troubled brain,
That her confessor now should choose
  An entrance to gain.

She knew there must be pressing need,
  Some strange event, or why
Would it the holy man there lead,
  And for her ear apply?

With visage pale, and trembling heart,
  She to the monk drew near,
To hear what he would fain impart,
  Or what had brought him there.

" My daughter !" said the holy man,
  Whose looks expressed concern,
And drawing near he now began,—
  "Thou must strange tidings learn !

" Compose thyself, and feel no fear,
  For joyous news I bring,
Tidings of love and sacred cheer
  Borne on an angel's wing !

" The heaven of heavens hath heard thy pray'r,
  My daughter, and I came
Thy precious feelings to prepare,—
  So listen to the same.

"This night I to the hospice went
  To pass a friendly hour,
As I have oft before there spent
  When evening shadows lower.

24

" While seated round the glowing hearth
    With other brethren there,
Joining in tales of woe or mirth,
    Two strangers did appear.

" They were of lofty rank I found
    From their address and mien,
And while the usual tale went round,
    Some change now wore the scene."

" Oh, holy father, speak! oh, speak !"
    The fair Zuona cried ;
While snowy paleness blanched her cheek
    Which beauty's mould supplied.

" Is it the prince? oh, speak, I pray !
    How frantic do I feel!
Hath Heaven shone across his way
    And changed his heart of steel ?"

" It is the prince, my daughter fair !
    Come, calm thyself, for now
Thou must with me to him repair
    Whose heart is steeped in woe.

" Yes, grief, my child, of purest kind,
    Sorrow for all that's past,—
Religion fills his noble mind
    And claims him heir at last.

" I chanced to name thy hapless fate,
    As other tales went round;
The hour as yet, not being late,
    And thus the prince I found.

" How was my soul astonished, when
  The tragedy I named,
Or pictured I the worst of men,
  The prince the feature claimed !

" Frenzied, he started from his seat
  With looks so deep and wild,
That when he did his tale repeat
  It made me weep, my child !

"And further listen, pray attend !
  Albaddin he is well !
He is the prince's bosom friend,
  Doth constant with him dwell !

" They at the kindly hospice wait
  For me to bring thee there ;
Then come, my daughter, 'tis not late,
  We thither will repair."

"Ah ! holy father, how can I
  Endure this interview ?
It will my very heart-strings try,
  Perhaps will break them too !"

" Nay, nay, my daughter ! this is wrong !
  Thy pious feelings sure
Should be with moral courage strung—
  Thou must the scene endure !"

Now on his aged arm she leans
  While thither they proceed ;
A gloomy pathway intervenes
  But does not mar their speed.

And long it was not ere they stood
    Before the hospice gate,
Were welcomed to the kind abode
    By those who for them wait.

But who can paint the coming scene?
    All efforts would be vain;
'Twas only such as to be seen
    And ne'er forgot again!

With eager heart the prince had flown,
    In shame and wounded pride,
And soon his form was prostrate thrown
    Before his injured bride.

Swelled was the quivering lip that strove
    To break the chain-bound spell;
One scream told poor Zuona's love,—
    She on his bosom fell!

"Adored Zuone! my well-beloved!"
    The prince in anguish cried;
"A vile and murderous wretch I've proved,
    And should thy curse abide!

"How have I torn thy precious heart,
    And grieved thy soul with pain?
How canst thou one kind look impart
    Or meet me e'er again?

"But thou art holy, and will not
    Resent my former deeds,
Yet will them from thy memory blot,
    While mine own conscience bleeds.

" But let me hear thee speak the word
    That tells my heart forgiven ;
'Twill be like music sweetly heard,
    Or echoed back from heaven.

"Yet shouldst thou but despise me, I
    Will bear the fatal blow
Just long enough to weep and die,
    A victim to my woe !

" Then, dearest, speak ! and tell me too
    What thus thy life did save,
When I had thought, or seeming knew,
    Thee 'neath a watery grave ?

" By what strange miracle wert thou
    Preserved from death's dark doom ?
I cannot see in nature how
    Thou hast escaped the tomb."

" 'Twas Heaven, Zubadah, saved my life !
    It knew my wrongs, and sent
A rescue to thy injured wife,
    That thou mightst yet repent.

"When thou didst from that fatal tower
    Commit me to the deep,
There was a holy, wakeful power
    Did to my danger leap.

" It chanced, as thou didst madly throw
    Me from thy fearful hold,
A sapling from the rocks below
    Caught in my dress some fold ;
        24*

"And thus suspended, there I hung,
    Nigh dead with fear and grief,
Till some kind fishermen had sprung
    In time to my relief.

" Not distant far their nets were cast,
    For they had fishing been;
They saw the tragedy that passed,
    And hurried to the scene.

" They placed me in their boat and bore
    Me to their humble cot,
Which every charm of comfort wore,
    Though rustic was their lot.

" Exceeding ill for weeks I lay,
    Dependent on their care,
Yet over-generous were they
    With all their simple fare.

" I charged them well, to never name
    The dark and solemn deed,
To see how time would rule the same
    Since I from death was freed;

" With promises of kind reward
    If they would silent be,
Nor name by single hint or word
    My hapless destiny;

" Believing through prophetic skies,
    Before thy frantic view
My spirit's innocence would rise
    A ghost to pierce thee through.

" The most I feared was that our page,
　So faithful, kind, and true,
Had fallen a victim to thy rage,
　And that from torture too !

" But thanks to sweet ordaining Heaven,
　It was a tragic dream!
And happy thou art now forgiven,
　And life may glide serene.

" 'Tis well Albaddin lives to see
　This night of joy arrive;
Wert thou his murderer, naught with me
　Could former love revive !

" I never could with Christian aid,
　The warmest and the best,
Again upon thy heart have laid,
　Or held thee to my breast.

"A murderer ! no ! and thus I sought
　A refuge for awhile,
Where sweet religion's ways are taught,
　And love and friendship smile.

" That shielding convent was my home,
　Where I have lived in prayer,
That Heaven would avert thy doom
　Of misery and despair.

" Trusting that time would tidings bring
　To my confiding heart,
With joy and healing in its wing,
　And sovereign peace impart.

"And thus hath Heaven heard my cry,
    And brought this happy hour ;
Thus may we Christians live and die,
    And sin, my love, no more."

" Come to my arms, sweet life, again !
    For thou art all to me !"
Zubadah cried; " how blest the pain
    Of meeting—ecstacy !

" From deep conviction I was bound
    To some known convent near,
To mourn thy fate in gloom profound,
    And live a life of prayer.

" Till this event of Heaven's own
    Hath brought thee back to me,
What changeless mercy hath it shown
    To set my conscience free !

"A slave to every guilty fear
    I had been doomed to live,   .
Didst thou not, love, now reappear
    And every wrong forgive.

" But now, back to the palace we
    Will hasten, and prepare
A banquet, for all guests most free
    Who shall our rapture share.

" The country round shall ring with joy
    At this, our bridal feast;
And may no cloud the bliss destroy
    Of each exulting breast !

" The tower, that sepulcher of ill,
   A chapel now shall prove,
By Heaven's kind ordaining will
   To firmer join our love.

" Mass every night shall there be said
   While our blest lives shall last,
There every grateful vow be paid
   For future and the past.

"And this, our own Albaddin here,
   Shall ever be our guest;
He is our bosom friend sincere,
   The very truest, best!

" But wealth and title are his claim;
   He is our page no more,
A dukedom shall enroll his name,
   And honors are in store.

" My sister Alrianna is
   Most beautiful and fair,
A princess, too; she shall be his
   With all her virtues rare.

"A marriage gift so nobly great,
   I deem a just reward
To one who thus pursued my fate
   And all my sorrows shared.

" We'll hail the pleasing jubilee
   In one united band;
This day that gives thee back to me
   Shall join them hand in hand."

Now knelt Albaddin at their feet,
  And blessed them o'er and o'er,
There did his constant vows repeat,
  And Heaven's decrees adore!

———————

HOPE.

THE sweet smile of Hope! what a bright little treasure,
  What a comfort to those that are sad!
It is, we e'er know, the sure index of pleasure
  Which lightens and makes the heart glad.

It whispers sometimes little things very kind,
  Which we fain would have true without fail;
Yet while it thus pleasingly buoys up the mind,
  It proves oft a "flattering tale."

Each fairy illusion, like some glowing scene
  Transferred to the canvas appears,
When meddlesome fate slyly steps in between
  And clips up the whole with her shears.

Yea, Hope! thou art light and as fickle as air,
  Yet comforting still in the main,
For while e'er coquetting like some giddy fair,
  Thou wilt fly off to come back again.

And thus thou art ever a kindly guest,
  Although disappointments appear,
Since thou canst roll back the dark clouds from the
      breast,
  And wipe off the sorrowing tear.

THE SPEAKING FLOWER.

Oh! what a beauteous flower, Jane!
  Its colors, they are soft and clear,
And while I gaze on every vein
  I see a hundred graces there!

Its azure blue like yonder sky,
  Its stems of velvet green;
On every leaf I cast my eye
  The Author's name is seen!

JANE.

Why, Anna, sure you rave, my child!
  The flower, I own, is fair
As any other growing wild;
  But name—I see none there!

But you can always find a charm
  In everything you see,
To kindle admiration warm,—
  It is not so with me!

A weed, a plant of any kind
  Has some delight for you;
You'll turn it over till you find
  Its worth and virtue too!

The other day, the little vine
  That shades our cottage door,
You saw in it such beauty shine
  As ne'er you saw before.

The gentle breeze that whispered by
   Was music to your ear,
And little birds that warbled nigh
   Caused on your cheek a tear.

Now, Anna, this is strange to me!
   Why you should look so sad
When Nature all looks charmingly
   And every heart seems glad!

ANNA.

Ah, dearest Jane! it was not grief
   That caused the gushing tear;
But while I gazed on every leaf
   I saw God's beauty there!

There's not a lovely flower that blows
   On nature's fertile soil,
But what His matchless wisdom shows
   As well as sacred toil.

And when I look around and see
   His glories spreading wide,
A thousand thoughts encompass me
   My feelings cannot hide.

His precious love and tender care
   Hath marked my youthful days;
He wanders with me everywhere
   And guards my trembling ways.

Then can I gaze on all around
   With cold and senseless heart,
Nor love, nor gratitude be found
   To act a generous part?

Ah, no! dear Jane, that must not be!
  I would inferior prove
To this sweet silent flower you see,
  Which speaks its Maker's love!

Though no broad name is written here,
  Its lovely virtues show
There is a God we should revere
  And early learn to know!

All things in nature speak His praise,
  E'en this retiring flower;
Then let us walk in wisdom's ways
  And bless and love Him more!

JANE.

You're right, dear Anna! now I see
  How dumb I've been indeed;
And since you've made all plain to me,
  A different life I'll lead!

I am ashamed! so many years
  I've heedless passed away,
Nor saw 'mid all that bright appears
  Their grandeur till to-day.

But now I have much wiser grown,
  Things different will appear;
And since you've made God's wonders known,
  I'll praise Him, Anna dear!

25

THE FORFEITED KISS.

" COME, pretty coz! you well remember
  This is the first of old December;
  And now it's just one year ago
  Since you made me a bet, you know,
  That if a riddle I should guess,
  You'd pay the forfeit of a kiss;
  But like a little prude, as yet
  You never have relieved the debt;
  And since twelve months it now is due,
  I frankly think you owe me two!"

" Go 'long! you silly torment, go!
  Why do you always treat me so?
  It seems you never will grow steady,
  Though twenty years you've seen already,
  And by this time, a clever span, .
  You ought to be a nice young man!
  Nor come with silly tales like this,
  And say I owe you now a kiss!"

" Nay, nay! I say you owe me two;
  The other is the interest due!
  I've waited now a year for pay,
  And must receive them both to-day!
  Don't think you, coz, my pretty tease,
  I'll let you do just as you please!
  So now we'll see who is the stronger,
  Since I'm resolved to wait no longer!

Look out there! here is one, two, three!
That is a sad mistake, I see!
Oh! pardon, coz! nor think me vain;
Come, take the other back again!"

"Go 'long! you sure have crazy grown!
Why will you not let me alone?
Take that! you good-for-nothing pest!"
Said Kate; "you are too bad at best!"
And while she blushed with maiden grace,
She slapped him gently in the face,
And pouted in such pretty mood
That Ned would further fain intrude;
And vowed by Cupid and his quiver
She should that day be his forever.

"I cannot say!" said prudish Kate;
"I have a mind to make you wait!
It would be nothing more than right
For putting me in such a fright;
Just see now, through your silly whim,
My hair is in an awful trim!
Indeed you better grow more steady
Before you are for marriage ready;
And all for taking kisses three,—
Now, mind, you get no more from me!"

"Ho, ho!" said Ned; "my pretty coz,
Now don't toss up your little nose;
For since you are disposed to pout,
We'll fight the silly matter out;
For there is luck in lover's sprees—
They bring a wedding on the breeze;

And now, my darling little maid,
Although you think the forfeit paid,
So sure as I am second cousin,
When we are wed I'll have a dozen !'

———※———

THE LITTLE CRIPPLE.

" Come, brother dear ! don't run away !
    I cannot walk so fast as you ;
My little limbs, you see how they
    Are sadly warped and shrunken too !

" It was not thus some time ago,
    Ere dreadful pain and sickness came ;
I then was blithe and gay, you know,
    And did not dream of being lame.

" But here I am a cripple now,
    And scarcely can I go alone !
Ah, brother dear ! I wonder how
    I'll be when I am older grown ?

" Poor mother daily grieves to see
    My little, weak, and shrunken form,
And while she fondly blesses me,
    I feel her tears fall fast and warm.

" She feels I am a helpless child,
    And very little use indeed ;
Yet day and night how has she toiled
    To keep us both from woe and need !

"Ah, me! she is so good and kind,
  We never hear her heart complain,
And hard she must the duty find
  Us both to shelter and maintain!

"I wish I could a little earn,
  If only but a mite or two;
But then, alas! I cannot turn
  My hand a single thing to do!

"But then I still will hope and pray
  My feeble limbs may stronger grow;
If this should be the case, I may
  Some comfort to her heart bestow!

"But now I just go creeping on,
  And wearisome I must appear;
Give me your arm to lean upon,
  And take me home, my brother dear!"

———⸙———

THE HERO'S GRAVE.

THE war drum was still, and the battle was o'er,
  The silence of death held its reign;
All hushed was the sound of the cannon's deep roar,
  And strewed was the field of the slain.

The battle-axe lay by the warrior's side,
  His sword and his shield stained with gore,
All told that the hero had nobly died,
  And would wield them in triumph no more.

25*

But ere the brave chieftain relinquished his breath,
   The glory of victory won
Gave joy to illumine the shadows of death,
   For he knew that his warfare was done.

" Huzza to my country ! huzza to the brave !"
   Was the language that fell from his tongue;
" I smile o'er the trammels of death and the grave
   Since the peal of our victory has rung!

" The grave of a soldier ! where else should it be
   But on the dominions of war?
If he dies, from the bondage of slavery free,
   And under a conquering star !

" Huzza to my country ! huzza to the brave !
   Huzza to bright victory's name !
'Tis glory to die my loved nation to save,
   And see her enameled with fame !"

Thus spoke the brave chieftain, and now
   A halo of triumph was seen
To illumine his breast and his brow,
   On the pillow of life's closing scene.

And now there's an emerald spot
   On the isle where the battle was known,
That will never through time be forgot,
   For 'tis carved on eternity's throne !

For who will not think of the brave,
   Wherever their relics may lie,
Who have fought their loved country to save,
   For its freedom and people to die ?

NATURE'S SOLITUDE.

WOULD man to holy thoughts aspire
  To lead him in a humble vein?
Let him in solitude inquire
  Of every valley, wood, and plain;
Where he may see the heather bloom,
  The violet peep from mossy bed,
Those gorges wild, where all assume
  A grandeur most sublimely spread;
The music of the silver rills,
  And whispering leaves that hang above;
The silence from a hundred hills
  May all awake his heart to love.

Not morbid love of selfish earth,
  Those passions of depraved delight,
But holy thoughts that life give birth
  And lead the longing soul aright.
Ask of the winding, babbling brook,
  Coursing along the forest glade,
Whence it its mirrored beauty took,
  Or who its flowery borders made;
Or mossy shrines, that silent rear
  Their pigmy heights on every side;
From each and all a voice I hear
  That tells who hath the whole supplied.

The tumbling cascade, rushing down,
  Amid a world of foam and spray,
The rocks that towering mountains crown,
  Whose depths ne'er meet the light of day;

And silent caverns, dark and deep,
    With many a beauteous sculptured wall
Formed by the drops that endless keep
    A tinkling music as they fall;
Ay, music such as silence woos
    When wrapped 'mid nature's works profound :
Vain man his finite self may lose
    In every whisper, every sound.

E'en to the crisp unfolding flower,
    Whose tender buds flash to the light,
In gorgeous beauty painted o'er
    To dazzle and exalt the sight,
A charm is breathed, a speech is given,
    In every germ or leafy spray,
Which mutely speaks of holy Heaven
    And offers homage in its way.
Hear but the choir of tuneful birds
    Who early wake their morning song;
It needs not finite power of words
    To tell who thus inspires the throng.

There is a depth of mystic awe
    That wraps the soul in dreamy mood,
When we to sacred haunts withdraw
    To woo the bliss of solitude;
The sighing of the gentle breeze,
    The twittering of some insect near,
The whispering of the forest leaves
    All sweetly rest upon the ear;
There, 'mid the dark and cooling shade,
    The mind drinks in the blessed calm,
Can soar in thought to Him who made
    The glorious whole, the great "I AM."

THE IMPATIENT SWAIN.

DEAR NELL! what a nod, nid, nodding you keep!
Are you acting the traitor, or are you asleep?
For here I've been knocking so long at the door,
That my fingers are weary and knuckles are sore!

And then I've been calling so long on your name,
My throat is quite hoarse and my lungs are the same;
If this is the way, Nell, you treat me, I ne'er,
On the word of a rover, will come again here!

I have watched you at least, my dear girl, for an hour,
With your head drooping down like a rose in a shower,
Then once in awhile you would bob back again
As though you had caught a new thought in your brain.

You never have kept me so long here before,
And I felt a great notion to knock down the door,
Nor could you well blame me, dear Nell, as a man,
If I had gone off like a flash in a pan.

NELL.

Ah, Rubin! dear Rubin! forgive me, I pray!
I really forgot you were coming to-day!
And then you'll believe me, till morning's gray peep
My eyes were not blest with a wink of sweet sleep.

Then is it a wonder I dropped in a doze,
Nor should waken e'en had you screamed under my
        nose?
There's nothing that makes one look more like a fright
Than to be kept awake a whole day and a night.

RUBIN.

And is there no reason, my own pretty Nell,
For this staying awake? now be candid and tell!
For if I should judge from the looks of those eyes,
At the bottom of this there's a mystery lies.

Nay, you blush, my dear girl, and hang down your head;
I fear on your toes I now slightly tread;
But tell me the truth, and I vow and protest
I'll freely forgive you, my sweet little pest!

NELL.

Well, Rubin, dear Rubin! I'll tell you outright;
I went to a quilting and sat up all night;
The beaus were so merry, the girls full of play,
So they kept up the party till broad, beaming day.

Nay, do not be jealous! for no one was there
For whom your own Nell did a single pin care;
Then away with that frown, or, I tell you quite plain,
As a piece of revenge I will go there again!

RUBIN.

Then come here, you puss! for it won't be amiss
To give me as make-up a good hearty kiss;
For sure as you don't, there is Debby and Bell
Will be proud of the honor, you know very well!

But as we're engaged, my dear Nell, to be one,
I feel far too modest to such a risk run;
So hold up your lips, so ruddy and bright—
There's one, two, and three! my sweet girl, that is right!

SHUN THE CUP!

THE cup! the cup! the tempting cup!
You say it lifts the feelings up!
It is a poison and a snare!
Oh, shun the draught! beware, beware!

'Tis like some dark and prowling foe,
Haunting your steps where'er you go,
Chaining you by its tyrant spell,
And fain would lead you down to hell!

Look not upon the sparkling draught;
'Tis safer never to be quaffed;
For like a viper's deadly sting
It will upon your vitals cling.

Then from the hydra monster turn,
Nor let its power consuming burn
Your mortal frame, your reason's throne,
And make you victim of its own.

Yea, bravely shun the fearful vice,
Ere life's dread forfeit be the price;
Let strength in giant beauty bloom,
And nobly shun the drunkard's doom!

DESPAIR NEVER!

How oft, in life's exulting morn,
    Our hopes delusive rise!
We paint our joys without a thorn,
    Nor dream of troublous skies.

While fancy aims by magic spell
    To hold the luring chain,
The direst scenes hath oft befell
    To shroud those joys in pain.

Well is it for the mortal mind
    The future lies concealed;
We could not bear life's woes combined
    Were they to us revealed.

But Providence hath kindly dealt
    With all His creatures here,
That more shall not be seen or felt
    Than we can mostly bear.

True, sometimes crushing ills oppress
    The heart with care and pain,
And while we wish our sufferings less,
    Are prone to oft complain.

But let it be well understood,
    Those earthly trials given,
Are wisely ordered for our good,
    To win our hearts to heaven.

FRIENDSHIP A TREASURE.

It is a saying, old as true,
　That friends are rare indeed;
Yet while we pass life's journey through
　We often feel their need.

For sympathy is sweet to share
　With actions meek and kind,
And some such generous friends there are,
　Though difficult to find.

However, when a heart we meet,
　Unselfish, pure, and brave,
A soul untainted by deceit,—
　What more need mortal crave?

It is a boon of social bliss,
　The soul may fondly cherish,
For in a world so cold as this
　Devotions often perish.

For ever since the days of old,
　The warmest zeal extended,
Has been known often to grow cold,
　And sweet affections ended.

But 'tis a pleasant thing to claim
　A true, unshaken friend,
Whose merits do not live in name,—
　Hearts faithful to the end.

26

Be such a sacred treasure mine,
   Nor time nor fate can sever;
A love so holy and divine
   I fain would hold forever!

———

SUMMER IS GONE!

BRIGHT Summer has departed! for the germs within
    the bower
No longer show their shining buds and sweet exulting
    flower;
The leaves appear to dusky grow, inclining to the sear,
Revealing to the moral mind that Autumn now is here.

The birds they whistle through the wood the same as in
    the spring,
And merry bee and butterfly continue on the wing;
But then they have a way to go to find their honeyed
    store,
Since flowers they no longer bloom as they have done
    before.

The farmer he is weary, yet his harvesting is done,
And glowing stacks of yellow corn stand ripening in the
    sun,
And mellow fruits and golden grain are careful stowed
    away
To bless his honest heart and brow when comes old
    Winter gray.

The lowing kine look neat and trim, and oxen in the
    stall,
They seem to think there is enough for master and them
    all ;
Their wholesome breath is pure and sweet as any new-
    mown hay,
When they return with cheerful pace just at the close
    of day.

Upon the rustic maiden's brow a happy smile is seen,
When comes the hour of milking time upon the cottage
    green ;
And when the apple-paring time comes gayly round
    again,
You'll find her at the village church with some young
    gallant swain.

Oh, happy is the farmer's life! as seasons take their
    round,
What pleasure thrills his noble heart while tilling up his
    ground !
A thousand pleasing hopes foretell abundant crops will
    rise,
Before the charming year has flown, to bless his honest
    eyes.

Give me the charms of rural life, its pleasures and its
    toil:
The proudest hearts that ever throbbed were yeomen of
    the soil ;
The bravest sons that ever raised a hand to strike a foe
Were honest freemen of the land, who loved to reap and
    sow.

Ay, give me but a cottage neat near some green mount-
　　ain side,
Where rivers flow and fountains leap; or by the ocean
　　wide,
Where pearl shells glitter on the strand and wild the
　　billows roar,—
This, this with humble competence, on earth I ask no
　　more.

———❦———

PROFANE THOU NOT THE LIVING GOD.

PROFANE thou not the living God!
　　Take not his holy name in vain!
Lest, touched by his chastising rod,
　　Thy lips may never speak again!

It is a fearful thing to stand
　　In froward might before the Lord,
With outstretched arm and daring hand,
　　Regardless of his power or word.

Look on the dark recording page,
　　As onward rolls departing time,
And see in every gone-by age
　　The judgments that have followed crime.

God hath resolved in holy writ,
　　Penned by inspired saints of old,
If we rebellion will commit
　　We never shall his face behold!

Appalling thought! yet true as dread!
   We often see destruction fall
Upon the reckless swearer's head
   Ere he can once for mercy call.

'Tis then the knell of solemn doom
   Breaks on the closing, dying ear,
Saying, "Welcome, sinner! welcome home,
   To endless regions of despair!

"Thou hast the living God abused
   And long insulted to his face,
His loving offers hath refused
   And scorned his pardon and his grace.

"His spirit grieved hath turned aside,
   Thou fearful son of wrath and boast,
And left thee to destruction wide,—
   Thou art among the doomed and lost!"

Lost! oh, solemn, fearful sound!
   To be recalled in judgment never!
It tells a home the soul hath found,
   Shut out from light and God forever!

OUR MOTHER.

WE miss thee, oh! my mother dear!
   And yet how much we cannot say;
For since thy voice no more we hear,
   A gloom around our hearth-stone lay;

26*

For now when evening shades appear,
  And we in social circle meet,
Our eyes fill up with many a tear
  To see thy loved, yet vacant seat;
Alas! it looks so sad and lone,
And tells, dear mother, thou art gone!

I think I see thy placid smile,
  As when we once beheld thee there,
So patient, knitting all the while
  And chatting, in that old arm-chair;
Each gentle look thou gavest then
  Is treasured in fond memory deep,
For there are sacred moments when
  We love to think of thee and weep;
For all is dreary now, and lone,
And tells, dear mother, thou art gone!

How oft affection calls to mind,
  When pain and sickness venture near,
Thy tender, soothing, accents kind,
  Which strove our drooping hearts to cheer!
Thy hand touched light our fevered brow,
  And smoothed the pillow with such care,
Alas! alas! 'tis not so now,
  When we the pangs of suffering bear!
Nay, nay! all now is dread and lone,
And tells, dear mother, thou art gone!

How oft, when silence reigns around,
  And dreamy thoughts come looming o'er,
We almost think we hear the sound
  Of thy dear footstep on the floor!

For still it seems it cannot be
  That thou must absent e'er remain;
We fain look fondly round for thee,
  And list to hear that voice again!
But, no! ah, no! we are alone,
And feel, dear mother, thou art gone!

———◦———

A SONG TO THE OCEAN.

OLD OCEAN, I love thee! what wonders untold
  In thy mystical depths lie concealed,
O'er which thy proud billows for ages hath rolled,
  Nor will e'er in time be revealed!
Thy surges, how wildly they beat on the shore!
Yet music, sweet music, is heard in thy roar.

When hurricane winds come with noisy breath,
  And clouds big with tempest arise,
And the sea-bird is heard, like the omen of death,
  As she speeds on her way through the skies;
Yet wild as her scream trembles over the sea,
In her voice there is music, sweet music, for me!

When lightnings are flashing and thunders loud roll,
  And nature seems quaking with dread,
And the storm-king is showing his august control,
  With his pinions of midnight outspread;
Yet his hoarse, wailing voice, as he beats through the
      air,
Brings music, though mournfully wild, to my ear!

And then, if I listen, dear Ocean, to thee,
   When nature is beaming and bright,
And the white-crested billows go dancing and free
   In the sun's grand and glorious light,
And leap to the shore with a magical bound,
A cadence of music is heard in the sound.

Oh, yes! I look on thee with wonder and awe,
   Thy mighty expanse and thy power;
What hidden creations that man never saw
   Must lie in thy depths evermore!
Yet still from thy gorgeous domains do I hear
Sweet sounds that are music, though wild, to my ear.

THE REFORMED GAMBLER.

DARK, dark was the night, and the tempest rose high,
Not a star was there seen to illumine the sky,
But the voice of the storm broke aloud on the ear,
And forest trees rattled and creaked in the air,—

When Morach, with mantle wrapped close round his
     form,
Left his desolate cottage, nor heeded the storm.
"Dear Minda!" said he, "I must go, love, indeed;
I am now rather late, but must quicken my speed.

"Go now to thy pillow and rest thee awhile,
   Perhaps, love, the morning may dawn with a smile;
   A kiss on thy forehead and I must away;
   My promise is given—I cannot delay."

"Ah, Morach! and must I alone here remain,
  And know not how soon I shall see thee again;
  With naught but my dreaming boy, beauteous and fair,
  To gaze on in sorrow when thou art not here?

" The voice of the tempest is thrilling and wild;
  Though it rocks our frail cottage it wakes not our child;
  And canst thou impress his fair brow with a kiss,
  And leave us alone on a night such as this?"

"Ah, Minda! these notions I cannot endure!
  Thyself and thy infant are warm and secure;
  Perhaps on the morrow at home I shall be,
  With thyself by my side and our boy on my knee!

" Till then, say no more! By the powers of light,
  There is naught shall detain me from going this night;
  My promise is given, I vowed to be there,
  And Minda and hail-storm shall not keep me here!"

Thus spoke now young Morach as onward he flew,
While his broad, heavy mantle around him he drew;
Yet a thorn of remorse barbed his soul and his mind,
For too well he knew he had spoken unkind

To one who was purest on earth to his view,
And worthy his love and his tenderness too,
Whose beautiful brow like a diadem shone
To reveal all those virtues and graces her own;

A being, who once was a parent's delight,
And the pride of those circles gay wealth could invite;
But love's fickle dream tore her heart from a sphere
Where filial affection and friendship were dear.

Young Morach had once a gay mansion, 'tis true;
But gaming brought changes most gloomy and new,
And poverty now, with its pitiless power,
Shed sorrow and woe where delight was before.

Now owing to deep disappointment in play,
He revels his cheerless existence away;
He mourns o'er the ruins of fortune and fame,
While conscience devolves on himself all the blame.

"Ah, Minda! my Minda!" he frantically said,
    While he beat through the storm that howled round his
            head,
" I feel in my heart it is madness to me
    To injure a being so lovely as thee !

" I have torn thee from friendship, from love, and from
            joy,
    And like some foul demon hath dared to destroy
    The last ray of bliss that could gladden thy brow,
    By scattering mildew and blight o'er it now. -

" Vile wretch that I am ! roll on, tempest, roll,
    And mingle thy voice with the night dragon's howl!
    Thy music rings loud through the valleys below,
    And seem like the horrible wailings of woe !

" But, hold! this night is the last of my sorrow;
    I'll live and be happy, or die on the morrow;
    I'll turn to the heart I have injured and broken,
    And prove every feature of love's dearest token !"

Thus Morach resolved as he turned himself round,
And soon the dark pathway unerringly found;

With feelings much lighter, through wind and through
 rain,
He sought his own ruinous cottage again.

But, hark! ere he raises the latch of the door,
He listens to sounds that he ne'er heard before;
What is it that breaks on his soul and his ear?
Can it be, holy Heaven! his Minda at prayer?

It is! and she prays that the guardian of power
May shield and protect him from dangers that lower.
" Save him, Father!" she cries, "through the gift of
 thy Son,
And among thy dear children, ah! make him as one!

" He is treading the pathway of ruin and woe,
And knows not the blessings thy love can bestow;
Ah! then in thy pity and mercy hang o'er him,
Shine broad in thy beauty and brightness before him!

"Then soon would this cottage, so lonely and drear,
Be a smiling and sweet little paradise here;
Then for this blest moment I plead, nay, implore,—
Grant this, holy Heaven! I ask for no more!"

" Thus, thus shall it be!" said Morach, as now
He rushed into the cottage and kissed her fair brow;
In the dream of his rapture he hung o'er her form,
While they mingle their prayers with the breath of the
 storm.

Are they happy? let reason with candor declare
There could not be found a much happier pair;
The heart that he bruised with unkindness before
He blesses in triumph a thousand times o'er.

The walls of the cottage seem gladdened with joy,
And the rose blush is seen on the cheek of the boy,
Whose beautiful fingers, so playful and fair,
Sport through the dark ringlets of dear papa's hair.

And soft as the voice or sweet music of spring,
When the lark in the morn shakes the dew from her
    wing,
Are the lispings the little one breathes in his ear,
Saying, "Papa, how good and how kind you appear!

"Before the green, pretty leaves came on the bough,
  It was not just then as it is with us now;
  For often I noticed, although but a child,
  That poor mamma wept, though she scarce ever smiled.

" But now she is smiling with joy all the day ;
  And even the kitten looks merry and gay,
  And the beautiful vines, that were faded before,
  Some creep in the window and some at the door."

"Ah, dear one ! thy heart is a stranger to all
  The events that throw mildew o'er memory's scrawl ;
  In life's future day, should kind Heaven allow,
  Thou shalt learn what I was, and what I am now !"

THE GOUTY UNCLE.

OR THE WAY TO GET TO A BALL.

A GOUTY uncle sat one day
  Close by the fireside ;
His feet upon the fender lay,
  All up in flannel tied.

And ever and anon a stitch
  Of angry pain would be
Resolved to make him madly twitch
  And slap his muffled knee.

A pretty niece, of merry wit
  And lovely, laughing eye,
Would often by his arm-chair sit;
  To soothe him she would try.

Fair Clara had a sparking beau,
  A youth in manners bland,
Who had just called to let her know
  A ball was now at hand.

Next night it was proposed to be,
  And said that he would call,
All dressed, in time, that he might see
  Her safely to the ball.

And now she to her uncle flew,
  But dreaded much to name
What she was fearful, if he knew,
  Would staunch oppose the same.

And how to manage the affair
  Poor Clara did not know,
She puzzled sense almost threadbare
  To plan a way to go.

Her uncle was so very cross,
  From spasms of the gout,
She feared her efforts would be lost
  To bring the thing about.

27

But hitting on her usual plan,
   She drew close by his side,
And soon her little tongue began
   In loving tones to glide.

" Dear uncle! you are much in pain!
   Let me once more repeat,
Or bathe with balsam warm, again,
   Your swelled and aching feet!

"And let me fix this cushion too
   More easy in your chair,
And with cologne, that's fresh and new,
   Perfume and comb your hair!"

"Go 'long! you little, prattling pest!
   I'm raving, sick, and mad!
I cannot have one moment's rest—
   I vow it is too bad!

"Murder! twitch! there it goes!
   Fire! scissors! gal!
Clear to the ends of my poor toes,—
   I shall go mad, I shall!"

" Dear uncle! do yourself compose!
   I will do all I can!"
Then swiftly to the cupboard rose
   To bring the wine-filled can.

" Here, here! dear uncle! do take this!
   It will compose your mind;
I never knew it yet to miss,—
   Relief you'll from it find!"

" Ha, ha ! you little, wily jade !
　　You know which way to please !
The gout is sure a tyrant made　．
　　To torture and to tease !"

Then twitch, twitch ! just as before,
　　Slap, slap ! goes on the shin ;
"My dear, just pour me out once more !
　　Such suffering is a sin !"

Again she hands the sparkling wine ;
　　His spirits they revive,
And Clara, pleased to see the sign,
　　Her hopes began to thrive.

For soon her uncle threw aside
　　His pouting, grunting tone,
And scarcely thought the gout to chide,
　　For angry thoughts had flown.

Now kind Sir Hubert did not make
　　A practice to taste deep,
He only would a·little take
　　To give him ease and sleep,

And put his spirits, when in pain,
　　Into a cheerful mood;
But reputation e'er to stain
　　By drink he never would.

So Clara thought it best to get
　　Her uncle calm and kind,
And then to work her heart she set
　　To change his fretful mind,—

Well knowing, when in cheerful tone,
  No kinder soul could be;
Each one could plan a way their own,
  And quite content was he,—

Except in matters highly vain,
  Extravagant, or wild;
These things he would resist right plain,
  Lest danger round them coiled.

And thus poor Clara felt a fear,
  Her dreams he would oppose,
Unless in more than common cheer
  Her uncle's feelings rose.

So now she thought the proper time
  To gain consent or not,
Or while the iron was in prime
  To strike while it was hot.

" Well, well, dear Clara! I protest,"
  Said he, " you are most kind;
Of nurses sure you are the best,.
  Or else I must be blind !

" Why, girl, I feel so smart and brave
  I scarcely can complain;
Since that last glass of wine you gave
  I feel as well again !

" Suppose I take a little more !
  Wine is a precious drug;
This I found out, though, long before,—
  Indeed, I feel quite snug !"

" Yes, yes, dear uncle ! and again
  Let me your cushion place ;
I cannot bear that horrid pain
  Should cloud your darling face !

"And here's a kiss ! a childlike kiss !
  Now I have cured you quite !"—
" Ha, ha ! you little rogue ! in this
  There's something wrong or right !

" You have some scheme now in your mind ;
  That I am very sure !
I thought you were uncommon kind
  My gouty pains to cure !

" You cunning puss ! now what's abroad ?
  Come tell me quick, and plain ;
And if consent I can afford,
  Your asking won't be vain !"

"Dear uncle ! my dear uncle ! you
  Have heard the latest news !"
" Yes, yes, my child ! but all's not true ;
  Such tales you must refuse !

" I s'pose you mean that I am bound
  To wed that stiff old maid ;
In truth, I'd rather go and drown
  Than have the crooked jade !"

" Oh, no ! dear uncle ! that's not it—
  Of that I nothing know—
Pray keep your patience just a bit,
  I other views will show !
        27*

" There is to be a splendid ball,
   And I am asked to go ;
Dear Edward said that he would call,—
   Then, do not say no, no !''

" Ho, ho ! so Ned is in the scheme !
   I see now how it goes !
There's love in some shape it would seem,
   And I must not oppose !

"At first, my child, I thought you had
   To rumor given ear ;
A tale that made me tip-toe mad
   When it I came to hear !

" Now in a little court of mine
   I there a tenant have ;
And going for my rent, in fine,
   To private gossip gave

"A little chance to spread a fib
   Of mean and silly kind,
And which, my child, I early did
   To strangle feel inclined !

"And she, the minx ! among the rest
   Now wants it to appear
That I my earnest views have pressed,
   Which met her willing ear !

"And has impatient now become
   Herself with me to tether,
And vows if I don't have it done,
   She'll show me stormy weather !

"Did anybody ever hear
  Such impudence and folly?
It is enough, my Clara dear,
  To make an old man jolly!

" To think, for sixty years or more
  A bachelor I've tarried,
And now, when over old threescore,
  The folks would have me married!

"And so, my dear! this wicked tale
  My temper somewhat tried;
Such news as this could never fail
  To be with force applied.

" But since all matters are no worse,
  Why you shall share the ball;
I give consent to this of course,
  So Edward he may call!"

THE WARRIOR'S DREAM.

'Twas night! when silence o'er hamlet and hill
  Threw its voiceless triumph around;
The trumpet's loud blast and the war drum was still,
  And hushed was the tumult of sound,—

When the warrior, weary from battle, reclined
  On his pillow encircled with fame;
A thousand gay visions danced over his mind,
  For valor now blazoned his name.

He thought of the present, the future, and past,
    As each picture arose to his view,
Till the dreaming god bound him in fetters at last
    To paint other visions, and new.

On wings rapid fancy soon wafted him home,   ·
    To his kindred and dear native isle ;
His fair Arrodell to meet him had flown
    With affection's caress and a smile.

His dear aged parents, to see him once more
    Could scarcely their rapture restrain;
While his sweet blooming sisters a thousand times o'er
    They kissed him again and again.

Each object that met his now favoring sight
    Held a claim on his memory and love,
While merry hearts joined in some festive delight
    Their home-chaste affections to prove.

The mansion illumined with tapers soon threw
    Their glory and brilliancy round,
And beauty and fashion in ecstasy flew ·
    In circles at music's sweet sound.

And Arrodell, fair as the goddess of spring,
    Appeared in the fanciful throng,
As light as a paradise bird on its wing
    When the orange grove rings with its song.

He gazed on her form in a triumph of bliss,
    While he clasped her with joy to his breast,
And thought in a moment of rapture like this,
    No warrior e'er was so blest.

Rich garlands of posies were scattered around
　　And woven in letters of fame;
Bright mottoes of valor and praise strewed the ground,
　　That were graven in gold with his name.

But, hark! what is this? there are martial alarms
　　That break on his slumbering ear;
With the trumpet's loud blast, and soldier to arms,
　　Arise! and for battle prepare!

He dashes the fetters of sleep from his brow,
　　And wildly starts from his bed;
Ah! where are those visions of happiness now,
　　That late o'er his pillow were shed?

"'Twas a dream!" said the hero, "too madly flown!"
　　As sadly his forehead he pressed;
"What a vision to break o'er my soul's dearest throne
　　To leave me a victim unblest!

"Proud phantom! how have ye bewildered my soul
　　With taunting delights so untrue!
When I thought in my spirit with magic control
　　I held every dear feature in view!"

The morning's gray mist hung over the vale,
　　The sun had not risen on high,
When the warrior, clad in his blood-sprinkled mail,
　　Did again to the battle-field fly!

The clangor of arms, the cannon's deep roar,
　　And the war drums were heard from afar;
And "*freedom or death*," were the mottoes he wore,
　　As he mounted the ramparts of war!

The trophies of valor again are unfurled
   And floated aloft in the breeze;
And newly-won honors again had empearled
   His forehead, he proudly sees.

But, ah! ere he turns from the field of the slain
   To join in triumphant career,
Some envious foe, who in ambush had lain,
   Sent an arrow of death through the air!

The warrior's temples the weapon received;
   From his war-horse he quickly fell,
But soon an avenger the traitor perceived,
   When he died on the point of the steel.

But, oh! what a change from the beautiful dream
   That had broke o'er his slumbering mind,
Was the sad, bleeding picture of life's closing scene
   O'er a bosom so noble and kind!

The deep, muffled drum, the march of the dead,
   Now told that the hero was gone;
Yet fame has a monument placed o'er his head,
   Which the deeds of his valor had won!

And oft as the summer her flowers unfold,
   And violets peep from his grave,
Shall the story by wandering minstrels be told
   As a dirge to the true and the brave!

A TALE OF THE CRUSADES.

Do you see that castle peeping just beyond the mountain
    side,
With ivy darkly creeping o'er its turrets far and wide?
I'll tell you now a story that happened long ago,
While the crusaders were passing through the valley far
    below.

There was a lovely princess, Esbatena was her name,
Who to see her lordly uncle to the stately palace came ;
She was a maid of beauty, and of sweet, engaging mind,
And many were the suitors who to wed her felt inclined.

But then fair Esbatena cared for none among the throng,
Though many great and wealthy did to the train belong ;
All thought her cold and haughty, though beautiful
    withal,
And wondered that among the whole, none could her
    heart enthrall.

But then there was a reason ; for the maid had seen be-
    fore
One whom her young and gentle mind could honor and
    adore :
It was a gallant stranger-knight, a hero on the way
Toward the fields of Palestine,—below the army lay.

She saw him at the tournament her lordly uncle gave,
Without the stately castle walls, to try her suitors brave,

When suddenly the stranger-knight, with tall and grace-
    ful mien,
With visor closed and golden spurs, appeared upon the
    scene.

He tilted with the greatest lords, although to all un-
    known,
And with such ease and bravery that many a knight
    was thrown ;
All wondered who the hero was, rich clothed in gold and
    gray,
Who came up from the crusade band that in the valley
    lay.

Some thought he was a mighty prince from neighboring
    realm or power;
Such prowess they had never seen in lord or knight be-
    fore ;
And some thought him a goodly monk, of noble kith
    and kin,
Whose zeal was leading him away to the walls of Pales-
    tine.

The lovely Esbatena gazed with fond, admiring eye
Upon the noble cavalier when he came riding by;
He sat upon his charger bold with proud and gallant
    air ;
She thought the visored youth a prize for any lady fair.

He saw the triumph he had won upon the maiden's
    mind,
For long, in secret, he had loved this creature chaste
    and kind ;

Yet little did the princess dream who was the warrior
    brave
Who now among the suitors came her favoring smiles
    to crave.

Yet more than charmed, we have to say, the lovely
    maiden felt,
When as a victor he approached and at her feet he
    knelt;
She thought had she a realm to give, a crown to then
    bestow,
The whole she would most freely give this visored youth
    to know.

"Fair lady," said the gallant knight, with modest air
    and bland,
While through his half-closed casque he spoke, and
    kissed her snowy hand,
" Your beauty I will ne'er forget in danger's darkest
    hour,
And thoughts of you my arm shall nerve to victory
    and power.

" I'm going to the holy wars on the plains of Palestine:
In victory, or life, or death, dear lady, I am thine.
Should e'er the joyous hour come to favor my return,
Then, lady, who your slave is now your gentle heart
    shall learn !"

Then quickly vaulting on his steed he left the gazing
    throng,
'Mid wondering eyes and valorous shouts that lasted
    loud and long;

And soon he joined the battle ranks and led his army on,
Those honored soldiers of the cross, to death or victory
    won.

But from this hour the maiden's cheek grew sickly, pale,
    and wan,
She mourned because the gallant youth to the crusade
    war was gone;
His prowess and his noble mien dwelt in that heart of
    hers,
And well she knew she loved the knight with the casque
    and golden spurs.

She thought could she have only seen the warrior's
    manly face,
The better in her memory his dauntless form to trace,
It would have been a holy bliss to cheer her youthful
    heart
While war, with all its brooding ills, should keep them
    thus apart.

And oft at evening's stilly hour the princess would re-
    pair
To the turret walls to lonely muse and breathe the genial
    air,
And far her eager eyes would roam along the vales
    below,
Remembering when her crusade knight there led his
    army through,—

And wondering, now the war was o'er, if he would soon
    return,
For still her heart more anxious grew the hero's fate to
    learn;

And much she longed the time to see that would his
    name reveal,
Or like a gallant suitor come and again before her
    kneel.

Three years had sped their weary way; the summer
    reign was o'er,
And autumn tints began to glow with sweet and gor-
    geous power,
When Esbatena, lone and sad, upon the turrets strayed,
And saw a lonely horseman wind along the mountain
    glade.

Though weary, still the rider sat most nobly on his
    steed,
With coat of mail well dusted o'er, yet lagging was his
    speed;
The princess thought that stately form she'd seen before
    that day,
With the visor of his helmet closed, and suit of gold and
    gray.

How did her gentle bosom throb, what visions filled her
    brain,
As she saw the noble cavalier approaching once again!
What nameless thoughts, what anxious fears her every
    passion stirs,
As she sees alight from his panting steed the knight
    with the golden spurs!

Scarce had she gained her garden bower when there the
    warrior came,
And kneeling, kissed her snowy hand and gently breathed
    her name:

" Fair lady, I have come, you see, as a true and valiant
  knight,
  My promise to redeem with thee, though worn and
  weary quite.

" Three years and more of battle toil on Asia's burning
  plains
  Hath bronzed my brow, but hath not quenched the
  ardor in my veins.
  I love thee still, sweet lady fair, as faithful knight
  should love,
  But whether I thy smiles shall share my presence now
  will prove.

"Alas! though valorous I have been, nor felt one coward
  fear
  When death and fury round me raged, I feel a coward
  here!
  Lady, when I shall breathe my name and be made
  known to thee,
  Though thou hast loved, I know it all, thy soul will
  shrink from me!

" Yea, I have heard, when far away, of thy wan and
  faded cheek,
  Of the power I held o'er thy gentle breast which now
  thy looks bespeak.
  But let the blow of fate descend, as a knight of the
  cross I stand;
  Lady, it is Guzpero seeks the honor of thy hand!"

" Guzpero!" screamed the stricken fair, whose cheek
  grew ashy pale:
" The gods are false that brought thee here; thy presence makes me quail;

The murderer of my father here! this is too much to
    bear!
My doom is sealed; I now shall die the victim of de-
    spair!''

"Nay, nay, dear lady! say not so! think well of what
    has past!
Remember, I am penitent! crime will not always last.
If sorrow for my guilt can wash the fearful stain away,
Then, lady, I have borne enough the solemn debt to
    pay!

"I love thee, noble lady fair, with knightly truth and
    zeal,
And all the pangs remorse can give I have been taugh
    to feel;
A thousand worlds I'd freely give could I revive once
    more
That honored father, brave and kind, thou dost so
    much deplore.''

The princess shrank with nameless dread; her heart
    was in despair;
To wed her father's murderer! the thought she could
    not bear.
Her cheek grew blanched, for horror spread its gloom
    upon her brow,
And much she wished ere that sad day her heart had
    been laid low.

To think that she had loved so true, and hated with
    such hate
Two beings, who now both proved one—how wretched
    was her fate!

28*

One she had loved as gallant knight and soldier of the
    cross ;
The other hated as a fiend who caused her father's loss.

She gazed upon his beauteous form in all his manly
    pride,
For now the hero stood revealed, his casque was thrown
    aside ;
She saw his melancholy air, his mild and pensive brow,
And thought a youth so perfect ne'er had yet redeemed
    a vow.

But then she quickly turned aside, she could not let
    the charm
Of beauty and of manliness her gentle soul disarm ;
Though she had loved as none could love, still holy
    honor bade
Her treat with scorn the foe who had her thus an or-
    phan made.

" Fly not, fair lady !" cried the knight, as now he seized
    her hand ;
"For one brief space I must, indeed, your gentle ear
    command !
    Your angel heart is steeped in tears at mournful
        changes past,
    But when the truth of all you hear you'll blame me
        not at last !"

" Would to the gods !" the maiden said, " this thing were
    even so !
    It would a blissful rapture give that well might heal
        my woe ;

For I have e'er been taught to feel a terror at thy
name,
Since by thy hand, I have been told, my father's death-
blow came."

"It did, dear lady! but the fault, his dying lips confessed,
Was all his own, since sternly he the case of honor
pressed;
His fiery zeal gave an offense no man of soul could
brook,
And sure a craven I had been on such to calmly look.

"Words brought on words of angry tone, which soon to
frenzy grew,
And while insulted honor bled, he aimed to pierce me
through;
Maddened with vengeance, then I rose; and, lady,
need I tell?
A challenge passed between us, when thy honored
father fell!

"But, lady! three long years or more of penitence and
prayer
I trust hath proved my holy zeal, my faith and love
sincere;
It was for this I left my home for the wars of Palestine,
That I might claim thy heart at last, and joyful call
thee mine.

"Now tell me," said the noble knight, as at her feet he
knelt,
"Fair lady, as a warrior brave, could I else then have
dealt?
And since it was a deep affair for honor to decide,
And I thy father's pardon have, wilt thou not be my
bride?"

"Thank holy Heaven!" the princess cried; "this is a
    feature new:
Far different has the tragic scene been painted to my
    view.
Convince me now of this, sir knight, that thou dost
    bear with thee
My father's pardon, and I vow thy own true bride
    to be!"

"'Tis here!" the joyous knight replied, as in her hand
    he placed
A scrawl he from his bosom took which had been rudely
    traced;
And what was now the maiden's bliss as these words
    met her eye,—
"Guzpero, thou my pardon hast, and blessing, ere I die!"

The princess knew her father's hand, though traced
    with trembling frame,
Nor needed she a fairer proof than his own strange
    style and name.
Next moment was her soul in tears, her form in her
    lover's arms,
And the hero of the holy wars was the owner of her
    charms.

Such joy before was never known within those castle
    walls:
For days and nights was music heard resounding
    through its halls;
But soon her lord bore her away in gorgeous pomp
    and state,
When speedily she found her knight as truly good as
    great!

THE FISHERMAN AND HIS SON.

A TALE OF THE SEA.

Upon a mossy cliff there stood,
   Whose height o'erlooked the sea,
A humble fisherman's abode
   In peerless majesty.

The snow-capped waves, in every form
   Of grandeur and of grace,
Curled playful in each swelling storm
   Around its coral base.

The mighty winds that swept the shore
   Threw out their murmurs wild;
But music was the surges' roar
   To this brave ocean child.

His castellated home, though rude,
   Defied the pelting blast,
And in this sacred solitude
   He many a year had passed.

But there no merry vine had flung
   Its laughing branches round;
Yet seaweeds, rich with coral strung,
   And pearl shells strewed the ground.

And on this isolated spot
   This child of nature dwelt,
Contented with his humble lot,
   Nor fear nor danger felt.

But think not he was all alone,—
  No, no! two beings dear
Were there to fill affection's throne,
  Affection's claims to share.

An angel wife and darling son
  Were subjects to impart
Delight when daily work was done,
  And soothe his aching heart.

The boy was fair, was chaste and kind,
  To every virtue given;
Bold honor centered in his mind
  Like some sweet star of heaven!

And ever would he nobly brave
  The dangers of the deep;
He loved to be upon the wave
  And o'er its bosom sweep.

And oft as rosy morn would spread
  Her beauty o'er the skies,
The father and the son would speed,
  Or to their labors rise.

Yes! scarce the sun would glorious rise
  Above the raging main,
When these two beings, good as wise,
  Were on its waves again.

Their little bark they'd launch away
  Upon the waters deep,
Returning at the close of day
  To climb their craggy steep;

When Angellett, with fond caress,
　Would hail them home with joy,
And many a welcome kiss impress
　Upon her fearless boy !

And soon a cheerful meal was spread
　Of sweet and savory kind,
Of fish, wild fowl, and home-made bread,
　To bless each weary mind.

And oft some deep and thrilling tale
　The fisherman would tell,
Enough to make the heart turn pale
　While on them he would dwell,

Of dangers they did often brave
　When on the roaring sea,
When tempests swelled each mighty wave
　As high as mountains be.

Thus Angellett would ever fear
　When they were far away,
If clouds of threat'ning would appear,
　Or darkness veiled the day.

High on the cliff this wife would stand
　As evening shades drew near,
With lantern in her trembling hand
　To guide their vessel there.

And often has the beacon proved
　A bright and friendly guide,
To bring those beings, dearly loved,
　In safety to her side.

But on a day the clouds rose high,
  The sun its glory veiled,
Blackness and storm hung o'er the sky
  Soon after they had sailed.

All nature looked in sable gloom
  As onward hours rolled;
The roaring from the ocean's tomb
  A knell of horror toll'd.

As night approached, a thousand fears
  Oppressed the anxious wife;
'Mid storm, she to the cliff repairs,
  At risk of death or life.

There on the frowning brow she stood
  Above the foaming surge;
Lashed by the winds, the rolling flood
  Sent forth a solemn dirge.

Long, long she gazed upon the deep,
  Till horrid darkness fell
In gathering clusters at her feet .
  As though by demon spell.

To leave the spot she could not bear,
  Though dangers gathered fast;
Her heart clung to those beings dear
  Who on its waves were cast.

She wept, and wrung her tender hands;
  Her piercing cries were vain;
No husband, son, before her stands,
  Perhaps will ne'er again!

She now her sentinel bugle blew—
   No answer met the sound ;
From this her wearied spirit drew
   The picture they were drown'd.

Again the bugle she applies
   With more than human power ;
Its voice upon the tempest dies,
   Or rolls along the shore.

Despair now flows in every vein ;
   The horn is thrown aside ;—
Hark! there's a sound! again, again !
   'Tis from the ocean wide!

Great God be praised ! the boat it nears
   The tempest-beaten shore,
And soon a signal voice she hears
   Amid the surges' roar.

" List, list ! all's well! all's well!"
   With joy she hails the sound;
And meeting accents loudly tell
   The deep-mourned lost were found !

THE FALSE-HEARTED.

PUBLISHED MANY YEARS AGO. REPUBLISHED BY REQUEST.

WHEN first I saw thee in thy youth,
   There shone such sweetness round thee ;
Thy lips they spoke that promised truth
   As though fair virtue crowned thee.

29

Thy azure eye beamed peace divine,
  Yet still thy tongue deceived me;
For none could doubt such vows as thine,
  And I, too soon, believed thee.

For when thy vows my fancy led
  To judge by Heaven were truly plighted,
Such dreams of bliss their radiance spread
  That all my hours with peace united.

But thou hast proved severe, unkind,
  And hours of bliss have now departed;
And from the sigh and tear I find
  That thou hast left me broken-hearted.

But, go! thou false, deluding man!
  Perhaps 'tis best those ties should sever,—
Though joys endured so short a span,
  Still painful memory lives forever!

Think not I ever can forget thee,
  Although we part; affection still
Shall prove a refuge to protect thee
  From censure's unrelenting will.

Then fare thee well! and yet forever
  Still this heart shall fondly glow
With purest feelings, ceasing never
  Choicest blessings to bestow.

THE FALL AND DEATH OF POMPEY.

OH, ROME! thy name upon the classic page
   Stands like a motto carved in human gore!
While all the horrors of the darkened age
   Rush to the mind in deep, revolting power!

Those days of yore, when war and carnage rung
   O'er Thessaly's plains, by Roman armies trod,
When swift and sure the battle-spear was flung,
   And proud ambition steeped their steps in blood.

Recorded age of civil strife and woe,
   When Roman heroes fought for lofty sway,
When kindred legions fell on kindred foe,
   And streaming o'er the battle-field they lay.

Hark! from the Forum peals are ringing loud—
   " Down with the cause of liberty!" they cry;
While Cesar's name resounding from the crowd—
   'Tis Cesar must the regal throne supply!

But Cesar's foe, brave Pompey, e'er the great!
   With Cato's valiant and decisive power,
Resolved to mar the pride of royal state,—
   Would have that tyrants trample Rome no more.

He, the bold conqueror of proud legions strong,
   The pirate's terror and the traitor's fear,
Beneath whom Mithridates fell ere long
   A vanquished hero, in his bright career;

He, the proud star of Roman glory, see !
    First in the field amid the battle's rage,
Then in the Forum, eloquent and free,
    The light and honor of the classic age !

But now the contest on Pharsalia's plains :
    Two armies meet, all mailed in armor bright,
Their pennants waving, while deep martial strains
    Proclaim the conquerors ready for the fight.

Cesar and Pompey with their legions come;
    The war shouts ring along Enipen's shore ;
Each heavy phalanx rushes to its doom,—
    To bravely conquer or to rise no more !

The clash of arms, the timbrels, trumpets sound,
    The clarions ring with loud and noisy swell ;
While fifteen thousand veterans strew the ground,
    Like warriors fought, like Roman heroes fell !

But now the voice of triumph on the gale
    Swells loud and long,—'tis notes of victory won
Comes o'er the vanquished with its madd'ning tale :
    For Cesar basks beneath a conquering sun !

Pompey had fallen ! yet though unsubdued,
    His lofty soul sought refuge swift in flight,
Till force and valor were again renewed,
    And mightier legions aid him in the fight.

For hope and chivalry hung o'er his brow,
    Bright as a meteor from the throne of Jove,
Believing slavish tyranny must bow
    Before the sway of liberty and love.

But true, his august mind was wrecked with scorn
    To see his faithless troops desert his cause;
'Twere worse than death their treachery to mourn,
    And see them fly from honor's sacred laws.

Yet the bold warrior lifts his potent mind
    That had nigh drooped in anguish and despair;
Mounting his war steed, sought a home to find
    Secure from foes who craved his life-blood there.

Night came; the moon in softened grandeur rose,
    As now brave Pompey, with a chosen few,
Left the sad plains of slaughter and his foes,
    His journey onward quickly to pursue.

Three days and nights he onward sped his way
    Along the mountain crags and rivers fair;
And now within a fisher's hut he lay;
    The rudest couch his noble form must bear.

The morning dawns; a flimsy barge is seen
    Launched on the waves by his remaining band;
'Tis void of splendor, seeming low and mean,
    But now it bears the vanquished chief from land.

But there are beings holy to his view;
    A wife, a son, now sharers of his fate,
Are on the deck, with feelings chaste and true,
    Resolved to follow and his doom await.

Cornelia, daughter of the Scipio brave,
    All beauteous as the summer's genial smile,
And Sextus, his own son, now share the wave
    That bears him o'er to some protecting isle.

Some days elapsed; 'twas but a transient while,
  Joined by some galleys of a chosen few,
Now scarce two thousand, anchored in the Nile,
  And Egypt's shores burst on their straining view.

Now on the prow the noble warrior stood,
  His corslet gleaming in the morning light,
His jeweled breast, reflecting in the flood,
  Gemmed with the richest pearls and diamonds bright;

His brazen helmet pressed his lofty brow,
  Decked with a plume of oriental grace;
While something like a smile of triumph now
  Lit up his manly and heroic face.

Firm on the vessel's deck his classic form
  Stood, like a brave Apollo of the age;
He hoped, he trusted in no coming storm
  To throw a cloud on life's historic page.

His gentle wife, Cornelia, near his side,
  His arm around her slender waist was flung,
While eloquence affection could not hide
  Fell from her lips, like music from her tongue.

It was in warnings from her gentle heart,
  A thousand fears sprang up within her mind,
Lest they should be forever doomed to part,
  And foes instead of friends now early find.

And why? ah! see yon legions from the shore,
  Those turbaned hosts with burnished deadly spears;
And loud is heard the barbarous music's roar,
  The wild tympanum, as the army nears.

The clashing cymbals and Egyptian bells,
    The rolling bugle and the cyntrum's note,
Now on the breeze of morning proudly swells
    And o'er the Nile in martial numbers float.

While from the shore a barge is seen to move,
    Bearing toward them with the utmost speed,
And turbaned warriors now advance to prove
    Their souls well worthy of a bloody deed.

But Pompey, with a mind unchained by fear,
    No coward impious thoughts invade his soul;
He deems a rescuing friendly army near,
    Nor dreams from thence of human treachery foul.

Watching heroic from the vessel's prow
    The mighty hosts that thronged the Egyptian coast,
He kissed his wife, and said, " Fair angel, now
    Thy Cneius can of certain victory boast !

" Those turbaned warriors and those noble steeds,
    See how they prance and curve the ambient air;
They seem prepared for war's determined deeds,—
    Those Ptolemies are heroes brave and rare.

" Yes ! such a host with Cato's valiant band,
    A good ten thousand, we can soon efface
The solemn blot from fair Pharsalia's land,
    That fills my heart with festering disgrace."

"Alas ! my Cneius !" the fond Cornelia said,
    With pleading look and anguish in her soul,
"Some deep, dark snare for thee is surely laid,
    I feel from thoughts I cannot well control !

" Some hovering gloom, of sad foreboding kind,
     Steals o'er me like a sea of sudden woe.
I would, my love, this visit be declined ;
     I pray thee, dearest, stay! ah, do not go !''

" Tush, tush ! my life ! my more than dearest, thou
     Dispel these fears ! why look so trembling sad ?
Cheer up ! let hope set on thy gentle brow,
     For joys triumphant surely may be had!

" Have they not oft, by former acts and deeds,
     Gave me to feel their constancy and power?
I've been their friend, and this it is that leads
     Me to believe they are the same this hour.

" I trust my life by all the rules of war
     To their high honor, and I hope to find
Help and protection 'neath fate's guiding star :
     Be as it may, my heart must bow resigned !''

"Alas ! my husband ! shall I doubt thee true ?
     Remember those all dearest to thy heart :
Our noble boy, our valiant Cato too,
     With daring Cicero ! canst thou from us part ?

"Afranius, Labienus, are all in arms,
     Thy bravest friends, a host of proudest blood !
And wilt thou, 'midst the direst of alarms,
     Thus leave us ?   All bodes to thee no good !

" See, look ! my husband ! at that humble yacht ;
     No royal ensign on its mast appears !
It is an insult, and a sad fiat,
     Not such as monarchs send for noble seers !''

"And there!" cried Sextus, while the blush of scorn
  Mounted his proud, his manly Róman brow;
" Their royal crafts I see are yonder borne,—
  'Tis insult, father, they would offer now !

" Oh ! hear the pleadings of thy anxious son !
  Let Fabius and others swiftly bring
Their pikes and spears, and bid them now begone,
  Ay ! quick as rain drops from the sea-bird's wing."

" Peace, Sextus ! 'Tis the brave Achilles ! he
  The leader of the army ! and, behold !
The king's preceptor ! highly honored we
  May deem ourselves, though not of this foretold !

"Avaunt with scrupulous notions ! see, they smile,
  And fain would give us tender greeting, boy !
I little care for silly forms of style;
  They thought, perhaps, 'twould give but meager joy."

It nears ; the salutations pass in formal state :
  "All hail, brave Pompeius!" cried the dark-skinned
      foe;
"All hail ! thou whom the world calls vastly great,
  And who hath laid the strength of armies low!

" Thy slaves, great Pompey! friendly greetings bear
  To thee from their devoted, mighty king,
Who now invites thee royal claims to share,
  And bid us thy most noble self to bring!

" He waits thy presence, most exalted sage!
  We will conduct thee to his royal tent,
And courteous thou wilt find him, we engage,
  Since for his benefactor we were sent !"

" Hail to Achilles!" was the prompt reply ;
    "To Proteus! Theodotus, ever brave!
I greet you welcome! draw, I pray you, nigh!"
    And Pompey each the hand of friendship gave.

" Thanks to your noble liege and august sire
    For making thus his goodly pleasure known !
To other favors I would fain aspire,
    And will attend you to his regal throne !"

" Nay, nay ! my husband ! noblest, bravest, best !
    Thou lovest Cornelia ! thine own faithful wife !
If thou wouldst see thyself with glory blest,
    Go not, I pray ! oh, save thy precious life !

" Methinks this is a greeting strange and new,
    So void of every honor and display ;
While royal barges gilded lie in view,
    The king, my lord, more courtesy should pay !"

" Silly, my love ! drive off these idle fears !"
    The husband said ; " I cannot bear this gloom !
Come, let me kiss away those anxious tears—
    Let hope and peace thy gentle brow illume !"

Yet while he spoke he found his courage fail ;
    Philosophy was trembling on its throne ;
His loving gaze now told a madd'ning tale
    More keen than what his generous lips could own.

He pressed her to his broad and throbbing breast,
    And on her brow sealed many a fervent kiss ;
" By all my hopes, Cornelia ! it is best
    For me to go in such a time as this !

"I must away! thou art a suppliant fair!
  But duty calls me now from friends and home!
To say thee nay, like daggers on me bear;
  Before love comes the safety of proud Rome!"

And now Achilles spoke with haughty smile,
  Indignant at her rising doubts and fears:
"And so, Cornelia!" said this friend of guile,
  "Thou art opposed, as plainly now appears!

"Thou doubtest, ay! the honor of our king!
  Ptolemy is brave! but, mind thou well,
Could we not, lady, mighty legions bring,
  And thy liege lord immediately compel

"To go with us, without one favoring word,
  On board our craft? but we are men, nor care
To be too over-nice, though we have heard
  Some like in gorgeous etiquette to share!

"No need of so much form, we should suppose;
  'Twere loyalty and kindness we mean:
Our noble king these better movements chose
  To give more friendly freedom to the scene!

"Thinkest thou three Roman galleys e'er could brave,
  Well-manned, such as they now appear to be,
Yon hosts that we could launch upon the wave,
  Not half of which the roving eye may see?

"But now 'tis well! thou doubtest us in truth!
  We can return to our most royal sire!
Yet much we think thee proudly wrong forsooth,
  Though darest, as slaves, thy beauty to admire!"

"Insolent wretch! barbarian vile! away!"
  The fearless wife in deepest anguish cried;
"Darest thou to Roman daughter thus reply?
  Foul dastard! thou hast meanly, basely lied!"

"Peace, Cornelia! now thy Pompey hear;
  Sure terror hath dethroned thy lofty mind;
Thou shouldst afford our friends more happy cheer,—
  They sure will deem thee haughty and unkind!

"But thou wilt yet, in future, better learn.
  Come, kiss me, love! again! I must away!
Ere sets the sun I shall to thee return;
  No longer, dearest, can I now delay!"

Then springing from her gentle, kind embrace,
  Thus spoke the warrior from his ardent soul:
"My wife! my Sextus! blood of my own race!
  Let honor, glory, all your acts control

"In all the future! may the gods descend
  Upon your path, and virtue be your aim!
May Heaven prove your constant guiding friend,
  And make you worthy of a lofty name!"

Again he clasped them to his throbbing breast;
  Again he charged them wait his glad return;
Breathing—he thought it surely wisest—best
  As glory might his future fortune earn.

"Yes," said Achilles, while his sable face
  Gleamed with a most unearthly savage smile,
"Thy noble self, brave Pompey, we will place
  In glorious splendor in a transient while!

"Greatness and pomp await thee on our shore,
  Or we would not thus come in humble barge;
But shallow waters would not grant us more
  Than this light craft to bear thy form in charge."

Enough! the hero gave the parting kiss,
  One more adieu he waved to son and wife,
Then sprang on board with hopes of future bliss,
  Trusting foul tyrants with his precious life.

Oh, fate! didst thou not do thy impious worst
  To thus delude so bright a star of Rome,
And leave him with those wretched souls accurst,
  To share a vile and ignominious doom?

Light skimmed the galley o'er the dimpled stream;
  The oars were plied with swift but measured aim,
While Pompey stood, wrapped in affection's dream,
  Gazing on those more dear than life or fame.

Not long they see his lingering look of love,
  As now upon the fatal deck he stood,
For those surround who would his murderers prove,
  And soon his form is bathed in crimson blood.

Yea, while the hero gave the cordial hand
  To some vile traitor recognized too well,—
A foul betrayer from his native land,—
  He through their blows a slaughtered victim fell.

For at a signal that Achilles gave,
  The fatal weapons thick around him flew,
Sprinkling with blood the proud, the mighty brave
  Who stood most firm and dauntless in their view.

One look soon told him treachery was there;
   He saw at once his solemn, bitter fate;   `
A captive now within their hellish snare,
   Doomed he must fall a victim to their hate.

He saw the mark of dark, designing Cain
   Stamped on their false and hell-devoted brows;
And as they struck, he bid them strike again,
   Nor moved nor swerved from their descending blows.

But soon his pale and lifeless body fell
   Down to the deck, all steeped in purple gore;
While naught but death cast round its solemn spell
   To tell the world that Pompey was no more.

TO THE DEITY.

To THOU, whose glory decks the skies,
I would some sacred anthem raise;
For bright as sunlit glories fall,
Thy love can gladden memory's scrawl.
Thy beauties rise before my view,
To wake some dream of rapture new;
And dull must e'er the vision be
That loses, Lord, the sight of thee!
For all thy wondrous works declare
Thy spirit lingers everywhere:
If upwards I direct mine eye,
Then thousand glories deck the sky,

To cast a charm o'er reason's throne,
While viewing all those worlds thine own;
If in the bosom of the deep
The human vision dare to creep,
Each hidden wonder there could tell
Thou dost 'mid voiceless silence dwell.

What though romantic poets dream,
And wake in tune some fairy theme
Of mermaids sporting 'neath the wave,
'Mid many a sparkling diamond cave,
Or wandering through each coral grove
To hold their voiceless feasts of love;
This one thing doth my spirit know,
Thou art a God, above, below,
That walks serene, 'mid calm and storm,
In all thy mystic, glorious form.
The seasons change at thy command,
And sweetly thy majestic hand
Is over every feature drawn—
From towering wood to verdant lawn,
From craggy cliff to ivy bower,
All still reveal thy sovereign power.

Far down in depths where human aid
Hath no inroads from venture made,
Or science with her magic rule
Sought out as yet, 'mid nature's school,
Those hidden wonders, great and wide,
Thy matchless wisdom hath supplied;
Yet there, 'mid august silence, we
May study thy immensity!

But hoary Time is on the wing,
And must ten thousand advents bring ;
And though for slumbering ages past,
The earth's broad tomb hath envious cast
Her midnight shadows o'er thy toil,
The march of mind shall wake the soil,
And myriad wonders be revealed
From human vision now concealed,
To blazon Time's historic page
In that propitious future age,
When every nation shall agree
And own the world is full of Thee !

THE END.